The Albigensian Treasure

The Albigensian Treasure

by
Maurice Magre

Translated, annotated and introduced by
Brian Stableford

A Black Coat Press Book

ISBN 978-1-61227-686-1. First Printing. December 2017. Published by Black Coat Press, an imprint of Hollywood Comics.com, LLC, P.O. Box 17270, Encino, CA 91416. All rights reserved. Except for review purposes, no part of this book may be reproduced or transmitted in any form or by any means, electronic or mechanical, including photocopying, recording, or by any information storage and retrieval system, without permission in writing from the publisher. The stories and characters depicted in this novel are entirely fictional. Printed in the United States of America.

TABLE OF CONTENTS

Introduction

This is the ninth volume of a twelve-volume set of translations of Maurice Magre's prose fiction. It contains translations of the novel *Le Trésor des Albigeois* (1938) as "The Albigensian Treasure," and the collection of vignettes "Communication avec la nature" from *La Beauté invisible* (1937), as "Communication with Nature."

Volume One, *The Marvelous Story of Claire d'Amour and Other Stories*, contains translations of early short stories, including the collection *Histoire merveilleuse de Claire d'Amour suivie d'autres contes merveilleux* (1903) and six other stories from various sources published between 1901 and 1913.

Volume Two, *The Call of the Beast and Other Stories*, contains translations of his first three works of prose fiction in volume form, *Les Colombes poignardées* (1917), as "Stabbed Doves," *La Tendre camarade* (1918), as "The Tender Comrade" and *L'Appel de la bête* (1920), as "The Call of the Beast."

Volume Three, *Priscilla of Alexandria and Other Stories* contains translations of the original version of the story collection *Vies des courtisanes*, first published in *Oeuvres Libres* 23 (1923), as *Courtesans' Lives* plus the additional story added to the version published in volume form in 1925, and the novel *Priscilla d'Alexandrie* (1925), as "Priscilla of Alexandria."

Volume Four, *The Angel of Lust*, contains translations of the novella, *La Vie amoureuse de Messaline* (1925), as "The Love Life of Messalina," the novel published as *La Luxure de Grenade* (1926), as "The Angel of Lust," and the chapter from *Magiciens et illuminés* (1930) entitled "Christian Rosenkreutz et les Rose-croix," as "Christian Rosenkreutz and the Rosicrucians."

Volume Five, *The Mystery of the Tiger*, contains translations of the novella *Le Roman de Confucius* (1927), as "The Story of Confucius," and the novel *Le Mystère du tigre* (1927), as "The Mystery of the Tiger."

Volume Six, *The Poison of Goa*, contains translations of the novel *Le Poison de Goa* (1928), as "The Poison of Goa," and the prose poems contained in *Le Livre des lotus entr'ouverts* (1926), as "Lotus Blossoms."

Volume Seven, *Lucifer*, contains a translation of the novel originally published under the same title in 1929 and the novella *La Nuit de haschich et de l'opium* (1929), as "The Night of Hashish and Opium."

Volume Eight, *The Blood of Toulouse*, contains translations of the novel *Le Sang de Toulouse* (1931), as "The Blood of Toulouse," and the chapter from *Magiciens et illuminés* entitled "Le Maître inconnu des Albigeois," as "The Secret Master of the Albigensians."

Volume Ten, *Jean de Fodoas*, contains translations of the novel *Jean de Fodoas: aventures d'un Français à la cour de l'empereur Akbar* (1939) as "Jean de Fodoas" and the chapter from *Magiciens et illuminés* entitled "Le Mystère des Templiers," as "The Mystery of the Templars."

Volume Eleven, *Melusine*, contains translations of the novel *Mélusine, ou le Secret de solitude* (1941) and the collections of vignettes "Le Côté d'ombre des âmes" and "Révélation des mondes invisibles" from *La Beauté invisible*, as "The Dark Side of Souls" and "The Revelation of Invisible Worlds."

Volume Twelve, *The Brothers of the Virgin Gold*, contains a translation of the novel *Les Frères de l'or vierge*, first published posthumously in 1949.

Maurice Magre's particular revision and detailed description of various episodes of the Albigensian crusade had produced an exceptionally fine historical novel in *Le Sang de Toulouse*, the text of which, among many other things, provided a mechanism for the material related by its narrator to have survived into the twentieth century in spite of never having been written down. Whether or not that mechanism could be taken seriously, it helped to dramatize emphatically the continuing relevance of the story told by the historical novel, particularly to its author. It was not at all surprising, therefore, that he went on to employ some of those background details, and his personal association with them, as the foundation for a very different text: the deliberately-enigmatic mystical allegory *Le Trésor des Albigeois*, which begins some three hundred and fifty years after the end of *Le Sang de Toulouse*, circa 1600.

The Toulousan physician Michel de Bramevaque is not explicitly represented as a reincarnation of Dalmas Rochemaure, and hence as someone who shares a continuing soul in common with Maurice Magre, but it does not take an excessive stretch of the imagination to see him in that light, and to view his quest for the Holy Grail as a symbolic transfiguration of the author's lifelong search for "the ideal." *Bramer* is the French term for the calling of a rutting stags, while the verb *vaquer* refers to being on vacation or idling; Magre used the surname again in *Les Frères de l'or vierge*, where the last two descendants of the line are decrepit, senile, and have fallen on hard times, but still have moral credit with the Rosicrucians because of their ancestors' involvement with the Grail.

Although it is not a not a novel of action like *Le Sang de Toulouse, Le Trésor des Albigeois* does involve Michel de Bramevaque in a number of dramatic confrontations, including a stressful interview with the remorseful ghost of his accursed ancestor, partly responsible for the loss of the Grail, and a celebration of the Mass of Saint Sécaire, a version of the black mass featured in Gascon legend. He is not a fighting man of the same stripe as Dalmas Rochemaure, however, and his heroism is a quieter kind, most conspicuously displayed during the epidemic of bubonic plague that he unwittingly lets into Toulouse while doing a good deed. That meek heroism, however, represents a significant step in the long spiritual evolution that Dalmas Rochemaure was still destined to go through, in the course of numerous future incarnations, at the end of *Le Sang de Toulouse*. Michel de Bramevaque's own philosophical self-development remains similarly and necessarily incomplete, even after he has located the Grail, but he remains on the right path toward his eventual fulfillment.

The narrative strategy of the novel is, to some extent, a recovery of the fragmentary method the author employed in *Les Colombes poignardées* and *La Tendre camarade*. He had presumably employed it then because those novels were pieced together from units written in short bursts, probably not in the order in which they appear in the finished text, and probably not all intended initially to be components of the texts as published. Having fund that the improvisation worked, however, it is not surprising that he turned to it again, either because it seemed artistically appropriate or because illness was making the circumstances of his literary production more difficult. All Magre's fiction tends to the episodic in any case, but in spite of his poor health, he was still perfectly capable of maintaining a long coherent story—as he did in *Jean de Fodoas*, set in the same time-period as *Le Trésor des Albigeois*, during his healthier intervals—and he never stopped writing, even when suffering.

The narrative artifice employed in *Le Trésor des Albigeois* is also reflected in the manner of composition of the curious near-contemporary hybrid volume *La Beauté invisible*, which consists of three sets of vignettes that mingle personal anecdotes, prose-poems and brief philosophical essays, just as *Le Trésor des Albigeois* and the subsequent work of fiction *Mélusine, ou le Secret de la solitude* do, except that in the anecdotes in *La Beauté invisible* the author speaks in his own voice—deceptively, as the great majority of those pieces are clearly fictitious—and in *Mélusine* he uses a close simulacrum of his own voice, whereas he uses Michel de Bramevaque's fictitious voice in *Le Trésor des Albigeois*. The partial solution to his philosophical predicament that Michel de Bramevaque eventually discovers, however, is exactly the same one that the authorial voice claims to have found in the first series of vignettes in *La Beauté invisible*, "Communication avec nature," and its simulacrum discovers in the plot of *Mélusine*, and a comparison of the three supports the notion that the same fundamental voice is speaking in all three cases, in spite of the fact that Michel de Bramevaque's is hypothetically distanced in time as well as the specific symbolism of his quest.

Further evidence for the close identification of Michel de Bramevaque with the author might also be seen in the curious chapter in which, having returned temporarily to Toulouse, he goes past the house in which he left his wife behind. Although insisting to his companion that they are just passing by, and that he no longer has any moral right to react to what his wife is now doing, the glimpse nevertheless evokes forceful memories, and new feelings that he cannot entirely suppress. It is surely tempting to suspect that the incident and its evocations reflect, at least to some extent, Magre's retrospective reflections on the unfortunate fate of his own marriage to Jeanne Rosen—with whom he presumably in touch again, since she was living in the south of France not far from where Magre was then living, and that she was present at his deathbed in 1941.

It is possible, too, that *La Beauté invisible*, with the aid of longer insight, casts more light on the whole endeavor of Magre's life than his previous volumes of autobiography, in spite of the evidently fictitious nature of many of its anecdotes. The remarkable opening paragraph of the preface of the book, reproduced here along with the text of "Communication avec nature," might be especially revealing, in its forthright announcement not only of the author's personal *désespoir* [despair], but his conviction that the despair in question is the general human condition, and his defiant declaration that he is glad that he has it—or, at least, that he has had it, since he goes on to assert to assert that he has now conquered it, or at least learned to live with it contentedly, and the hope that the book's contents can inform others, if they care to listen and make the effort to understand, how they can do likewise. That claim impressed some readers, at least; the book was awarded the Grand Prix de Littérature de l'Académie Française, the most important of the literary awards that Magre author won during his lifetime.

It would not have come as a surprise to anyone who had bothered to follow Magre's literary career from the beginning, that he was a deeply troubled man, whose writing, in all genres, not only included both an attempt to express and analyze that fundamental disturbance, but comprised an attempt to counter it. His first collection of short stories, *Histoire merveilleuse de Claire d'Amour suivie d'autres contes merveilleux* (1903) was remarkable in being the most downbeat and despairing of all the tales of disenchantment written in the genre of *contes merveilleux*, setting new standards in pessimism and lamenting desperately the conclusion that the irresistible light of amour was a lure that was not only unattainable but essentially destructive. Having got the expression in question out of his system, the author then set about trying to find a way to repair the situation. After an interim in which he tried existential solutions whose immediate literary spinoff was limited, he eventually returned to using prose fiction explore, analyze and express the solutions he had tried, and those he was still in the process of trying out. *Le Trésor des Albigeois* is one of the quirkiest of these explorations, but it is also one of the most determined and most heartfelt.

What Magre meant by *désespoir* has something in common with such clinical terms as *depression* and such philosophical terms as Martin Heidegger's *angst*, but is probably more apt to liken it to terms used by other writers, such as Robert Burton's *melancholy* and Charles Baudelaire's *spleen*, in that those authors, too, had not only used literary work to express and analyze their perceived predicament but had used literary endeavor as part of their coping mechanism, as a form of self-medication. There are not only similarities between the feelings that they were trying to dramatize but in the narrative strategies those that their endeavor encouraged, and, in particular, their powerful attraction to the fantastic. That attraction is natural, because the phenomenon that Magre called *désespoir* is essentially an excess of realism, which insists on seeing life as is, with all its essential nastiness, brutality and brevity. If it is to be escaped, or even survived, it has to be done by means of the exercise of an adventurous creative imagination.

Some of Magre's readers might, of course, have doubted the fundamental assertion made in the opening sentence of *La Beauté invisible* that if there are any human beings who escape despair, they are very few in number. Doubtless there were readers, too, who could not understand why Robert Burton was banging on at such enormous length about melancholy, why Martin Heidegger thought that human life was essentially cursed by angst, etc., etc. Even Magre, in one of the mini-essays in "Le Côté d'ombre des âmes" (translated in Volume Eleven)—a set of humorous essays on the weak points of great philosophers who sought solutions to the human predicament—asserts that Buddha exaggerated in saying that life was essentially evil; he suggests instead that it is really only two-thirds evil and one-third good, and that most people would be quite satisfied with an even smaller proportion of the good. It is undeniable that many people think of Magre's problem as something rare and abnormal, just as naïve psychologists have a tendency to consider depression as a kind of "mental illness" rather than a variety of sanity

Perhaps those people are right and Magre was wrong, and it is only a minority of people rather than the vast majority who are living lives of quiet despair. Perhaps, on the other hand, it is simply that a great many people are in denial: that they are, in fact in despair, but cannot and will not admit it, even to themselves, and are hence suffering from the only authentic disease of reason, optimism. That is obviously far too big a question to debate in the present introduction, but it is worth pointing out that it does have a particular relevance to fiction in general, and fantastic fiction in particular, because it has a considerable bearing on the nature of the literary appetite and certain peculiar features of that appetite, including the liking for the fantastic and, most of all, the avid, compulsive hunger for what are generally called "happy endings."

If one takes a philosophical sidestep in order to take a more distanced look at the phenomenon of literature, and the nature of reading as a mental activity, recognizing their fundamental bizarrerie, one would surely be tempted to come up with the hypothesis that it is not merely authors of fiction who often using that endeavor as self-administered therapy to counter their mental troubles, but their readers as well, consciously or unconsciously. Most of those readers, of course, most of the time, like their tales of enchantment to be far less nihilistic than Magre's story of Claire d'Amour and far less enigmatic than his account of Michel de Bramevaque's quest for the Holy Grail, and many of them would deem Magre's constant aversion to conventional happy endings—which even extends to his most buoyant texts—to be disappointing, or even perverse. Perhaps, though, that is merely a side-effect of their denial. The reason that Magre wrote in the manner he did, rather than in the conventional manner engendered and controlled by the tastes of the majority of the reading public, is that he was not only in despair but knew it, and wanted a better solution to the problem than the endless ritual repetition of the kind of story that ends with a marriage and an inheritance.

Whether such a solution can be found is, of course, a debatable point. The answer that such literary predecessors as Burton and Baudelaire tacitly reached, in the end, was simply negative, but that does not mean that their endeavors were not heroic, just as Michel de Bramevaque's and Maurice Magre were.

Between *Le Sang de Toulouse* and *Le Trésor des Albigeois* there was a seven-year gap in Magre's production of fiction, which is unusually long in the context of the later phases of his career. He was certainly not idle during those years, of course; he published several non-fiction books, including the philosophical tracts *La Mort et la vie future* [Death and the Future Life] (1932), *L'Amour et la haine* [Love and Hate] (1934) and *À la poursuite de la sagesse* [In Pursuit of

Wisdom] (1936) as well as his second popularization of his version of the hermetic tradition *La Clé des choses cachées* [The Key to Hidden Things] (1935). He also produced two books that Jean-Jacques Bedu classifies as fiction, although Magre never did, and they are probably better regarded as collections of journalistic articles: *Pirates, Flibustiers, Négriers* [Pirates, Filibusters and Slave-Traders] (1934) and *Les Aventuriers d'Amérique du Sud* [The Adventurers of South America] (1935). It is possible that he was also writing fiction that did not reach print; at least some of the components of the sprawling portmanteau novel *Les Frères de l'or vierge* might well have been written, or at least begun, during that period, given their obvious kinship with the dramatized documentaries contained in the last-named volumes.

What is certain, however, is that during the interim in question, Magre took a major step in his personal quest for a solution to his despair, by making a pilgrimage to Pondicherry, in India, in 1935. Magre undertook that voyage in order to consult a Hindu sage who called himself Sri Aurobindo Ghose, whose philosophy Magre likened to that of Lao-Tsu in an article in the *Mercure de France* that he subsequently wrote about his journey, and subsequently incorporated into *À la poursuite de la sagesse*. Sri Aurobindo was a former teacher of French, which facilitated his communication with his new disciple, and helped Magre to put flesh on the elusive educators previously featured in his hypothetical fictions. When the author returned to France he produced another volume of apparent hackwork, *Inde, Magie, Tigres, Forêts vierges* [India: Magic, Tigers and Virgin Forests] (1936), which is entirely fictitious although it pretends to be a memoir—for which reason Bedu classifies it, rather inaptly along with two pseudonymous accounts of *Magie à Paris* [Magic in Paris] (1934) and *Le Magie aux colonies* [Magic in the Colonies[(1935), both signed "René Thimmy," as an element of his "oeuvre Philosophique."

Typically, however, Magre's initial enthusiasm for the spiritual rewards of his pilgrimage soon waned, and he found the prospect of taking the advice he had been given—essentially, to seek solitude and meditate, after the fashion of Olympios in *Priscilla d'Alexandrie* and Lao-Tsu in *Le Roman de Confucius*—not only familiar but still difficult to put into practice. He had not hesitated in *Priscilla d'Alexandrie* to represent Olympios as a happy man, nor to represent Lao-Tsu's eventual lonely but hallucinated death as a transcendent triumph, and he had been equally wholehearted in representing Albigensian perfecti and their alleged successor Christian Rosenkreutz as supremely joyful and successful philosophers, in his fiction and scholarly fantasy alike, but it was one thing to make that statement in scholarly fantasy and imaginative fiction and another actually to try to live it.

Nevertheless, by the time he published *La Beauté invisible* and *Le Trésor des Albigeois*, Magre seems to have been able to convince himself, at least momentarily, that he had found the key. That key, he had decided, was beauty: not the beauty of women, which was essentially deceptive, a kind of trap set by carnality in order to drag men down into the murky depths of their inferior selves, but the beauty of nature. It is via a particular solitary communication with nature that Michel de Bramevaque and the unnamed narrator of *Mélusine* contrive to find their personal *consolamenta*. Both of them are endowed with the temporary gift of being able to understand the speech of animals, and thus to understand the true situation of animals hand human in the hierarchy of creation.

Magre lays claim to the same gift in the fantasized essays in autobiography contained in the section of *La Beauté invisible*, translated in the present volume allowing him to conclude, in one of the exercises in visionary symbolism translated in Volume Eleven, that "the lake of despair is not far from the mountain of serenity"—always provided, of course, that one can find the way from one to the other. *Le Trésor des Albigeois* suggests that the journey is not an easy one, and that most of the signposts encountered along the way are bound to prove misleading, but it maintains the valiant conviction that serenity is ultimately achievable, if one has a friend like Isaac Andréa, and a garden like his.

The translation of *Le Trésor Albigeois* was made from a copy of the 1985 edition published in Rennes-le-Château by Philippe Schrauben. The translation of "Communication avec nature" was made from a copy of the 1937 Fasquelle edition of *La Beauté invisible*.

Brian Stableford

THE ALBIGENSIAN TREASURE

INVOCATION

By the four marvels of Toulouse,[1] by the beauty of its bell-towers and the youth of its gardens;

By the Comtes Raymond Bertrand, Pons and Taillefer who are sleeping in the three stone tombs of Saint Sernin but wake up every night, it is said, and stroll around the Basilica, chatting;

By the wisdom of the eight Capitouls, by the memory of the Knights Hospitallers full of courage, by the presents of human Saints, those who re revered in the churches and those who were called heretics and burned in the Place Saint-Georges;

By the Garonne, blue daughter of the mountain of Aran, by its song and by its shingle;

By Clémence Isaure, the virginal and the protective, by Pierre Goudoulin of the beautiful songs, by the Hôtel d'Assésat with the beautiful sculptures;[2]

---

[1] Author's note: "At the end of the sixteenth century, the four marvels of Toulouse , for the inhabitants of the Languedoc, were the Church of Saint Sernin, la belle Paule de Viguier, the mill of Bazacle and the violinist Mathali." The list appears to be quoted from an 1844 *Recueil de l'Académie des jeux floraux*, where the nickname of the violinist Gailhard Tailhasson, usually rendered Mathelin, is given in that form. Paule Viguier, who was reputedly called "la Belle Paule" by Francois I, became legendary in consequence.

[2] Clémence Isaure was the legendary founder of the annual Toulousan poetry competition held by the Academy of Floral

By the melancholy of the cloisters, the curves of the bridges, the doors of the leprosaria;

By the purity, by the resignation, by the solitude;

I, Michel de Bramevaque, declare that I shall only write veridical things in the delectation of words and the love of beautiful thoughts. Having accomplished actions that appear insensate to men, I am content now to watch the sun set while elevating my soul toward the unknowable world.

I live in a house with a cloister and a garden, which are the vestiges of an ancient abbey. They belong to Isaac Andréa, a man of great wisdom, who welcomed me when I was a wanderer. Thus, I have realized simultaneously the vow to have no possessions and that of knowing the constant amity that gives more joy than the light of the stars over the Garonne.

Amid the box-trees and the ivy and under very old cypresses, there are the tombstones of unknown dead people. Isaac Andréa has told me that those dead people date from an era anterior to the abbey, anterior to Christianity. The monks only came here because it was a place of predilection for meditation and prayer. And it is, I believe, those ancient dead who have advised me, in the very subtle manner in which such advice is given, to put in writing the things that have happened to me.

I am not writing in order to provoke admiration. I prefer not to be admired. I am not writing in order to be useful to my neighbor. My experience has taught me that all work accomplished by human beings is immediately denatured. Separations are also set in stone. The love of ignorance is profound and everyone is content with it, like a pig in filth.

I am writing in gratitude for the grace that had penetrated me. I am tracing characters on parchment in order to perpetuate a praise that is in my heart. Having lived in darkness, light has come to me. I have had the experience of that which is veritable, as one touches the blade of a sword. I have felt the

---

Games mentioned in the previous note. Pierre Godolin (1580-1649) was an Occitan poet born in the city.

chill of an unalterable metal that has traversed my breast. And that is why I am evoking the episodes of my life before they are effaced, like the towers of a city in the mist.

May the invisible powers guide my trembling hand! I call to my aid the spirit of the ancient Druids and the ancient Minerva to whom the Tectosages erected a temple with seven columns on the sunlit hill that overlooks the Garonne! I call upon Abbé Saturnin, who was dragged by the bull, and Marie the Golden, who is also known as La Daurade![3] I call upon the Albigensian[4] saints who received the wisdom of the Orient and the inspired Troubadours who were initiated by the birds of the Pyrenees! I call upon the Pure and the Perfecti, those whose names are unknown because they remained voluntarily obscure, those who died silently as everyone ought to die, face to face with their invisible star!

May they give my words the rapidity of well-launched arrows, the savor of ripe fruits, the warmth of blazing embers, the music of singing trees! May they sow golden spangles in

---

[3] Although the name of Notre-Dame de la Daurade does derive from the Latin word for gold, the Marie whose icon was displayed there before being stolen in the 15th century was a "Black Madonna."

[4] Author's note: "There is often mention of the Albigensians in the course of this book. I have abstained from developments on Albigensianism, given in other works. I shall content myself with recalling, in a few words, what everyone knows. The Albigensians were heretics who, in the thirteenth century, professed in the Languedoc a wisdom of Oriental origin that had close links with Buddhism. The last Albigensians were exterminated in the Château de Montségur, in the Ariège, where they had taken refuge. The sect then became very secret. There were still traces of it in the sixteenth century, since the Papacy became sufficiently anxious to carry out an investigation in its regard." The most significant of the "other works" to which Magre refers are, of course, *Le Sang de Toulouse* and the essay reproduced as an appendix to it in volume 8.

the water of the story! May they spread there, like a dust of the light of the setting sun, a little of the winged, celestial, ineffable beauty that one sometimes glimpses in dreams.

THE SUMMONS OF THE VOICE

It was more imperative than a trumpet of the Last Judgment, than an order given by Jesus Christ in person to someone designated by his finger of light.

In the nocturnal silence, between the columns of my bed, I heard my name pronounced three times.

"Michel de Bramevaque, get up!"

Once would have been sufficient. But the gods are doubtless like old men and children; they like to repeat themselves.

The voice then said: "Walk in the Toulousan lands. Find the Grail that is hidden there, and men will be saved!"

That happened one night in September, in Toulouse, not far from the Porte Arnaud Bernard, while the moon as still adolescent, and there was a favorable wind that orientated the weathervane of my natal house southwards.

I call it that not because I saw the light there in the form of a child, by the complicated mystery of generation, but because many dreams with white wings were born there under the old beams, charmed me with their presence and then flew away.

That house had only one story, but it was a great marvel of form and comfort. The beauty of dwellings diminishes with the stories and there is already a heavy weight on the back a house that has a single upper story with its oak doors and its furniture with somber panels.

And I said to my wife with the swan-like neck and the incredulous face: "Give me my long staff, the one with copper nails that is slightly curved like a crosier and possesses a certain magical power."

She laughed at the idea of that power, because she did not believe in it. I refrained from talking to her about the voice that had just resonated; she would have laughed even louder, and laughing at a divine voice is something other than laughing at a magic staff.

"I want to go far into the Toulousan lands to study people and living creatures." And I lowered my voice to add: "I sense their dolor in me and I want to share it by knowing them better."

She laughed again, and I thought that a precious porcelain had fallen and broken. I had often formulated projects of a chimerical and humanitarian order that I had not put into execution.

"Give me that maroon cape too, which has a hood for the rain and makes me resemble a monk of a mysterious Order that does not accept the Pope. It will be useful to me when I go to the Château de Bramevaque in the mountains."

There was something like a crystalline rain around me. The Château de Bramevaque had fallen into runs in the Pyrenees and I had said a thousand times that I wanted to go to meditate there and rediscover the thoughts of my ancestors.

I looked at the Bible printed by Gutenberg that my grandfather had acquired, the Ortelius Atlas that was generating much talk in the world, the Latin and Greek books and the Arabic manuscripts that I had from my master Isaac Andréa and in which there were secrets related to the body and the soul. I looked at the parchments attesting to the Capitoulat of my father, an honest and wise man. I had no regret in me, and a surge of delight penetrated me at the thought of the mission with which an Invisible Power had charged me, by means of a curt—and, in truth, rather vague—order.

In the distance, beyond the ramparts, the bell of the Minimes chimed twelve times. I heard the footsteps of the soldiers of the watch. They were marching with precaution, for thieves were numerous and redoubtable. The lantern of the Porte Arnaud Bernard cast a ruddy light.

How silent and inanimate the dolor of creatures was! And yet, that dolor was not asleep. It never rested. I was marching toward it but I did not perceive its breath. I knew that it was present, however, ever present and living in all the places inhabited by human beings.

TORNEBUT

Tornebut was a carpenter by profession, in the Saint Cyprien district, and he possessed a great treasure, the extent of which he was unaware. It was his faith in everything. And most of all, he believed in me. He carried out petty tasks for the people of his neighborhood, but he did not like work much. He preferred listening to people talk and giving his approval. But for him, words were all the more beautiful when he did not understand their meaning.

One never accomplishes a great deed if one has not created it first in the mind by recounting it to someone who believes; for a point of support is necessary for any realization, and faith is the most solid.

I therefore went to find Tornebut.

I found him on his doorstep, as he was getting ready to go and fetch water. The sun had scarcely risen. A little dew was moistening my hair. The waves of the Garonne could be heard recounting the beauty of the forests of firs on the Pyrenean slopes to the shingle of its banks. The air was filed by an odor of freshly-sawn wood.

Tornebut had never heard mention of the Holy Grail, but he nearly fell to his knees when that phrase struck his ears. When I told him that I was going away to search for it, he looked by turns at his empty bucket, his workshop, where his tools were shining, and me, leaning on my staff in the form of a crosier, and he said:

"Every morning, I went to fetch my water from the fountain near the ramparts. I found all the local housewives there because, no one knows why, women have the specialty of water. Water is for women; stone and wood are for men. They made fun of me because of my square shoulders and my hairy chest. But my solitude was light. What does it matter if the day goes by in material labor, if the spirit rises in the evening with the beauty of conversation, and rises very high? O my master, what will become of me if you leave?"

25

And as I knew the force of consolation that substance conceals in its fibers for a man who manipulates it with his hands, I showed him the wood cut by his saw, the shavings like scattered tresses, and the living planks with their years circularly inscribed, for there is no wood that is dead.

But he shook his head and went to fetch his leather jacket, which he put on, along with a bizarre bonnet with two wings, somewhat similar to a donkey's bonnet.

"I'm going with you, O my master! Was it not said by the master who walked in Galilee: *You will leave your father and your mother to follow me?*"

"I'm not the Christ, Tornebut, but a sinner."

"And I have neither father nor mother; I have no one to leave."

He locked his door with a large key and placed a load of sawn wood on his back.

"An old woman who lives in that low house at the street corner asked me to saw her logs for the fireplace. I'll put them outside her door and I'll have finished my work, because it's a slack time."

And that was what he did. We walked for a while and he asked: "Today is Friday the thirteenth of September. Do you think it will be the most prosperous of the days of September, and ought to be chosen for the departure?"

I did not reply, and remained perplexed.

"I'll let the old lady off the six liards she owes me," Tornebut went on, "So today is prosperous for her in the proportion of six liards. But in what proportion will it be for us?"

"Alas, one can only judge the luck and the prosperous character of days on the last day of one's life."

It was then that a flock of birds flew over our heads. A feather was detached from one of them. It descended in a spiral, for feathers are deprived of weight and do not fall as simply as stones. I seized it and I put it in my cap, saying: "It's a white feather! We shall go in the same direction as those birds."

THE HANGED MAN OF AVIGNONNET

When we arrived in Avignonnet, the entire town was abuzz because a man had committed suicide.

Oh my God! I thought, immediately. *As long as he's not the man I'm looking for.*

On the threshold of the inn where we were staying, the master of the place was sniggering with men of evil appearance under an extinct lantern; but his face could be distinguished by the light of the interior rooms shining through the windows. He lifted up a pair of shoes, saying: "I made haste to grab his shoes and will burn them in the fire on the spit. When one burns the shoes of a suicide, you all know that a smoke thicker than other smoke escapes, which chases away evil spirits."

And all the listeners affirmed that they were very familiar with the evident power of such smoke. The joker of the assembly permitted himself to say that the roast would stink of suicide's foot, and sketches of laughter put grimaces on the faces, but were quickly effaced, because that was a godly matter about which it was not appropriate to laugh.

And the one who was holding a long pole with a tallow candle at the end said in his turn, with a sideways glance: "I've received an order from the Inquisitor. I won't light the lanterns tonight. It's necessary that a soul in the torment of the wicked has no light to guide it. It will grope its way through the streets, searching for its route without finding it, for who knows how many years!"

And that miser of light lowered his pole and blew out his tallow candle, for fear that it might serve as a reference point for the soul in torment.

"It's a bad augury for the children who are about to be born," said one.

"That's because the Devil has his eye on us," said another.

"The suicide hasn't put a child into the world to bear his sin," said a third.

"I can make out thin ghosts with bald heads outside his house," said a man with big eyes, like flies ready to take off.

The house in question was of modest appearance and radiant with simplicity, by virtue of the mystery that makes edifices resemble their inhabitants.

Then I went forward and said: "Who is the man who had committed suicide?"

The innkeeper replied, with a hideous expression of disgust: "He was an intellectual!"

At that word, a breath of hatred passed through the group.

"He read books! He had them brought by colporteurs. He once said that he understood different meanings of the Bible, and another time that animals have souls like humans."

"How did he commit suicide, then?"

Then everyone spoke at the same time.

He began by fasting on certain days of the week. Then he had stopped eating, and when he was no longer anything but a shadow, a living specter, he hanged himself from a beam in his ceiling. His shadow was seen from the street. He was so thin that the wind was swinging him like a tree branch. His perverse joy in dying was so great that when the rope was cut he seemed to be smiling, and scornful of those who cut him down.

"Where is his body now?"

"The Inquisitor of Avignonnet gave the order that it be suspended from the gallows like a criminal. Big Ferré dragged it there. It didn't give him any trouble, he pulled it one-handed. The body bounced with a rattle of bones."

I was about to ask more questions, but I saw the circle of faces turned toward me angrily. And like a man lost in the mountains standing up to irritated wolves, I held them in respect with my gaze while they questioned me.

"Say, did you know him by any chance, that intellectual?"

"No, I didn't know him."

"You're as pale as those who don't drink wine and don't eat meat. Aren't you one of the band of intellectuals?"

"I'm certainly not!"

"One might think that you resemble him. Aren't you a member of his family?"

"In truth, I'm not."

They finally dispersed. The lantern-lighter started singing as he drew away. I walked through the dark streets.

Then I wept bitterly. I had just had news of one of the men I was seeking. He was dead; he had been suspended from the gallows, and I, like the disciple devoid of courage, had denied him three times.

ALPHONSE URRAQUE, THE DOMINICAN

Alphonse Urraque, Inquisitor of Avignonnet, was a man who lived in the past. With ardor and amour, he sought Calvinists and Lutherans in order to hand them over to the secular arm. But with what more joyful ardor, and with what more terrible amour, he tried to discover in the human soil of the Lauragais the severed roots, the still-living and secret roots, of the old Cathar heresy! For he knew, as I knew myself, that in the triangle formed by Toulouse, Foix and Carcassonne, Albigensians were still born, and, as if they had a sign on the forehead, the invisible sign of God, they recognized one another.

Alphonse Urraque, the Dominican, by virtue of a mysterious return to things past, incessantly revived in the Château d'Avignonnet the death of other Dominicans who had perished horribly three centuries before under the heretics' daggers.[5] He suffered from that ancient crime as if it were him who sensed the blade in the heart, not the Dominicans of old, and he could not forget it. He would have liked to resurrect the guilty parties in order to torture them, but he did not know the secret of such necromancy, and did not believe that it could be found, for God had buried it with triple darkness because of the wickedness of men.

Then, in dominant Avignonnet, he had extended his nets in order to find he children of the murderers and try to discover some hidden sin in their lives susceptible of punishment. He had gone upstream in the rivers of genealogy; he had enquired into destinies; he had drawn up a chart of marriages and the

---

[5] The murder in Avignonnet of several Inquisitors in May 1242 by a group of Albigensians who came from Montségur and returned there, led by Raymond d'Alfaro, provided the pretext for the siege and destruction of Montségur, described in *Le Sang de Toulouse*.

childbirths that ensued. Did he suspect that they were the same souls, reincarnated in their descendants?

Personally, I had understood immediately when I had learned that the suicide of Avignonnet, the man of simply and solitary life, the reader of books and drinker of water, was named Raymond d'Alfaro, like Raymond d'Alfaro the violent, who had guided the murderers of the Inquisitors from Montségur, and had struck the first blow. Who knows whether he did not have within him the obscure remorse of a crime once committed and whether, after three centuries, the violent had not become the solitary? I had understood why Alphonse Urraque, unable to subject him to any terrestrial torture, had condemned his remains to be suspended from the gallows with highway brigands and criminals.

That Dominican, the inquisitorial judge mysteriously attached to a past epoch, was an ascetic, like me and the last of the Alfaros. He slept in a narrow cell, fasted and prayed frequently, and for him the things of the world were of mediocre interest and scarcely seemed real. The true reality dated from olden days, from the time when holy Romanists had gone into battle against the accursed of the Languedoc. And the Château d'Avignonnet was only a true château, built of admirable stones, because behind its walls the Dominicans had meditated the punishment of the accursed and assured the victory of Jesus. But although those walls had been washed by abundant water in the course of the centuries, he could see bloodstains, bloodstains invisible to everyone else, the blood of eleven murdered monks, and he wanted to erase those stains.

And when, having requested an audience, I penetrated into the château, when I had traversed three rooms as silent as tombs and passed under three Christs of black wood, behind a monk guide, when I was introduced into the presence of the judge in a room where there was a fourth Christ sculpted in the same somber oak, I nearly uttered a loud cry, thinking that I was hallucinating.

For the head of the inquisitorial judge of the Faith was sculpted in a block of bone analogous to the one that formed

31

my own skull. The same sculptor of nature had caused the cheekbones to stand out, emaciated the chin and hollowed out the eyes. I saw a face of icy parchment that resembled me. I was like a brother in the presence of his brother, but the brother I had before my eyes must have been raised by a pitiless father in a distant world, a planet of cold stone where all beings were virtuous and pity was unknown.

THE TWO BROTHERS

Alphonse Urraque the Dominican listened with extreme attention to what I had come to ask of him. He looked at me for a long time, and instead of replying to me he said: "Michel de Bramevaque, I've heard mention of you."

He took parchments from his table and riffled through them with his marble hands; then he put his index finger and one of them, leaned over it, read what was written there and murmured: "You are not a son of the Church."

Suddenly, he stood up, and I saw his eyes turn toward the south, looking through the window wide open to the autumn, in the direction of the mountains of the Ariège, where the Château of Montségur once stood.

"It's by that winding road that Raymond d'Alfaro the impious led a troop of men toward the Château d'Avignonnet."

"You're doubtless talking," I said, softly, "about Raymond d'Alfaro the bailiff, who was in command in Avignonnet more than three centuries ago?"

"He had with him Pierre Roger de Mirepoix, a most celebrated sinner, whose story is well-known; the Catalan Montagnol, who had lost an eye in his brigandage, one-eyed in his visage, blind in his soul; Pascal Malpinasse de Laurac, a man of war, who did not believe in God or the Devil, who had been paid to come because of his great love of killing; Porphyre de Lacabarède the troubadour, who had a musical instrument and a bloody sword in the same belt; and the wretched Espalion, who called himself a perfectus and was the most cowardly of all. When the time for punishment came in the prisons of Toulouse, he denounced so many accomplices that it would have been necessary to imprison all the inhabitants of the Ariège and the Lauragais."

"I believe that was done, Monsieur le Juge. Carved stones could no longer be found to build solid prisons. Those times are long dead, fortunately."

"The times of justice never die. Raymond d'Alfaro made his men drink before killing the guards by treason. Assassins often lack courage and they need to be in the darkness of intoxication in order to kill."

"That happened three hundred years ago and more, Monsieur le Juge Inquisiteur."

"Great crimes become more alive as time passes. Eleven monks, including two of my Order, were killed by night in this château, killed standing before the registers of the Inquisition, like warriors at war."

"Those registers of the Inquisition contained in their parchments so many deceitful denunciations, having welcomed hatreds as eagerly as proven verities, that many innocent people were burned in consequence, and the good Christians of the day considered them as books of injustice and death."

"When the pillage commenced, after they had broken down the doors, Guillaume Arnaldi, the man of God, ran through the rooms and appeared in the midst of the assassins. 'Is there one among you who will dare to strike me?' he said. And they all recoiled, fearfully. And perhaps they would have gone away, with a great shame in their souls. It was Raymond d'Alfaro who first spilled blood, by striking Guillaume Arnaldi in the heart. And it was the actor, Porphyre de Lacabarède, the troubadour of Mirepoix, who set fire to the registers of the Inquisition with his torch."

"To the reports of calumniators, the lists of those condemned to death."

"They dragged the bodies of the eleven along stone staircases, and the blood spurted very high."

"Monsieur le Juge Inquisitor, in those days, hatred possessed souls. From the blood of tortures, murders are born."

"Among the murdered eleven there were four envoys of the Pope, who holds the power of God himself."

"Among the men who struck there were some who would not have wanted to strike, but were sickened by injustice."

"Woe to those who committed the crime."

"Monsieur l'Inquisiteur de la Foi, they were tortured in Toulouse, they died horribly in the hands of the executioner in the Place Saint-Georges. And it was more than three hundred years ago! Where, then, is the dust of their bones? I have come to talk to you about a man of today, who has done no harm to anyone but himself."

"The sons shall be punished for the sins of the fathers, it is written in the book. There are sins that extend to the end of generations, and when the trumpet wakes the dead, all the progeny of the evil will be condemned."

"Never any remission, Monsieur le Juge Inquisiteur?"

"Never any remission. I will not take down the carcass of that descendant of a murderer, as you ask."

Alphonse Urraque had moved around the oak table that separated us. We were face to face. He was the same height as me and I saw the strange similitude of our faces even more clearly. The evening breeze came in through the window and dispersed the parchments, but he did not think of reassembling them. The wind had the odor of the soil of the Lauragais, an odor of maize and calcined stone. To the two men who were living in a dead past, it sang the living present and the eternal future.

Alphonse Urraque's eyes were too close to mine, and I understood by the terrible hardness of their steel what he was entering into my soul and seeing there.

"And why are you asking me to remove Raymond d'Alfaro from the gallows where he is swinging and commit his body to the earth?"

"Not in holy ground, Monsieur le Juge Inquisiteur, but in the common earth of men, which is blessed by no one, and where trees nevertheless grow."

"You are not of Alfaro's family, and if you are related to that suicide, it is only intellectually. Suicide is a great crime in the eyes of the Church."

"I know that it's a crime in the eyes of the Church Monsieur le Juge Inquisiteur."

"But perhaps you're one of those men who think that in killing oneself one saves oneself from the Hell that the earth is, and escapes to the hands of God."

"I think that there's no greater misery that what I see around me, and that there cannot be another world in which the hand of God has spread suffering more liberally."

"Monsieur descendant of Cathars, you're illogical with the principles of heresy. According to you, Raymond d'Alfaro the suicide has joined his brothers the Perfecti. What does it matter, then, that his wretched remains are swinging from the gallows of Avignonnet instead of reposing in the Christian cemetery? His soul is on high, his soul is far away."

"You're right, Monsieur l'Inquisiteur de la Foi."

Alphonse Urraque's hatred was palpitating around me like a devouring fire. I was certain that he could not contain himself, that he was about to start shouting in order to have me dragged away to some subterranean prison in the château.

I bowed before him profoundly and, in order to put an end to the scene and permit his fury to burst forth—for I no longer hoped to leave the place unharmed—I took a step toward the door. To my great surprise, he did not budge. I began to draw away; he remained as still as a statue. And I heard, while I walked under the weight of his gaze, that he took two or three steps behind me, and stopped on the threshold, on which he must have leaned, for the door did not close again.

I walked slowly. I reached the staircase, and every time my foot touched a step there was a resonant sound, as if age-old echoes were awakening. At the foot of the stairs I remained till for two or three seconds, under the magnetism of the eyes whose glare accompanied me. No order was shouted. No soldiers came running. I still advanced very slowly. A monk went past me without seeing me.

Finally, I went through the door. I saw the sunlight outside again.

THE GALLOWS

"The moon's rising now," said Tornebut. "There's a danger that the watchman on the ramparts will see us in the distance."

"The moon is rising to aid us. It isn't easy to recognize the living, and even less easy to recognize the dead."

The gallows were some distance from the road that goes from Toulouse to Carcassonne, in an old stone quarry. Not many people were hanged in the comté of Avignonnet, because the King's Seneschal was a man full of clemency. He had received the gift of tears, and anyone who was able to make him weep was set free.

The gallows were low and very ancient. They creaked when the wind blew and one wondered whether their old wood, eaten away by time, might collapse under the weight of the dead. Shaky and worn, with their ropes and their hooks, they resisted decrepitude, as simulacra of justice and symbols of punishment resist.

There were only three corpses suspended and Raymond d'Alfaro was like Jesus Christ between the thieves. Doubtless the executioner had stolen his garments, for his thin limbs and bare shoulders were visible.

The silhouette of the watchman was outlined on the ramparts.

As Tornebut climbed the gallows by means of the steps carved in the wood, the moonlight was suddenly extinguished. There was a sound of wings, and birds took flight, turbulently. The entire edifice of old beams started trembling and agitating, and I feared seeing it collapse, dragging the living and the dead with it.

"Don't make any mistake, Tornebut—cut the middle rope."

I heard his knife squeak against the rope, which resisted. It seemed to me to take a long time, but the dead man was finally detached, as if of his own accord, and fell silently, ending up sitting up in the stance of someone about to tell a story.

But he did not relate what he had seen in the realm that the dead traverse, nor the reason for which he had brought forward his hour, and he remained motionless, his hand seeming to indicate the mountains of the Ariège and the Château de Montségur to the south.

Then the moon lit up again. I could make out his face. Suspension by a rope does not deform the features any further if they have acquired *rigor mortis* beforehand. There is no torture for those who are dead. The inquisitor was mistaken. They only suffer the force of disaggregation that is within them, and which no one escapes. Raymond d'Alfaro was smiling: a smile scarcely sketched on his disenchanted lips; an infinitely sad smile. I regretted that he was not expressing joy and admiration because of the worlds that he had glimpsed at the moment when he quit the terrestrial region.

"How light he is!" said Tornebut, who had loaded him on to his back.

With the lantern that I had hidden under my cloak, I illuminated his footfalls in front of him, in order that he did not bump into stones.

"Be careful that light doesn't alert the soldier on watch," he said, again. "The spade on your shoulder looks like a musket, and he might mistake us for nocturnal thieves, one carrying the booty and the other the light and the weapon."

But the silhouette was as still as motionless as a scarecrow. We had taken a little path and I did not know where to go.

Then I heard the speech of two crows that were perched on a branch of a cork-oak. I sometimes understand the language of birds, but only on certain occasions, under the empire of an emotion, and as long as I say nothing about it to anyone else. Every time I pride myself on hearing the speech of an animal species, that speech ceases as soon as it becomes intelligible to me. I lent an ear, making a semblance of observing the direction from which the wind was blowing.

The first crow said: "Raymond d'Alfaro, the hanged man, would have been content to sleep in the shade of those old cypresses in which our dwelling is. He cherished the cypress wood, as he cherished crows. Men who hang themselves have such preferences for certain trees and certain birds."

And the second crow replied, assuredly for my benefit: "The old cypress where we dwell is situated to the right, next to the old stone wall that once enclosed the Alfaro estate. Men who hang themselves like to repose in what was once familial ground."

I believe that, by virtue of an incomprehensible mystery, birds know astonishing things, and possess truths that humans do not know. I made a sign to Tornebut to turn right and we saw a large cypress that was standing next to the vestiges of a wall.

Tornebut put the dead man down. I took the spade and we took turns to dig a grave for him. The ground was hard and stony, the work long and difficult, but the soldier on watch in the distance, did not budge in the nocturnal sky.

When the grave was dug, we laid Raymond d'Alfaro in it, and I put a cypress branch on his breast. We filled in the hole and erased the traces as best we could. For the dead are disinterred by ecclesiastical rancor as surely as by beasts of prey.

"We need to hurry, in order to get out of the comté of Avignonnet," I said to Tornebut.

We were walking rapidly when I heard an owl in a tree. It seemed to be addressing itself to me. Its snigger was ironic.

"Men who hang themselves are glad to feel their remains dried by the sun. Only their soul seeks darkness. And then, did he not sin in troubling the order of destiny?"

Perplexity filed my soul. I have learned from harsh experience that contradiction is not only in nature, but is the very essence of the divine soul.

THE QUEST FOR THE GRAIL

Certainly, many others before me had set out in quest of the Grail, but had not found it. If they had found it, humans would have begun to love one another. Cavaliers would have been seen on the roads announcing the good news. Animals would have been reconciled with their human brethren and birds would have come to peck on the tables of houses. But nothing of the sort was seen.

As certain people believed, the Grail could not have been transported over the sea to any other land of election. The soil of Toulouse is the most sacred, that which extends from Carcassonne with the towers of stone to the Pyrenees of the Seigneurs de Foix and beyond the Abbey of Comminges. It is there that the Celtiberians, bearers of hair that hung down to the ankles and which they braided at the base of their nape, had once brought the mystic riches of Delphi. In the inaccessible mountains of the Ariège, the Druids had hidden the Greek symbols along with the secrets that permitted them to deduce terrestrial events from the geometry of the stars. And it was to Carcassonne that Alaric transported the table of Solomon, the treasure of the original thought that the King of the Goths had taken from Rome, and which came from the temple of Jerusalem.

And later, four knights—no one knows why there are always four—came to the Château of Montségur, hiding under their cloaks the heritage of Joseph of Arimathea, the emerald in the form of a lily that contained the blood of Christ.

Why is it necessary that that part of the world should be the receptacle of all the talismans of divine order? Why did those who received the mission to guard them and transmit them think they would be safer there than elsewhere? That is a mystery that I cannot comprehend; but there are so many things that remain forever incomprehensible. Can one know why water is fluid and why fire is only manifest on certain occasions, in the wake of certain frictions?

It is reported in the traditions of the siege of Montségur that, during a stormy night, four Albigensians with courageous hearts were let down on ropes along the stony slopes, traversed the lines of the King's soldiers and escaped into the mountains. Those four men took away the Cathar treasure. It was not gold and precious stones, nor Church candlesticks and reliquaries, beauties made of metal, splendors made of silken thread and the damascened hilts of scimitars that the knights had brought back from the crusades. That treasure would have required carts pulled by all the oxen in Mirepoix and the valley of the Ariège, and it would have taken four long days for it to descend the flanks of Montségur. The treasure of the four nocturnal messengers was of an entirely different nature. It only required one man to carry it. And yet there were four, and the stories transmitted in the villages have retained the names of the four.

The first was Amiel Aicart; the second was named Poitevin; the third was named Hugues; and the name of the fourth was Alfaro. And tradition reports that while they were descending the ropes, Ramon de Perelha, the old man, and Pierre Roger de Mirepoix, the young man, who were in command of Montségur, the knights who fought under their orders and the soldiers who fought under the orders of the knights, and the Perfecti who did not fight and who prayed for the victory of the Holy Spirit, and the women in their white robes, and the old men tugging their beards, behind the broken crenellations, on the stone galleries, on the high towers of defense and the barbicans in the clouds, were all motionless, all leaning over silently, with the consequence that the château and its defenders—the entire mountain of Montségur—seemed to be struck by a enchantment.

And when, far away, on the other side of the valley, on the mountain of Bidort, a little flame sprang up to announce that the treasure was safe and that the four men who were carrying it had plunged into the impenetrable forests guarded by packs of wolves and long stone abysms, a great hymn surged from the breasts of the defenders of Montségur, a great hymn of gratitude, for now they could die, since the Grail was safe.

O Lord, the evil have triumphed and inexorable time has passed. But evil is never entirely the master, and even when it is believed to be victorious and the field is devastated and sterile, there is a small seed somewhere, a tiny forgotten seed, which awaits its hour to flourish and gives rise sooner or later to a tall tree.

And now it is me who has been chosen in order that the seed might flourish again. Is that because of the magical character of my staff, curved in the form of a crosier? It is impossible that it should be for that reason. Have I acquired great merit, unknown to myself, in caring for the sick or in doing good deeds here and there? But the good one does is a very small thing in the general economy and I am not even sure that it goes any further than only applying oneself to do good. The only virtue that is worth the trouble of being cultivated is the elevation of souls. But either for want of luck or because I have searched poorly, I have never encountered one elevated enough, any soul that merited receiving the divine fluid of the spirit.

However, the voice said: "Michel de Bramevaque, get up!"

It is up to me to find the lost Grail. There has been no further trace of it since the four Albigensians disappeared into the forests of Bidorta. What became of those four men? Did they have manor houses, castles or only shepherds' huts? Did they possess the secret of prodigious caves, or did they only dig a hole in there straw? Did they hide the Grail in an eagle's nest, or in a field, under a vine stock? In any case, the one who carried it on his breast must have lived for well over a hundred years, because of the force of life he had received. So that if, by questioning families and interrogating village traditions, one learned that a prodigious old man had lived far beyond the normal age, one might think that he was the one who, three centuries ago, had had the blood of Christ against his heart and had received physical life therefrom. Unless he was consumed by the incandescent effluvia emerging from the sacred emerald and he has been nothing but a little ash under the ground for a long time.

THE SIGNS ON THE EARTH

"You might tell me, Tornebut, that it is a singular thing that the Grail was hidden and that it is necessary to search for it with so much difficulty."

Tornebut nodded his head. He could have said that. It was pure chance that he had not said it.

"Alas, everything that is perfectly beautiful and immaculate, everything that is miraculous in nature, becomes a motive for covetousness for certain men who want to possess it, and a motive of hatred for others, who want to destroy it, in order that there should be less beauty in the world. But do you not think, Tornebut, that there will be signs, signs on the earth and perhaps in the sky, that will permit me to recognize its presence?"

Tornebut hastened to agree. He was certain that there would be manifest signs.

"Except that you might perhaps ask me, Tornebut, why the supernatural voice that ordered me to set forth in quest of the Grail did not inform me of its exact location, or at least give me some approximate indication."

Tornebut had not thought of asking such a question, but, in fact, since I mentioned it, his opinion was that the voice might have been more explicit, which would have saved us a great deal of trouble.

"Firstly, the spirit creature that gave me the order might be as ignorant as we are of where the Grail is to be found. Many invisible creatures see scarcely any further than humans. And if the one who addressed itself to me knew the location, perhaps it considered that the effort of the search was as indispensable as the success. There is no great deed without great difficulty. It is necessary to toil, with the body as well as he mind.

"Let us reflect, then, and be full of wisdom. If the blood of Jesus Christ has reposed for a long time in one place, there will be visible signs by which that place can be recognized.

What signs? A great miraculous force is attached to divine objects. The bodies of humans living in proximity with the Grail will be more perfect in form and attain a great longevity, and their souls will be excellent, endowed with more purity and charity than elsewhere. Thus, if we learn that there are astonishing old men in a village, and that men are better there than elsewhere, less harsh to their wives and more pious, we might think that a secret influence were acting in that place. For it is a well-known fact that physical matter stores the spiritual force of saints and that objects that belonged to great masters in times past retain a radiation of faith the approach of which gives faith to doubters and divine joy to those perspicacious enough to hope for it."

I saw that my words had cast Tornebut into an extreme disturbance. He agitated his arms and eyebrows like someone who has revelations to announce. And he announced them with a radiant visage.

"O my master, I can lead you straight to the place where the Grail is. For in that place, there was a man who was so good, and had a heart so pure that I've always thought that no one could be like that without some secret influence of divine origin."

"And who is that incomparable man? Can you take me to him right away?"

"Alas, he's dead." Tornebut's face filled with both sadness and pride. "He was my father. His father, grandfather and all our relatives were like him. All of them attained an extraordinary age, except for my father, who died in a fortuitous manner, for destiny willed it thus. It's in the village of Valentine on the bank of the Garonne that I was born. That village was full of astonishing old men with long white beards, and now that I think about it, I remember that that old age was abnormal and had an unexplained cause. I even wonder whether a certain number of those old men weren't immortal.

"Furthermore, in Valentine, everyone was good. The poor were helped. Children did no harm to birds. No stones were thrown at Saracens expelled from Spain, and the consuls even permitted several families of those bronzed pagans to settle on a stony hill and to sow wheat there, if it were able to grow. I left Valentine a long time ago, but I remember that all the girls were pretty, and that they didn't even lose that beauty with age. Now, as I've seen ugliness predominate over beauty everywhere in an overwhelming manner, I'm obliged to think that there was an extraordinary magic spell in Valentine that acted on forms to sculpt them marvelously."

"O Tornebut," I said, enthusiastically. "Let's not delay in going to Valentine."

THE VILLAGE OF VALENTINE

The village of Valentine displays its slate houses on the bank of the singing Garonne. The towers of Saint-Bertrand-de-Comminges and those of the Château de Barbazan are not very far away, and the traveler who arrives on foot along the road to Toulouse is struck by the blue tint that the shadows take on there.

"Places and people change rapidly," said Tornebut, "for I no longer recognize anyone. I left Valentine when I was fifteen years old."

Houses bordered the road to the left and the right. There were people on the thresholds but they were all middle-aged and had no appearance of immortality. Several women were exceptionally ugly. I looked at Tornebut from the corner of my eye and was struck by the sincere admiration reflected in his face. He seemed to be saying to me: *Well, you see! What did I tell you?*

I espied a man whose little eyes were shining and mobile beneath thick eyebrows, and who was sitting outside his door.

"What is that gray building on the hillside over which a crow is flying?" I asked him.

Unknown to me, that question made allusion to some burning local quarrel, for the man stared at me with irritation.

"Are you not an envoy of the Bishop of Saint Bertrand?" he said.

"Not at all—merely a traveler curious about things in Valentine."

"That gray building is the leprosarium that has been imposed on us by His Holiness the Bishop of Saint Bertrand. Valentine has been chosen to be a receptacle of lepers! And not only the lepers of the region but of the entire comté of Toulouse. For the Bishop of Saint Bertrand, Valentine is the leper capital! Once, someone wanted it to be the Saracen capital! Well, you can tell the Bishop, when you see him, that the lepers will have the same fate as the Saracens."

I raised my right arm and affirmed again to the old man that I had no connection with the Bishop of Saint Bertrand—but that arm was holding my long curved staff. Doubtless the ignorant man mistook it for an Episcopal crosier lent by the Bishop.

He had quit the little wooden bench on which he was sitting. A horrible joy dislocated his toothless jaw and made it rise up to an unusual height.

"You see that mountain that seems to be made of a single rock? When we were obliged to receive the pagans of Spain among us, our consul Magala said to the Seneschal of Toulouse: "We'll receive the pagans of Spain and we'll give them a mountain to cultivate, with grain to sow, on condition that they don't leave the mountain.

"They were given that rock, and they built their cabins there and they prayed to Mohammed. They were taken sacks of grain, and the entire village laughed. They sowed so many and so well that they all died. And behind the stone mountain there's a Saracen cemetery. Well, if you see crows above the leprosarium, it's because the lepers are in the process of dying there. And if you make a tour of that mount, you'll see that there's a cemetery of lepers there. For those are things that it would be good to let the Bishop know. The village of Valentine is made for the men of Valentine, born on the bank of the Garonne in the comté of Toulouse. Tell the Bishop that when you go back to him."

We continued walking among the houses and Tornebut led me along a narrow street to a place where a carpenter was working and where there was the trunk of a tree dead for a long time. The wood of the tree was entirely covered in little parallel lines. Tornebut considered it attentively and said:

"My grandfather and my great grandfather marked every year of their life on that tree with a little lines, so the track of their old age is inscribed in the wood. But children have amused themselves covering the entire tree with similar lines, so that it bears the signs of thousands of years, and the ages of my ancestors will be lost forever."

Suddenly, he fell to his knees and started pronouncing incoherent words, and I saw that his face was bathed by tears.

"What's the matter with you, Tornebut, and why are you striking the trunk of that tree with your head?"

"I'm weeping because of the harm I've done to my father. It's to this tree that he tied me in order to beat me for my sins. If I'd been laborious, if I'd done the work he gave me, I would have filled his soul with contentment and I wouldn't have obliged him to strike me."

"And did your father beat you hard?"

"Oh, hard and often. But the blows were in proportion to the faults."

"And did those blow leave traces?"

"Profound scars that are still visible. But it was necessary to get the evil out of my body."

We were interrupted by a snigger. The carpenter was on the threshold of his gloomy workshop and considering Tornebut, who was still on his knees.

"Certainly, his father beat him with a thick rope, in which he'd made a knot, and doubtless he deserved it, for a rotten seed gives birth to a seed even more rotten. That Tornebut, father of this Tornebut here, was the most evil man in the region, and he left Valentine between the Seneschal's soldiers to be hanged I don't know where."

Tornebut had stood up and he said in a loud voice: "He was the innocent victim of a false accusation."

"Tornebut the son can't be worth any more than Tornebut the father. I don't want the air I breathe to be sullied by the scion of such a line. Get out of here, or you'll repent of having returned to Valentine."

People had appeared at doors and windows. The name of Tornebut had rendered their faces menacing. A stone, and then another, were thrown in our direction.

"Come," I said to my companion, and hastened to draw him away.

When we were some distance away, and saw the Tour de Saint-Gaudens in front of us, I said to him, gently: "Perhaps the inhabitants of Valentine don't have the excellence of heart that you attributed to them?"

"One or two ewes aren't the flock," Tornebut was content to reply.

"Perhaps your father hadn't quite attained the great sanctity that you were pleased to recognize in him?"

"A great saint can be hanged. Wasn't Jesus Christ crucified?" Tornebut was content to reply—and he walked more rapidly, so that I had difficulty keeping up with him.

Then the light dawned within me.

"Don't walk so quickly, Tornebut—I'm having difficulty keeping up."

GUILLAUME AICART AND THE STORKS

Curés have certain registers in which they record marriages, births and deaths. Unfortunately, the Huguenots burned many of those registers, doing harm to genealogies and the knowledge of the past.

The curé of Tarascon in the Ariège was a wise old man who had fled when his church was pillaged, but he remembered the registers that he had consulted out of curiosity.

"The centuries are long," he told me, "And there are a great many men. I can't swear that I've seen the name of Amiel Aicart, but there were still Aicarts in Tarascon. Soon there won't be any more of them, though—the only one who still has that name is very old and has no children. He's a solitary and stubborn man; you won't get much out of him. He doesn't come to the church, nor does he belong to the reformed religion."

We were staying at the inn and we set out walk as far as the house of that Guillaume Aicart, a low house that was at the extremity of the town, on the bank of the Ariège.

The curé was right. There was so little to get out of him that I thought he was going to throw us out. But he did not have the energy. I came back several times. At hazard, in the end I made him party to the objective of my visit. Was there not in the Aicart family, to his knowledge, a spiritual heritage that was transmitted, and west back to the time of his ancestor Amiel Aicart, who had lived three centuries ago?

That question changed my interlocutor's attitude completely. He ceased to simulate deafness and gave evidence of keen hearing. And it was him who heaped me with questions. Why had I come? What did I want? What did I know?

That day, Tornebut had not accompanied me. On the way, I had perceived Guillaume Aicart on the bank of the Ariège, his head raised, watching the sky attentively. I had approached him, parting the bushes that enclosed his garden. His sudden animation betrayed his old age—for old age is sometimes hidden beneath the features, like genius beneath the colors of a master painting, and only appears if the elements are stirred by the effort of the soul.

Guillaume Aicart was older than I had thought and I understood that all the better when he began to talk to me about his youth. He spoke about it without joy, He cursed his family and the errors they had made him commit. He had been haunted by remorse all his life because of a sin of his youth. And that related to the questions I had just asked him, questions that resuscitated his remorse.

Yes, there was a secret that the Aicarts transmitted from father to son. His father, Martin Aicart, had been on the point of revealing it to him several times. He had hesitated, putting it off until later. He thought him to young, too frivolous.

"I was," he told me, sadly. "And by virtue of a singular state of mind, I was proud of it. Youth had such a price for me that I considered that any word coming from my father could not have any great importance. Then evil entered my life in the form of a woman. She was a Spaniard. It was sufficient for her to sing for me to go mad. A moment came when my father sensed that he was going to die. I was with him. But it was the very evening when it was agreed that I would accompany the woman to Andorra, where she was to go over the passes on the back of a mule.

"I had sent word to her not to count on me, that I would stay with my father, but she came along the road anyway, singing a refrain that was a signal for us to meet. My father had taken my hand. 'I have something to tell you,' he murmured. His voice was already like a whisper. I would have been able to hear him by making an effort, but I listened to the refrain on the road and calculated the distance that the woman singing it had to travel. My father spoke for quite a long time. I nodded to signify that I had understood—but I had not heard anything except the refrain.

"It was only much later that I felt the vanity of youth falling away from me like a garment. Then the secret came back to my mind, but too late. It had passed alongside me and I had disdained it. And that is why I cannot tell you anything."

Guillaume Aicart described his remorse to me all the more obligingly because he was conscious that no one could understand him. While he was speaking he stopped sometimes to look at the sky in a northerly direction.

As I was about to quit him he made me a sign to stay.

"One last hope remains to me. Oh, very vague…so vague…I hardly dare express it to you. Shortly before my father's death, an injured stork fell into the garden, at this point. It was the time when those birds migrate. That one had a broken foot. My father cared for it, and attached a small splint to the leg; he managed to cure it. He was absolutely alone then. All his contemporaries were dead, as all mine are now. I've told you that his son….

"He was smitten with a great affection for that stork. He spent every day with it. He told it stories, exactly as if he were dealing with a sentient individual. People who saw him from a distance thought he was mad. Only storks are like humans. When that one was completely cured, it flew away. It circled in the air above the garden and departed southwards. My father followed it with his eyes. I saw a tear run into his beard and he sat down at the place where the stork had the habit of standing, on one foot.

"Well, the stork came back. It was in spring, when vast numbers of birds pass over. There was another stork with it, almost the same size, and two others, very small. But the stork my father had cared for was quite recognizable, because it limped as it walked. My father's joy was immense. He had installed a sort of nest on the water's edge and he talked to them all the time, as if he were addressing humans. The storks spent one night there, but flew away in the morning all the same. They described a circle again, and then departed northwards.

"In following them with the eyes, it was easy to recognize the one that was leading the little troop, one of whose legs seemed to be longer than the other. I don't know whether they came back. I might not have been there to see it, and my father died immediately after their departure. But would you like me to tell you the idea I have? Perhaps you'd think that I don't have all my reason. That's possible, in fact, and of no importance at my time of life. Well, I think the storks took away my father's secret. I'm sure that he confided it to them, and almost sure that they understood.

"There's a great mystery in birds. Birds can even penetrate human thoughts, but only if those thoughts are of an elevated order. No one has ever been able to explain what the nightingale expresses. It attains the superior elements of the soul. It seems to go even further than humans. Naturally, it's only a few species of birds—not always those that have admirable songs. Thus, among us, those who are closest to God are not those who tell everyone so.

"Now, my father once told someone that storks were the most intelligent of birds, and perhaps the most intelligent of all creatures. He had a reason for saying that. For years he studied birds, but without ever depriving one of its liberty, even for a few minutes. I'm convinced that my father told the storks what his son had not even understood. And my unique hope before dying is that those birds might bring me, I don't know by what signs or what form, my father's spiritual heritage."

I was careful not to allow the slightest smile of doubt to appear on my face, for there is in every chimera, not matter how implausible, a consoling element. As I quit Guillaume Aicart, I even made a semblance of looking attentively at the part of the sky that I had seen him considering.

"We can go," I said to Tornebut, when I met him again. "We won't learn anything here." And I told him everything that Guillaume Aicart had said to me.

When we had been walking for some time, Tornebut, who had reflected, said to me: "It's possible that he's right. Birds live in the sky. Why shouldn't they have more knowledge than men of celestial things?"

THE CHEVALIER DE POUCHARRAMET

I had always heard talk of the Chevalier de Poucharramet as a man full of wisdom. People came from afar to consult him when a difference arose. He had a library with very ancient books. Protestants and Catholics alike said: "He's a man of God!" Even judges interrogated him. He possessed the measure of all things.

He had ended up growing old, to such an extent that one day, he died. But reputations have more duration and resistance than the men themselves. The absence of such a just seigneur was an inconvenience for the region. As he had a son similar to him in all respects, although a little younger, taller and more solidly built, with a red and slightly puffy face and a shiny pate, the qualities left disposable by the father were attributed to the son, and after a short interval the two Poucharramets were confounded into one: a seigneur filled with wisdom, red in the face and possessed of a large library.

I was not very sure myself that one Poucharramet was dead when I went to see him in his château, which was a good half day's march from Toulouse.

"You might find an indication in Poucharramet's library," Isaac Andréa had said to me.

I walked quickly, to be sure, but autumn preceded me along the banks of the Touch and through the hoary vines of the region of Rieumes and Muret.

The Seigneur de Poucharramet received me in front of a large fire that had only just been lit and whose flames gave his face the color of new wine. In the fireplace, which was as tall as him, there was a pile of large books as high as the mantelpiece. From time to time he picked one up by the edges of the pages and threw it into the flames.

When I displayed astonishment he said: "My valet Bourtoumieu is an idler. He leaves the fire without dry wood. I have to stand in for a slothful servant." And he burst into loud laughter.

Then I knew that the real Poucharramet was dead and that I was only in the presence of an unsuccessful imitation.

After a period of glory, the church of Poucharramet had known days of dilapidation. Poucharramet the father had left a large sum of money in order that the church could be restored and become once again what it had been when the Knights Hospitaller had built it.

The stained glass windows were falling apart. The great portal no longer closed. Owls had built their nests in one off the lateral chapels and one of those birds, dazzled, had once fallen on to the altar while the curé was saying mass, with a loud clatter of wings, at the moment of the offering.

However, Poucharramet the son said nothing about that. Something singular had happened to him. He had always been pious, orderly and slightly timid. Since the death of his father, however, a new man had been born within him. He lived in deregulation. He had started running after women, and a certain impiety had even become manifest in him. He had been heard to say things like: "One can pray as well in a church open to the wind as a church firmly sealed, and if Our Lord descends into the host, a flying owl won't put him off."

When he was going to Toulouse on his mare the color of wine-lees he said to his valet Bourtoumieu: "I'll be back tomorrow for supper." But days passed without him coming back. Then, he no longer quit the back-street behind Saint Sernin where the Saracen dancers were and women whose profession is to drink until morning. Once he stayed so long that people at Poucharramet became anxious. The consul Jean Nogarol decided to go to Toulouse in person to search for his seigneur.

"Don't worry, worthy people. I'll bring the chevalier back."

Days went by, and he consul did not come back.

"I'll go in quest of him myself," said the curé, who was a member of the Mascaon family and liked Poucharramet the son for his reputation for wisdom, but most of all because he liked a good time, as he did himself.

Days went by, and the curé did not come back. At Poucharramet there was no seigneur, no consul and no curé. Now, the time came for Cassuéjouls the fruit-merchant, who was nicknamed the Taciturn, to go to Toulouse to sell his peaches. He took his largest cart—he usually took a smaller one—and simply said to the people of Poucharramet: "When I've sold my peaches I'll bring all three of them back."

"But where will you find them, Cassuéjouls?"

"Oh, I know where to find them."

Because he did not say much, Cassuéjouls was thought not to know anything, so the people of Poucharramet were very surprised two days later, when he brought back the seigneur, the consul and the curé in the bottom of his big cart. The wine-lees mare was following behind, on the end of a rope.

"How did you do it, Cassuéjouls?" people exclaimed from their doorways.

But Cassuéjouls was not talkative, and was also discreet. "Don't worry about that. The essential thing is that they're back."

The Chevalier de Poucharramet only decided to undertake the work on the church when the Bishop of Comminges intervened personally. And then—no one knows why, perhaps to annoy the Bishop—he decided that the church that was to be reconstructed would be a fortified church, which required immense labor.

"But why a fortified church, Monsieur le Chevalier?" the consul asked him.

"Do you know that the Saracens once came knocking at the church of Poucharramet, and that the men of Comminges were able to hold them at bay because it was a fortress?"

The consul and everyone else were unaware of that. "But the Saracens are no longer to be feared!"

"In the time of the Albigensians, the church was still a fortress, and I can show you on certain stones the traces of bolts left by the evil Simon de Montfort's crossbows."

"Those days were a long time ago, Monsieur le Chevalier."

"Fifty years ago, in Pamiers, the Jesuits were massacred in their convent by the Protestants. What wouldn't they have given to have had a fortified church?"

And he started to draw up plans, with towers at the corners and deep ditches."

"The sum left by your father won't be sufficient," his alarmed friends told him.

"It's not a matter of that derisory sum. The consul will find the money! The Bishop of Comminges will find the money!"

And he summoned to Poucharramet a large community of construction workers based in Carcassonne—people who liked nothing better than building and destroying in order to build, people who had to other reason for being than the edification of monuments.

The works took on an extent so vast that anxiety took possession of souls. A fortified church! And no one knew who was going to pay for it? Would it be the Bishop of Comminges, on his treasury, the consul, by means of taxes, the seigneur who had launched the affair, or perhaps the King of France? It would be necessary to refer the matter to the Parlement de Toulouse, and it was well known that those who addressed themselves to the Parlement were doomed forever, on earth and in Heaven.

The constructors were installed as masters and turned the region upside down. They quarreled with the peasants and there was no poor man leaning over his plow who did not think, on seeing the immense scaffolding of the fortified church from afar, that the works were being carried out at his expense and that he was only laboring for them.

"The Chevalier de Poucharramet is such a wise man!" people said.

Everything depended on that wisdom. That was what permitted people to live with a residue of hope—but only until the day when Cassuéjouls the Taciturn, who as a man of common sense, said in the public square; "Eh! It was Poucharramet the father who was wise! Of that wisdom, he's only left his son the weight of an autumn plum of which the sun has eaten the flesh and caterpillars the stone."

Now, Cassuéjouls had to be a knowledgeable judge, having brought the chevalier back from Toulouse. From that day on, the fortified church became more menacing over the village, its shadow took on an extraordinary extent and covered the entire area, and everyone bore the weight of its bell-tower on his shoulders.

The culmination came when pride took possession of the soul of the Chevalier de Poucharramet the son. Seeing so many workmen at the old church, like bees around a hive, and seeing the upheaval he had caused and the orders of which people came to the château in search, an intoxication of an insensate character gripped him, and was manifest in a rather singular fashion.

The choir of the church was closed by very ancient statues representing, in a primitive fashion, Jesus Christ, the apostles and the characters of the passion. Over time, the arms and legs of some statues having been detached, the head of the Christ was only posed on his body, from which it had once been separated by the Saracens.

The Chevalier de Poucharramet decided to have the statues entirely remade. For that he summoned Thomas Capellan in person, the great artist of Toulouse. The latter set to work immediately, and by virtue of divine inspiration, he began with the head of Jesus Christ, which he sculpted marvelously, and into which he put the beauty he had conceived.

However, when the Chevalier de Poucharramet saw that head in the choir, he flew into a great rage. He seized it in his arms and threw it on to the paving stones some distance away—for he wanted the head of Jesus Christ to have his own features! He wanted to substitute himself for God in the church!

"Haven't I given you the order?" he said to Thomas Capellan.

He had, in fact, said that, but it was so implausible to represent Jesus Christ with the face of a fat, bald and red-faced seigneur that Thomas Capellan had taken no account of it and had sculpted in accordance with his inner vision.

The head had broken into several pieces and Thomas Capellan wanted to reunite them and replace them on Jess Christ's shoulders. He thought it was a temporary folly. But the Chevalier prevented him from doing so and ordered him to set to work to sculpt his own head. When Thomas Capellan refused, he drew his sword and, menacing him, he ordered him to commence immediately or say his prayers. Under the threat of the sword, Thomas Capellan was obliged to make a sculpted simulacrum. Leaving the pieces of the marvelous head of Christ, in which there was broken beauty, on the ground. When night fell he ran away to Toulouse, and was never seen in Poucharramet again.

It is impossible to know what might have happened if order had not returned, both to the region and the Chevalier de Poucharramet's head. It returned in an unexpected and mysterious form, from which I was able to obtain an advantage. This is how the Chevalier described the event to me himself.

THE FOUR NOCTURNAL CLERICS

It was very cold that evening, and I was sitting next to the fire, face to face with the Chevalier.

"I have a simple soul and I don't like enigmas," he said to me. "You've done well to come. Perhaps you can give me an explanation. You have the reputation of being a knowledgeable man and, I don't know why, the form of your staff gives me confidence in you. But who can one trust nowadays? People are afraid, and no longer dare venture anything. Valets become idle and renounce their work."

Having said that, the Chevalier de Poucharramet took a quarto bound in black, with chimeras on the cover, and threw it into the fireplace, where it almost stifled the fire at first.

"Seigneur," I cried, "If Bourtoumieu is hunting or collecting winter pears in the orchard, I'll go myself to look for firewood, but please don't destroy these precious books."

"I'd give them all to the Devil! My father wasted so much time consulting them, annotating them and—who knows?—perhaps reading them, that he forgot our estate and left our lands to lie fallow. And that's why the church is in the state it's in. But listen to what happened. It was a little while ago. One morning, Bourtoumieu said to me: 'There'll be four guests at supper this evening.' I thought he meant friends from Toulouse who had plotted some surprise, and, in order to let the surprise take effect, I didn't ask him anymore. Otherwise, I wouldn't have been surprised.

"'Bourtoumieu,' I said, make sure to have roast pheasants, and get out a few bottles of that old Saint Girons wine, the one that our curé prefers.'

"I noticed that Bourtoumieu was manifesting a certain anxiety, but when he replied: 'These guests only drink pure water,' I thought it was part of the joke and the plot of the jovial friends from Toulouse.

"When night fell—there are always coincidences in such cases—it was a darker night than usual, I heard the sound of a

61

horse and I perceived through the window the large silhouette of a unknown man. 'Is that one of the guests?' I said to Bourtoumieu.

"'Assuredly, that's one of them.'

"I saw a tall, thin man with a black capeline, with an air of importance, but that of a notary or a judge in the Parlement, a kind of man with which I don't associate, and who might indeed be a drinker of water. All four of them arrived successively, the four guests that I hadn't invited, similarly dressed in black, as grave as cypresses over tombs, and they stood in the great hall, stiff and silent.

"'Bourtoumieu, can you tell me who the devil these fellows are, these four nocturnal clerics come from who knows where?'

"'They're friends of your father—although friends might be saying too much. They came every four years or so to sup with him, and it was usually the Eve of Saint John. And that evening, when they didn't come, your father left on a journey, which made me suppose that he was going to sup with them somewhere else—but where, God alone knows.'

"The wine—no, the water—was poured; it was necessary to drink it. I made the four grave men welcome and I told them to sit down. They scarcely replied to me. The meal was taciturn, and I sometimes winked at Bourtoumieu. But the fellow served gravely, and with such great respect, that in the end I was intimidated myself, and the conversation, which languished, gave way to an oppressive silence.

"I was wondering why those water-drinking guests had come to have supper in my house, when they got up to leave. Bourtoumieu went diligently to fetch their cloaks, and I felt the formulae of politeness dry up on my lips.

"It was then that one of them, who hadn't opened his mouth but whose sparkling eyes I had noticed, placed his hand on my shoulder, as if I were a child. I have difficulty explaining, and have trouble believing, what happened. Exactly as if I were a young child, he reprimanded me severely for my conduct, and in the tone of a man who commands he gave me orders regarding the fashion in which I ought to live, the construction of the church that I had to complete and the head of Christ that ought to resemble Christ and not my own head, as had been my fantasy.

"Take note that he was a man without a sword, a kind of cleric, who wouldn't have weighed more than a feather in my hand. And if you tell me that there were four of them I'll reply that I've fought bodily with bears that come down in winter from Venasque and La Picade, and I'm not afraid of four men of war accustomed to fighting. But it wasn't a matter of that.

"I remained child-like before that man; I stammered I know not what excuses; I replied that I'd obey his orders. And he didn't utter a word. I believe, though, that he said: 'That's good.' Bourtoumieu had had the horses brought forward. The night was pitch dark, as I told you. They disappeared as people in a dream disappear.

"Well, I haven't talked to my valet about it since, and he hasn't breathed a word to anyone. There's an agreement between us, which we haven't made. Also, he heard a part of the remonstration, and I'd rather leave it at that. You can believe me if you wish, but I've given orders for the church. I've sent away the builders from Carcassonne. I would have liked, though, to have my head in the choir in the midst of the twelve apostles. The old head of Christ that the Saracens once cut off has been replaced, because—I don't know why—Thomas Capellan doesn't want to come back. I'm obeying those men in black, who might perhaps have been envoys of the Devil. Can you, who are a learned man, tell me anything about them? Do you know them? Are there people who know them? Why do they go to supper in châteaux, just like that, in order to give lessons and leave?

"Oh, I forgot—on the table, at the place where the one who had sparkling eyes was sitting, I found a cut rose, slightly crumpled: a large fresh rose."

LUCIDA DE DOMAZAN

I was sitting under a cypress and meditating on death, because that is an important subject with which it is appropriate to occupy oneself.

A demoiselle clad in white passed by, on a black horse with a white mane.

"Where are you going, Demoiselle, on this Pyrenean road, at an hour when the song of the torrents is melancholy and the wind descends along the slopes of the valleys slowly?"

"I could ask you what you're doing, Monsieur Traveler with a large staff, sitting alone under a cypress in a meadow strewn with immortelles—but I don't like questions. Since you want to know, I'm going to the Château de Bramevaque in the valley of Larboust, a valley that plunges into the mountains, ones that are so high and so charged with cold clouds that all the lakes there are frozen."

"That's an extraordinary coincidence!" I couldn't help exclaiming.

And I considered the demoiselle on the horse. Her beauty filed the soul with admiration. I'm not talking about the elegance of her body, whose forms were elevated by youthful ardent life, but a radiation that emanated from noble facial features, in which intelligence flowed. It required a penetrating attention to notice a certain emptiness in the admirable steel of the eyes.

"Do you know those ruins by any chance? In that case, can you tell me whether the valley of Larboust is really the one that is on the left when one has passed the village of Cazaril, which is suspended on the flank of the mountain like a clump of box on a wall?"

"The valley of Larboust will be on your left after Cazaril and after La Chapelle de Saint-Aventin. But one can encounter bad men on these roads."

"My horse is a redoubtable animal, which would bite anyone who attacked me. Nothing happens when one is not afraid."

"And the Château de Bramevaque is nothing but a ruin in the midst of the firs."

I was on the point of telling her that I was the Seigneur de Bramevaque. I strive to appear to be a vagabond for the sake of humility, but that is more difficult before a woman, especially—I don't know why—if she is on horseback. It is very little to be the seigneur of an abandoned château, but I could have added negligently that I had a beautiful house in Toulouse and that I cared for the sick there. And yet I said nothing.

The demoiselle's face brightened, as if a lamp had approached it. She made her horse rear up and said: "It appears that the master of that château is a sort of madman who is looking for something without knowing exactly what, something that he might perhaps have found by remaining in his château."

My words reentered into myself of their own accord, like servants who have been summoned prematurely. As the young woman thought that I had nothing more to tell her, and that I was just some man meditating under a cypress, she made me a sign with her riding-crop and drew away without haste. At a bend in the road I noticed that she turned back, making a little sign. For, although I am detached from women and have vanquished desire, I inscribe involuntarily on certain obscure tablets of my soul the sympathy of certain gestures and the quality of certain gazes. Those tablets are useless, but they are there nevertheless. In the same way, there are astronomers who note the movements of the stars in cosmological books that will never be of any use to anyone.

Tornebut, who had lain down behind a little stone wall to sleep, got up and said: "It seemed to me that an angel passed along the road."

"Angels don't travel on horseback, Tornebut."

65

"But they're dressed in white and disappear when one wants to contemplate them."

"Whence comes this knowledge of angels?"

"A man who works with wood has a vision of the angels of the wood. They're small in stature, no taller than a large boot. They're puerile and they're dreamers. One perceives them in the evening, but only if one hasn't done anything bad for a long time."

And suddenly, I remembered. The features of a woman I had only seen once returned to the surface of my memory. Thus, in certain deep rivers, there are victims of drowning who float with their hair trailing behind them, and sometimes they return to the light, only to disappear a little further away. Memory is like a river with traveling images.

That demoiselle on horseback was Lucia de Domazan.

"She's neither an angel nor a woman," I said to Tornebut, looking into the distance along the road, where there was a little cloud of dust.

"What is she, then?"

"I don't know."

THE EVOCATION OF THE DEAD

It was three years before, and Lucida de Domazan had been very young then. She had been three years younger, you will say—but no. Three years are only a rapid dream for an old man, but they are an interminable interval for an adolescent.

Now, that adolescent with the beautiful face, that Lucida, full of grace and enveloped by an enigma as if by a shawl with bizarre designs, was the daughter of the rich Domazan, loved by priests, who had a notorious commerce with the dead. He was not troubled for his necromancy because of his liberality to convents, his subsidies to Chapters and his individual gifts slipped into the hands of churchmen. He was a former King's Seneschal. Everything is permissible with that title. He had even acquired in growing of a certain reputation for sanctity and it was whispered in ecclesiastical society that he had a special permission from God to converse with those who were no more.

But there was a great mystery in that, denied by some, affirmed by others, and which was resolved in numerous masses. For not a week went by when Domazan did not make the acquaintance of some dead man, a great sinner when alive, who was demanding prayers. The masses were said in a little chapel of the Cathedral of Saint Étienne, which seemed specially affected to souls in torment, clients of the rich Domazan.

Now, one night in that year, Isaac Andréa had come on Domazan's behalf to ask me to be present at one of the rendezvous given to him—I have no idea how—by formless creatures in habitants of the afterlife. It was because of my medical knowledge that I was summoned to that meeting. For everyone knows that nothing but bad things can result, for the body and the soul, from commerce between the living and the dead.

When I went out, the wind being chilly, I put a garnache over my shoulders—a garment of our ancestors fallen into disuse—and I covered my head with an old-fashioned cloth hat, with the result that I looked like a man of a previous century.

We did not go to Domazan's dwelling, but went through the Porte Arnaud Bernard and walked across the waste ground outside the ramparts as far as a wooden gate at the extremity of a little path, which gave access to a courtyard surrounded by dilapidated walls. In the moonlight, I saw that the place was abandoned. An old gnarled fig-tree was near the gate. It could never have yielded any figs, and it seemed to say that there were only exceptional things in the world that evening, that the lantern hanging from one of its branches had only just been placed there, and that, ordinarily, everything around it was shadow, misery and solitude.

We opened the door of a single-story building and went into a room illuminated by a single lantern. Four or five men were gathered gravely around the former Seneschal, as well as a jaundiced and wrinkled woman in a cornet and wimple, the same color as her face. They were talking in low voices and in the corner, sitting on a chair, there was something like a little silver cloud—and that cloud was Lucida de Domazan.

Another very venerable individual arrived, who was the castellan of Bouconne and a member of the Parlement, the oldest and most rigid in that assembly. It appeared that the company was complete, and everyone declared that they were only present with a pious intention and with the aim of soothing souls in torment, for everyone feared being suspected of sin himself, everyone knowing full well that he was about to approach the diabolical region in which those abandoned by the Lord live.

The pious Domazan said a *Pater* in a loud voice, but it was a *Pater* that rang false, devoid of wings, which did not rise up. I saw Espinasse emerge from the shadows, who spoke Greek, Hebrew and Arabic too, and was not prevented by that knowledge of languages from being very thin, in the manner of those who eat very little, not out of penitence but involuntarily. He was proud of playing an important role and he extended his bony hand above Lucida's head.

I had heard talk of these gatherings and I knew that many gave no results. Everyone then went his own way to sleep. It was necessary to wait for a long time, but a moment came when I felt with my senses that invisible presences were gliding around us

Espinasse's special power consisted of permitting those creatures, which were deceased individuals that had been wandering for an indeterminate time, to express themselves through the mouth of the suave Lucida. The young woman's delicate lips then took on the accent of the dead person, even if it was hoarse and vulgar, beyond the possibilities of Lucida's oral creation. Everyone present shook their heads then, remarking that particularity as a marvel of the occult order.

The first words that resounded, transmitted by Lucida's throat, were words of terror. They were halting, and I understood poorly at first, because of my lack of familiarity with that transmission of language.

But Domazan lunged toward me and, to my extreme surprise, he snatched the cloth hat from my head and instructed me sharply to take off my garnache. The subtle spirits of the dead retain a confused visibility of the living. That one had perceived he silhouette of a man dressed as in his own time and was doubtless afraid of having to recommence life.

He calmed down, said other things—he or another, I don't know. For it seems that the discourse of the dead is often filled with mediocrity and scarcely merits attention, except occasionally, of course.

The scene was approaching its end when Lucida uttered a great sigh, so full of terror that the entire group approached her. I saw her then at close range, so beautiful but still a child, and I contemplated for a second the extent of the spaces of her eyes, in which there was depth, and perhaps stars.

She repeated: "No! No!" and writhed beneath Espinasse's extended hand. He gave me the impression of a torturer, but no one else judged him thus, for I heard around me:

"She's refusing to say something!"

"It's necessary to force her to speak!"

"Make her say what has to be said!"

In the end, Lucida seemed resigned, or rather, she was possessed by the entity that had something to say. The young woman stood up with a sudden gravity in her visage, her voice became profound, and it was herself that she summoned three times: "Lucida!"

Everyone was attentive. She looked into herself, and said: "Lucida! I'm giving you an order! Cease committing incest with your father!"

Espinasse's hand fell back. A great silence descended.

I put on my garnache and hat in haste, thinking that it would be better had the dead person been inconvenienced and those words had not been pronounced. The head of the castellan of Bouconne seemed to me to be suddenly elongated, and the face of the jaundiced woman even more jaundiced. I tugged Isaac Andréa's sleeve. Outside, we walked with a long stride. The church of the Minimes chimed in the tranquil night.

"It is imprudent to make the living speak," said Isaac Andréa softly, "and even more imprudent to make the dead speak."

THE CHÂTEAU DE BRAMEVAQUE

In the valley of Larboust, beyond La Chapelle de Saint-Aventin, the Château de Bramevaque stands at the place where the peak of Agude extends the tip of its shadow at noon. It would be more accurate to say that it perches. The wind that blows from the direction of Oueil has caused all the slates to fall from its tower, and that tower now seems to lean to the right, as if to attest that it is not a proud tower and only dominates henceforth an abandoned dwelling.

The Château de Bramevaque is reached by means of a long rising avenue of beeches—the very beeches that, in the time of my childhood, were afflicted by a disease specific to beeches, a strange malady causing the stunting and twisting of sylvan limbs, and a reddish tint in the leaves, as if their sap were carrying blood.

When I appeared in the avenue of beeches, I saw that they were no better, that they were as twisted as before, prey to that fiery disease of the vegetal realm, which knots and wrings, and gives an aspect for fury.

The hour was becoming crepuscular. Nocturnal birds were beginning to snigger in the nearby forests. The great shadows of the evening that descend from the mountains ceased to move and took on the terrible mobility that announces the advent of night. In the distance, shepherds were calling to invisible flocks in voices emerging from who knows where.

Oppressed by the desolation of the place, I asked Tornebut if he knew why we had come, and he replied that he did not know. I was accustomed to act in accordance with interior intuitions. Something had driven me to return to the château where I had spent my childhood. Perhaps I had some information to receive there, and sometimes, such information is received unwittingly.

We had arrived at the perron. Tornebut pointed out to me that several horses must have been browsing the vegetation.

The door had been broken a long time ago, but one of the battens had been moved aside recently in order to give passage to visitors who, reluctant to bend down, had only wanted to enter with heads held high.

And indeed, when we walked through the empty rooms, in which only the phantoms of furniture remained, we were able to distinguish signs in the dust that several individuals had passed through the ruin, seemingly so recently that I stopped several times to listen, thinking that I had heard the footsteps of the visitors in question resonated in some distant room.

But no—we really were alone with the shadows that entered and wandered here and there.

I waited for an inspiration, of the kind that come to come when necessary—but perhaps it was not necessary, for none came.

I cast a final gaze over the once-familiar but now dead rooms, and I said to Tornebut: "Once there were packs of wolves that came down all the way to the park of the château. Perhaps they've retained that habit. We'll go to the village of Saint Aventin to request hospitality from benevolent men who knew my father, the Seigneur de Bramevaque."

And as I darted one last glance at what had once been called the trophy room. I saw that there was a large freshly-cut rose on the mantelpiece.

I picked up the flower and we went down the avenue of beeches in silence.

Later, we saw a man sitting on the threshold of a thatched cottage. He was a man of the land, thickset, whose hair began at his eyebrows.

I stopped and asked him to tell me whether he had seen, since sunrise, travelers heading toward Bramevaque—for no human being haunted that solitary location and I was sure that if anyone had taken the avenue of dolorous beeches, it would have given rise to many comments, for a long time, around the hearths of Saint Aventin.

The man with no forehead made a great effort to direct his thoughts and permit them to take on oral form. Yes, he had seen a young woman dressed in white passing on horseback. She had come and gone again. Then he had seen four horsemen dressed in black. They had gone to the château, but they had not come back by the same route. He had perceived them on a dangerous path, in the far distance, above the Val d'Arun, in the region of the highest lakes. They were bound to get lost in the stone corridors of Crabioules, for there were eagles there to make you lose your reason and fall to the bottom of the abysms of the mountain.

A young woman dressed in white! Four horsemen in black! So others than me had been driven toward the ruins of Bramevaque.

We were approaching the lights of Saint Aventin. I said to Tornebut: "Perhaps this journey was futile. I found nothing at the château."

But he replied: "Don't you have a freshly-cut rose in your hand?"

THE NIGHT OF THE WOLVES

As I could not sleep in the barn in which the worthy people of Saint Aventin had installed us I got up silently and went out.

The moonlight designed the contours of the trees and the sinuosities of the path, and I walked with a long stride, sure of my goal, having the secret knowledge that I had to find myself alone that night, and not another, in the Château de Bramevaque. I traversed the avenue of diseased beeches and then the overgrown paths of the garden, and I uttered a sigh of satisfaction when I was on the perron of my ruined dwelling.

But immediately, I made the reflection that if I had some reason for hope, its cause was entirely unknown to me. And with a gripping rapidity and an extreme precision, certain memories of childhood returned to my mind. Those memories had to do with the presence of wolves in the neighboring forests.

Throughout the winter, they could be heard howling only a short distance from the house. But on one snowy night, they had invaded the garden in considerable number. My father had fired shots of an arquebus at them from a window, and when, in my childish ignorance, I said that it was necessary to go outside to fight them, my father assured me that even if we gathered all the servants, with weapons, there was a good chance that someone would be devoured.

That night, a large wolf succeeded in getting into the stable through the roof. It killed one horse, but another horse broke two of its limbs with kicks. The wolf was found in the morning on the dead horse, face to face with its energetic companion. I was able to see it once it had been killed. It was a beast with red hair, with an enormous tongue sticking out of its mouth. Its expression was so hideous that I had never been able to forget it, and I associated it in my mind with the idea of evil.

I listened, and it seemed to me that I heard, very far away, a few distant howls. But wolves were so numerous in the forests that not a night went by in which they could not be heard howling in the heights.

I tried to block the entrance with the debris of the door, but I saw that it would take too long to succeed in the task and I gave up. I had brought with me, at hazard, the source of light that had been suspended on the wall of the barn where I was supposed to spend the night. It consisted of a wick soaked in oil in a copper goblet. I lit it with my flint-and-tinder. The wick only gave me a faint light and I noticed that it was very short. With its aid, I reached the staircase, climbed it and arrived in the principal room, where I installed myself on the skeleton of an armchair.

"Why have I come?" I asked, aloud—which I regretted immediately, because my voice had an almost unknown resonance, and it seemed to me that rumors and inexplicable noises in the rooms replied to me that it really was here that I had to be at that moment. I decided to wait. I had no idea what I was waiting for, but that ignorance was the principal attraction of my expedition.

A little patch of moonlight bathed a corner of the room. I was very surprised by the number of wild creatures that I heard walking in the garden or flying between the trees. There were also slitherings and animal pursuits in the rooms. All of that did not worry me. Like a nail profoundly embedded in a wall, which it is impossible to extract, there was a fear of wolves in me. I sensed that they were part of myself and, on reflection, I told myself that that was not at all unreasonable. In any case, I observed, on lending an ear, that the howling of those animals had drawn singularly nearer and were resonating on all sides.

In spite of that, I let myself slide without realizing it, into a state that was neither that of wakefulness nor that of sleep.

I believe that such a state is indispensable for the manifestation that I am about to relate. The account in question will only encounter incredulity, but I am writing more for myself than for the few curious individuals who will read these pages. Among them, there might perhaps be two or three who have had an analogous experience. They will believe me, in referring to their own memory. Perhaps there will be one who will believe me without having made the experiment, by virtue of a natural desire to believe. It is for that one, primarily, that I am going to give the details of what happened.

I heard a voice—or rather, no: I had the perception of things thought, which did not attain the usual intermediary of words. Only those words, instead of being registered by me thanks to the organ of hearing, touched my mind directly without making use of the ears and their channels.

The voice expressed itself without paying any heed to my opinion and any response I might have made, and this is approximately what it said:

"It was tonight that it was necessary for you to come and you have been faithful to the rendezvous that was not given to you by anyone. I, Mathieu de Bramevaque, your great-grandfather, desire to bring you assistance, in the very small measure of my strength. I cannot explain the reason to you, not knowing it myself, but the humans of the region that I inhabit are submissive to unknown forces and they are not masters of being here or there, as they wish.

"There are other, brighter regions, and those that have reached them have more mastery of themselves and can see further. But with that mastery and that vision comes, at the same time, an indifference to terrestrial matters that distances them from the world of forms, with the consequence that the living hardly ever communicate with any but the wanderers and the blind, those who struggle in the fog in pursuit of their own interior light. That light, I believe I have developed within me. There is very little of it. Every sin obscures it, and mine were numerous. But the story, if I could tell it, would serve no purpose. Beware of sin, my child, and listen to what I am going to tell you.

"In the world where I am, I perceive your quest for the Grail and the intention of that search, as a light. You are of my

76

family and your light has something of mine. I would like to be able to guide you by the hand, but the dead can do so little with regard to terrestrial life! They see less well than humans do with their eyes of flesh. They distinguish active hatreds like moving shadows, great hopes as luminous turbulence, but what they know best are the evil thoughts that are born in the region they inhabit, the thoughts of those who hate and who, in the world of shadows, strive to make hatred predominate.

"On the day when you set forth in search of the Grail, by virtue of correspondences between one word and the other, contrary forces were set in motion. They have stimulated unknown enemies who aspire to find the Grail in order to make use of it to their advantage, as a magic power. For all great materialized forces, even the blood of Christ, can serve both god and evil.

"Beware of a young woman named Lucida, whom men skilled in necromancy utilize to evoke the dead and extract their feeble knowledge from them. For the dead, summoned in accordance with the rites, are obliged to obey the will of the living. Beware of all those who have recognized in you the forgotten blood of the Albigensians. They have discovered what you did not know, that I, your ancestor, was one of the Knights Hospitaller charged with guarding the Grail. They have discovered that my shade, the receptacle of ancient desires, was condemned to return here on certain dates, to revive here the evil deeds whose images are suspended in the ambient air.

"Those evil men you will encounter again on your route. If only I were able to protect you from them! If only I were able to guide you to your goal! But it is not given to me to see it. Between it and me there are the tableaux that retain me in this dwelling."

There was an interruption then in my ancestor's words. Was it caused by the evocation of one of those images that obliged him to haunt the place? I got up and went to the window. The bushes in the garden were full of a singular agitation and I recoiled precipitately on hearing the call of the wolves, so close at hand that they seemed to be addressing me directly. There were so many of them prowling round the house! The thought occurred to me that, in sum, nothing prevented them from reaching me, and I felt the frisson given by an abrupt apprehension of a danger of a horrible nature.

With a bound, I crossed the room and ran as far as the staircase. There I stopped, open-mouthed with amazement, experiencing a particularly dolorous terror, because it was mingled with attraction, like that experienced on the rim of a vertiginous abyss. And I really was on the edge of an abyss from which evil spirits were calling to me.

At the bottom of the stairs, forming a semicircle of a mysteriously geometrical regularity, the wolves were grouped in the uncertain moonlight. I could distinguish their eyes like animate embers. Almost all of them were seated on their behinds. Their heads were turned in my direction, their tongues dangling. They were thin, bristling, and frightful. And at the same time as their bestial odor, I perceived that there was a desperate sadness in the depths of their souls.

At first I thought of fleeing, of barricading myself in a room—or trying to do so, for all the doors had fallen into pieces. But I told myself that since they had not come up, having scented the odor of prey, something must be holding them back, obliging them to that semicircle. Perhaps wolves could not climb stairs! Perhaps the spiral of the stairway was contrary to their primitive spirit! Unless a protecting emanating from the beyond had traced a magical line to defend me. A scorpion, and even a chicken, can be imprisoned by a line drawn in chalk. But I knew how illusory belief in hidden protection is.

The sight of me had provoked an increase the howling of the wolves. But none of them ventured on to the stairway. I thought that it was better not to confront them and I beat a retreat. With fragments of furniture that I was able to gather together, I even made a fragile barricade.

Time went by. I saw with alarm that the moon was descending and that I would soon be in complete darkness. I had resumed my place between the hard bones of the armchair, and gradually, I fell back into the same intermediary state that partly bathes the first phases of sleep.

The voice then resumed speaking to me, but in a very different, more uncertain fashion.

"Oh, my child! Pray for me. Ask with your innocent heart the powers that rule us that I should no longer be condemned to relive what I have done. Pray, request, try to obtain that. It isn't God that it's necessary to address; he can do nothing! He doesn't even know! There are powers devoid of contours, devoid of faces! It's them! But how inexorable they are! And I would also like to aid you in order to aid myself, for there is a balance somewhere, a balance that has no pans, but in which actions and even intentions, are weighed.

"But how to see? There are false Grails and Evil guardians. The hearts of saints are stolen by night in the crypts of cathedrals. The damned go to place snake-venom in soiled reliquaries where there is no longer anything but caricatures of relics. So, do not remain alone. Evil is too powerful. Try to join the four men who are searching, like you. You'll encounter them, thanks to the rose. And with them, perhaps you'll find! You must find it. The true Grail exists. It is somewhere. If only I could tell you where! The faculty of sight has been taken away from me. By my own fault!

"There were twelve of us in the Château de Cucugnan: twelve Knights Hospitaller chosen for their courage and their faith. Courage is insufficient. Faith is insufficient. It requires purity. We were not pure enough. How did that happen? The knights died one by one without their deaths being explicable. Was it an epidemic or poison? The frightened servants fled. And yet the presence of the divine light should have filled us with exaltation and joy. Nothing of the sort. Those who were going to die began by losing their reason.

"In the end there were only two of us left, myself and Antoine de Cassagnavère. Then I mounted my horse and I said to my companion: 'It's necessary, before dying, for me to sleep for one night next to Bérangère de Bramevaque. I'll ride flat out through the mountains. Wait for me for three days.'

"He said to me: 'Don't lose any time.'

"Night fell and as I was at the foot of the slopes of the château I saw him at the postern. He was holding the Grail and he had placed it over his heart. But I didn't return after three days, as I had promised. Woe betide the man who is bound to a woman by the flesh. By the specter of the flesh, by the specters issued from my criminal action, I am now enchained here.

"When I returned to the Château de Cucugnan, it was too late! Antoine de Cassagnavère had gone mad. But his tomb was not beside the tombs of our ten companions. He had departed on horseback, taking the Grail with him. But no one knows in what direction. In vain I asked on all the roads whether an insane rider had been seen to pass. And in my turn, I died. And I have found roads more obscure than those I followed when I was alive. And all of them end here."

The voice fell silent, either because my ancestor had nothing more to say to me, or for some other imperious reason unknown to me. The moon was about to reach the level of the horizon, and was on the point of disappearing.

I stood up. It seemed to me that there was a wave of silence over the world. I advanced without making any noise to the head of the staircase. I saw red gleams lighting up and going out, the eyes of wolves—full of impatience! Suddenly, one of them uttered a desperate, interminable howl that chilled me with horror. At the same time I had a rapid, fulgurant vision, as if a veil had torn, permitting me, for a second to see what had happened in another time.

A man whose beard was divided into two points, a man who resembled me—although I scarcely dared formulate that to myself, so rapid was the apparition—was going down the stairs. He was clad as a Knight Hospitaller and there would have been grandeur in him if anger had not altered his features. He was dragging behind him a wounded or dead woman whose long white chemise was covered in blood, and he was making the gesture of throwing her to the wolves—not to the same wolves that I could see, but to other, more numerous wolves, spread over the snow, over the snow of a dream, in the midst of icy trees: the wolves of the past, dead a long time ago.

As if a curtain had closed, the vision disappeared. The living wolves, still sitting in a semicircle on their backsides, responded to the one that had howled first with equally desperate howls, which succeeded one another. They did not attempt to climb the stairs; they remained motionless in their despair.

Had I glimpsed momentarily a part of the drama that my ancestor was obliged to relive? The veils that separated me from the past fell back, and did not open again. I had lost the appreciation of time and I did not know how many hours had passed.

I heard the voices of men in the avenue of beeches and recognized the accent of Tornebut's voice calling to me. At the same time, I perceived that the light of morning had replaced the darkness. There was no longer any trace of the wolves. Had they returned to the forests, or had they dissipated in time, like the man with the beard with two points and the woman covered in blood?

THE CARPENTER OF SAINT-BÉAT

We were passing through Saint-Béat at the foot of the mountains, and I perceived that I was walking alone; Tornebut was no longer by my side. I retraced my steps and I found him in a posture of ecstasy before a vast hangar filled with logs adjacent to a workshop where a carpenter was working. For a long time I had sensed that he was possessed by the nostalgia of wood and I knew that that there is no greater attraction than that of a métier that one has loved.

"O my master," he said to me, "the sight of wood renders me drunk, as when one has partaken of a fermented beverage. I was born to saw and shave, and I can no longer live without occupying myself with things related to wood.

And I replied: "A destiny falls due for everyone and it has been fixed for thousands of years by the actions of former lives and the entanglement of causes and effects. You are linked to wood and its working. Don't waste time delaying what has to happen. Ask that carpenter of Saint-Béat, a bearded man with a gaze full of malice, if he cannot take you with him—for there's an evident disproportion between the quantity of logs in that hangar and his solitude.

Tornebut did so, and went into the carpenter's workshop. There was a discussion, and after a time, in which I saw cunning measuring itself against naivety. Tornebut came back toward me. He had a face in which there was joy on one side and sadness on the other. The sadness came from the fact that he was about to quit me, but I saw immediately that the joy was predominant.

"The carpenter of Saint-Béat will take me as an apprentice, and I'll only have to give him twelve sols a day."

"Apprentice? But Tornebut, are you not an expert carpenter?"

"He doesn't know that."

"Why didn't you tell him?"

"It's never good to appear to know too much."

"And why are you paying twelve sols when, in general, the man who works receives a salary instead of giving one?"

"It's for nourishment and lodging."

The carpenter had approached us, holding his beard in his right hand. He saluted me politely, but not without malice. He had an excellent air, but perhaps that was in the measure where excellence is compatible with pettiness of soul.

He had heard the last words.

"I ought to tell you that the meals are uniformly composed of a soup—an abundant soup—in a bowl."

"I like soup," said Tornebut, without noticing the quantitative restriction implied by the bowl.

"And as I have no bedroom, you'll sleep in the hangar on a bed we'll set up this evening between the logs."

"Between the logs! That's perfect."

"I ought to tell you that custom dictates that the apprentice gets up an hour before daybreak in order to clean the house and the workshop."

"Good."

"The apprentice has to saw the primitive wood and reduce the tree to logs when it is entire."

"Very good."

"Winter is coming and there will be days when it's necessary to go up the mountain to roll tree trunks down the slope."

"I like mountains full of trees."

"But sometimes there are no slopes and it's necessary to load the trunks on his back."

"My shoulders are vigorous."

"And not to slip, if the ground is frozen, for if one falls, one risks being crushed by the weight of the trunk."

"I won't slip and won't be crushed."

"And in the evening, after supper, under the lamp, there are still small jobs to do."

"Jobs with wood?"

"Of course."

"That's perfect, then."

The two men shook hands.

"And you'll pay twelve sols a day for that work of a slave?" I said to Tornebut, who had accompanied me to the bridge and was hesitating to bid me adieu.

"What wouldn't I give to sleep in the midst of piles of logs?"

There was a part of his soul that was weeping, but wood was his true master. I drew away rapidly in order not to permit our weakness to become manifest. I had been walking for a long time without looking back and I knew that he was still in the same place on the bridge. I knew that if I had made a sign to him then he would have come running and would have followed me—but I did not want to compete against the love of wood.

I walked very quickly. Later, night fell. The mountains had never seemed so high to me, or the forests so inexorable.

THE ACCURSED CHURCH

Above the valley of Barousse there is an old dilapidated church lost in a fir wood. No path ends there and one wonders how the ancient builders were able to transport the stones necessary to build the church so high and so far.

In what distant epoch did those ancient builders come, and why did they build there, on that remote mountain? It is said that the Seigneur de Barousse, who went to the crusades with Raymond Saint-Gilles, once returned to Mauléon laden with miscellaneous spoils, the most astonishing of which, the one that impressed the inhabitants of Comminges most, the one that the seigneurs of the surrounding area came to see, was a huge snake with all its teeth and two large glass eyes, marvelously stuffed by skillful Syrians.

But the Seigneur de Barousse also brought back unhappiness. He had lost the ability to sleep. He was haunted, it was said, by the memory of all the pagans that he had put to death. Then, he climbed the heights that overlooked the valley of Barousse by night, and he was heard from afar uttering loud cries under the trees.

In the end he had vowed to build that church, which only served a single sinner, himself, and to carry there in his arms all that he had stolen from the cities where he pagans lived. And that was what he did. He spent his life there, like a hermit, and he rang the bell himself, and for recreation, he unwound the coils of the snake in front of the church. And in the end, he died. It was said that the church was haunted by pagan phantoms. No one dared go pray there. Then, with time, no one knew any longer whether the snake brought back from the crusades was alive or dead.

The years passed. The wind broke the portal of the church. The beasts of the forest made rounds under the nave. Evil and diabolical things were accomplished there, for the memory was retained that in the last century, a Bishop of Saint Bertrand forbade any ecclesiastic to go into that accursed church, under penalty of excommunication. The prohibition was remembered, but not what had motivated it.

Now, some fifty years before, a great-uncle of the present Seigneurs de Barousse, who was a singular individual, like all members of the family, took it into his head to utilize his ancestor's church as a studio for sculpture. He had become a misanthrope as he grew older and said that he preferred the company of men of clay to that of men of flesh and bone. He had been a companion of King François I and had fought at Cérisolles, a victory entirely due, he said, to his personal prowess, But the King had discontented him, had shown himself to be ingrate in his regard. He had resolved to create the companions of his existence by means of sculpture.

Having been a warrior during his life, he was scarcely expert in manipulating a sculptor's chisel; but he was proud, like all the men of his family, and like all men in general, and he thought that, since he had decided to be a sculptor, he could only be a great sculptor, and even the greatest of all those who had fashioned matter before him.

He had clay and marble brought, tools and pieces of wood for the pedestals, and he set about carving and sculpting. He commenced with Jesus Christ, the twelve apostles and the characters of the passion. He made Mary Magdalen, Joseph, Pilate and the soldiers. But it was scarcely possible to tell them apart. They were all formless creatures. The church was soon full. Then the Seigneur de Barousse sculpted in the open air. He imagined a long path on the side of the mountain, which he bordered with all manner of figures: knights, clerics, judges or peasants. But above all, it was King François I of whom it pleased him to reproduce the contours, and on whose face he tried to put the hideous expression of ingratitude.

He worked while incessantly singing hymns, and even by night the sound of his hammer on stone and his ax on wood could be heard a long way away. Then he started sculpting animals. They were almost similar to the humans—they could only be differentiated because they had four feet—and they all had beards trimmed like that of François I.

And in his turn, he died. The presence of the sculpted monsters added a maleficent character to the church. Time did its work. Plants corroded the statues. Some of them fell over, others disappeared under the growth of young firs. A population of crows chose the tower of the church as a habitation. Every evening a great flock of those birds was seen wheeling in the sky, like a magical indication traced in nature.

DOMITIEN DE BAROUSSE

There is a Château de Bramevaque in the valley of Barousse which belonged to one of my uncles, to which my father often took me in my childhood. As far as one can go back into the past, the Seigneurs de Barousse and Bramevaque were always quarreling, although in appearance they maintained a relationship of hostile courtesy. The people of the region had sided with one family or the other. So, when I took a room at the Blanche Épée inn in the Grand Place de Saint-Bertrand-de-Comminges, I was glad to learn that the innkeeper, Paulin Couloumiès, was linked to my family by mysterious bonds of sympathy.

"Beware of the Barousses," he said to me.

And the day after my arrival, as I was going past the Basilica of Saint Bertrand, at the conclusion of mass, a child of two or three, scarcely able to stand on his feet, and very ugly to boot, freed himself from the hand of a sort of governess clad in garnet velvet and ran up to me in order to prick me in the leg with a miniature sword—a toy, but a toy far too sharp to be given to a creature devoid of conscience.

The governess was content to snigger. I pretended not to have experienced any pain, and I heard a passer-by say: "That's the son of Estelle de Barousse, who's already delivering sword-thrusts."

Estelle de Barousse! I was sensible to that incident, and I had difficulty forgetting it—not for the prick, of course; but I had acquired the habit of examining and passing although a sieve the thoughts that emerged from the depths of the soul, in order to mutate their bad qualities into nobility. Now, I had initially experienced a bitter satisfaction in observing so much ugliness in the face of a child born a Barousse, even Estelle. Afterwards I had been obliged to repress an instinct that urged me to knock that hostile inhuman creature over with a kick, in the same way that one defends oneself against a dog that bites you. If it is dolorous to recognize that men are evil, it is even more so to put a finger one one's own evil instincts. The latest of the Barousses to arrive had unconsciously manifested the hatred of the Barousses against me, and vulgar reactions had emerged from the depths of my being that testified to a very ordinary soul.

The three bothers Barousse—for fatality wanted there to be three in order to augment my burden—hated me equally, with an irrational hatred. The youngest had been an officer in the King's army and now dedicated his life to chasing women. The second was a member of the Parlement de Toulouse and was reputed to be one of the most severe men in that redoubtable assembly. The eldest had taken holy orders. When young he had had crises of mysticism. He had spent a long time at the Court of Rome and longer still in a convent where the religious authority, it was said, had imprisoned him for faults relative to dogma. I had heard him once debating the Holy Trinity in ancient Greek with a monk who had come from Germany for that oratory joust. He had won the admiration of a very small number of Hellenists who were listening. Isaac Andréa had told me that he knew Hebrew as well as him and that he possessed all the arcana of the Kabbalah. He was a man of vast intelligence, but a bitter and destructive intelligence.

As I was going up a narrow staircase that led to the highest part of Saint-Bernard I suddenly found myself face to face with him. We had not spoken to one another since the days of our youth.

"You're climbing these steps very quickly, Monsieur de Bramevaque," he said to me. "You're young, still very young!"

It was to my physical youth that he was alluding.

I hastened to reply to him that we were very nearly the same age.

Domitien de Barousse was wearing a Dominican habit. The wind that was blowing lifted up his black cloak like a sinister wing whose folds hid the sunlight from me. He was thin, with a large nose and a mouth that allowed rotten teeth to be seen. He was tall of stature, and as he was placed above me he dominated me so entirely that I could not help feeling a sentiment of defeat. The tone of his voice betrayed the superiority that he attributed to himself. I knew, moreover, that he affected to speak to everyone with a voluntary hint of scorn.

"God certainly leads men toward one another at the necessary moment," he said to me, with a gravity that he attenuated with a half-smile, to mark that he was above the opportunity of an encounter. "I have a warning to give you."

"To me?" I said, although it could not be to anyone else, for we were alone on the stone steps, where the autumnal wind was blowing. And in that second I had a presentiment of that he was going to say to me, and was agape with astonishment that he had pierced my secret thoughts.

"Believe me, don't go any further. Go back to what you were, an honest physician of Toulouse. Devote yourself to saving bodies. For souls, the Church has traced the path. There are no others."

I opened my mouth to reply, but he stopped me with a sudden vehemence. "But above all, proud man, renounce the search for that which would kill you if you found it, for that which would kill you even for having the pretention to attain it. Men of a different temper than yours have died for having pursued the same chimera."

"I have nothing to fear from anyone. Neither the Capitouls of Toulouse, nor the King's Seneschal, nor the Catholic Church, can reproach me for anything."

"But heresy is as visible on a man's face as an ulcer on a leper's! It isn't necessary to be clairvoyant to recognize it. I have only to plunge my gaze into yours to know that Jess Christ is not sitting alone on the throne of your interior tabernacle. I see beside him all your delirious imaginations, the dreams of the ancient Albigensians. What do I know? Be very careful. The inquisitors are not as powerful as they once were, but don't too confident. They still build pyres. They still make heretics disappear into prisons. And they always judge, not on the facts but the intentions—and I know your intentions. They escape you like ill-guarded birds. Believe me, go back to Toulouse, Michel de Bramevaque! You only have the cloth of a well-intentioned man who does good in his quarter. Each to his role. Go back to the Porte Arnaud Bernard, good physician. I enjoin you to do it without delay, this very evening, before the sun sets."

I started to laugh to indicate that I did not take that extravagant injunction seriously. "But were you not suspected of heresy yourself once?"

He contented himself with shrugging his shoulders.

"And it's you who are giving me the order to leave?"

He pursed his lips. His eyes shone. "Yes, the order. Exactly." He lowered his voice. "And I'm not giving you that order in the name of a tribunal, in the name of the Church. I could. No, it's me, personally, who is giving you that order and in your interest."

He had passed before me with the dead expression that the gaze of a man acquires when he does not want to hear any sort of response to what he has just said. In the movement he made, because the stairway was very narrow, his face was very close to mine. For a moment, I respired a fetid breath, the odor of the putrescence of the dead.

He had descended three steps. He turned round, and the wind, which is often pleased to augment the theatricality of things, caused his cloak to fly up again. His features were rigid, as if they were carved in stone, and they expressed a mysterious hardness, so inhuman were they.

I would have liked to understand, to explain myself to him, but I experienced such a relief in seeing him draw away that I did not yield to the impulse to run after him. It seemed to me that, for a few minutes, I had been on the brink of a horrible abyss, from which the breath of his breast and teeth emerged: the same abyss where I had once heard the call of wolves howling mortally.

THE MASS OF SAINT-SÉCAIRE

Are there creatures of the abyss? An in any case, does the abyss exist? Is there a world into which evil beings strive to make us fall, because they have fallen themselves? The great force of degradation comes from the desire to destroy those who rise. It is said that is necessary not to linger, in the evening, in the vicinity of leprosaria. Men who were passing have sometimes been seized by the lepers and dragged away, to be subjected to touches and kisses that have the objective of communicating the disease. The equality that comes from below is a frightful temptation. Those who are voluntarily doomed aspire to doom their brethren who have resisted the attractive power of descent.

I know now a creature who does evil for evil's sake. But it is not the desire to cause suffering that animates him. Dolor is a very small thing.

The man of whom I speak and who has attempted to kill me might perhaps have been satisfied to know that I was happy in spiritual mediocrity. What causes his hatred is the faith that he senses in me, even if that faith might come to nothing, and not be useful to anyone. It is sufficient for faith to be illuminated in the solitude for the evil to join forces in order to extinguish it.

My God, defend me from their traps, their sorceries, and their poisons. I know that the more one advances, the more the path is filled with thorns, and the time comes when one has a lacerated face and hands. So do not take away from me the shield of pure metal, the unalterable faith in which the sublime resides. May I be eternally able, by closing my eyes, in life and in death, to contemplate and love that which is reason in human beings, the admirable body of a goddess and the light of the morning star, the blood of Jesus Christ.

O Tornebut, why were you not there? It is always better to be two. The lone man is without courage. He wonders whether what he is doing might be insensate. He needs the wink of an eye, the nod of the head, of a witness.

So, this is what happened one moonlit night; this is what I saw, thanks to a fortunate impulse of my nature—or rather, a deliberate determination of my invisible protector, for the man who knows the evil directed against him can combat it with the force of his soul.

On the eve of that malefic night I had gone or a stroll outside the town boundary I had climbed a ridge from which one can see between the firs the silhouette of the forbidden church once constructed by a Barousse: the church where mystery and desolation reign.

The moon had scarcely risen and I distinguished between the trees a sort of red eye of enormous proportions, which was staring at me. What could that solitary eye be? It was made by a stained-glass window of the church and its light was not coming from the moon but from an interior glow. There was, therefore, someone in the church at that nocturnal hour.

I thought that it must be a man of great courage, led there by a very powerful interest. Since the ecclesiastical malediction that weighed upon it, the solitary church exerted a terror so great on the entire region that people did not go near it even in daylight. Thirty years before a family of Bohemians, expelled from Saint-Bernard, had taken refuge here one stormy evening. The next day, the members of that family—there were six—were found dead in front of the portal. Doubtless the lightning, by the natural play of its force, had struck them normally, but the death had been attributed to stranger causes. Popular belief had even gone so far as to resuscitate the ancient serpent brought back from the crusade by the companion of Raymond Saint-Gilles.

I told Paulin Couloumiès what I had seen. He had a strong mind and a cunning difficult to deceive.

"I wouldn't say this to anyone else, for there's a risk in knowing too much, but when the moon is full, the Mass of Saint-Sécaire is celebrated in the Barousse church."[6]

"Who celebrates it?"

"I don't know, and it's better not to know—although, in truth, it would be easy to divine. In order to be celebrated, as everyone knows, the Mass of Saint-Sécaire needs a night of a full moon and a forbidden church. One has the night everywhere, but where can one find a forbidden church more solitary, where one is as sure of not being disturbed? And what a coincidence! Certain travelers arrive from Toulouse or elsewhere two or three times a year, just when the moon is full—and that's exactly when a vague light tints the windows of the church up there."

I could not get him to say any more, but from that moment on, I was burning with the temptation to see with my own eyes the faces of individuals voluntarily avowed to the Spirit of Evil and to know the rites by which that Spirit of Evil is enabled to emerge from the shadows—if, that is, it can materialize in form, and if it even exists.

I knew that my curiosity came from an evil source itself, made of the same substance of its object. I knew that evil is initially manifest as an appeal, that its presence is an attractive force, a void into which one is tempted to launch oneself, and which sucks you in. But I gave myself altruistic reasons. There

---

[6] The legend of the evil Mass of Saint-Sécaire was popularized in the 1880s by the French folklorist Jean-François Bladé (1827-1900) in the second volume of his massive collection of *Contes de Gascogne*, the fullest version of which is the three-volume edition of 1886. Magre was undoubtedly familiar with the work; Anatole France had earlier used material from it in some of his supernatural fiction, and Bladé was acquainted with several writers of the Symbolist school, including some—notably Laurent Tailhade—with whom Magre became acquainted. The legend had earlier been reported in an article in *L'Illustration* in 1852 signed "L. Laprade."

are weak individuals who are threatened, whom I might save, I said to myself, but it is necessary to know the danger in order to preserve them from it effectively.

I went to reconnoiter the area during the day and took reference points to guide me when night fell. Evening surprised me at the extremity of the strange avenue of stone bordered by the insensate sculptor's statues. Almost all of them had fallen over and hardly anything was distinguishable but elongated forms and confused masses. A few still remained standing in the church invaded by twilight and I saw immediately what I ought to do. By climbing on to a pedestal and remaining motionless, with my staff in the form of a crosier in my arms, I could give the illusion in the dark that I was one of the twelve apostles, if not Jesus Christ himself. I armed myself with patience. I drove away the image of the six Bohemians, the phantom of the snake and all the unknown phantoms that might inhabit the place, and I waited

I waited for a long time. The moon rose and its light shone through the broken windows, elongating the shadows of pillars, emphasizing the concavity of arches and enabling the silhouette of a large wooden cross above the altar to appear. Bats commenced a hectic round, circling under the nave, and birds came in, fluttered their wings and departed again, as if they had had a message to transmit from the neighboring forests.

Solitude, the fatigue of remaining standing and the oppressive character of the place eventually had an effect on my mind. I told myself that perhaps the gleams perceived the previous evening were only the play of moonlight on the stained glass and that I had lent too much credence to Paulin Couloumiès' imaginings. I was thinking about abandoning the wooden pedestal I was occupying and taking the path back to Saint-Bernard when I glimpsed shadows in the luminous section that comprised the portal and the paving-stones of the entrance.

There were three forms that slid silently, whispering, which I could not examine because they immediately plunged into the dark part of the church.

After a few seconds, there was a glimmer of light. I heard a man's voice complaining about the narrowness of a candlestick, into which a candle of excessively large dimension would not fit. Then two brighter gleams were animated and I saw that two candles were illuminating the altar.

Indistinct words became audible. I heard the rustle of fabric, and my heart suddenly began to beat more forcefully. The silhouette of a naked woman passed in front of the altar. She was slender and I could not distinguish her features. With an abrupt movement she stretched herself out on the altar. Then she propped herself up on her elbow, her hair falling all the way to the floor, in the pose of someone waiting.

The stones of the church had been deprived of any sanctification for centuries. It had become any place, haunted by the beasts of the forest. In spite of that, however it retained the form of a place of election that people devoted to prayer. I felt the emotion mingled with horror procured by the violation of what is spiritual by contact with baseness and evil.

Suddenly, the woman lay down, and the gesture she made to roll her hair beneath her head displaced the shadows throughout the nave. A tall man of whom I could only see the back then began to say the mass, while the third person, kneeling down, played the role of choirboy.

At first that partly-glimpsed scene did not seem to me to be so terrible. Rather, I saw the ridiculous side, especially when I heard the musical voice of the woman, who said, with a hint of amusement: "Look out! The toads have escaped!" and I was able to think that toads had been transported in some receptacle, as the necessary accessories of the rite and the pollution.

But my ears gradually grew accustomed to the muttering that emerged from the lips of the man who was playing the role of the priest and distinguished the words pronounced. The invocatory formulae were appeals to the spirit of darkness, to the evil force of the world, and its aid was requested for a work of death.

The death of whom? I could not tell. But I had enough knowledge of magic to understand that the magical ceremony that the mass is, composed with the objective of fraying a path for humans to the divine—a savant, ordered and efficacious ceremony—was being utilized inversely to attain the pole opposite to God and utilize the force of its radiation for the work of destruction.

And gradually, involuntarily, I was penetrated by the horrible character of what it was given to me to see. The sensation that I experienced was so violent that disgust prevailed over curiosity and I would have given a great deal to find myself outside that detestable place, under the firs of the mountains of Barousse.

When the moment of the elevation came, my head turned with the force of a weathervane activated by the north wind and my soul launched itself into the patch of light streaming under the portal like a diver into a tranquil lake. In accordance with the wise Albigensian doctrine, I did not believe that there could be a real presence of the divine being in the host, especially in the hands of an impure priest, but I saw the intention behind the act as if that intention were clad in material form.

And when the hand-bell of the assistant had resonated several times, doubtless at the time fixed by the rite, the priest lifted something in his left hand that had to be the figurine representing the bewitched creature for whom that mass of death was being said. His right hand held a blade that I saw glinting, and his voice suddenly swelled in order to pronounce the sacramental formula, invoking Lilith and Nahemah, the accused goddesses of the abyss, whose work consists of bring form to annihilation. It is at that moment that the ceremony becomes effective, and its action is realized in the invisible before materializing in the real. The invocation must be preceded by the name of the victim and the man proclaims that name in a resounding manner as if the name emitted augmented his will.

My blood froze in my veins, for I heard the syllables of my name, Michel de Bramevaque, repeated three times.

But with the same rapidity as the chill coursing through my bones, the active warmth of salvation possessed me, for a fortunate disposition of my nature has determined that in danger, presence of mind comes to my aid like a runner armed with a sword.

I knew that in such a rare occurrence, it is possible to destroy the effect of a conjuration by confronting it with the contrary conjuration and making it rise as high by an equal vocal resonance.

In an explosive voice, I intoned at the same time as the priest of evil the invocation of the beneficent angels.

"*Conjuro vos!*"[7] I cried, in a voice that touched the silent arch of the nave and caused the stained glass windows shaken by time to quiver. But while the priest, raising the useless figurine and the impotent dagger, appealed with a voice that amazement and alarm rendered faltering, to the infernal creatures, daughters of oblivion, abyssal larvae of the nameless kingdom, I pronounced the sacred names, Onelech, Sabaoth, Adonai, the ineffable syllables evocative of the seventy-two servants of the Spirit, from Vehuiach to Mumiah.

We arrived simultaneously at the final words of our two adverse conjurations, which are the same: "*Per omnia saecula!*"[8] The voice of the evil priest was quavering and inarticulate; mine aroused birds, previously immobile, and obliged them to beat their wings beneath the vault.

Beneath the chasuble and the stole, the man scrutinized the darkness of the church, and I suddenly recognized Domitien de Barousse, and I also recognized Lucida de

---

[7] In Latin, *conjuro* usually refers to an oath, but French verb *conjurer* can mean to exorcize, and that is presumably the implication intended here.

[8] i.e., Eternally—more usually rendered *Per omnia saecula saeculorum* [For ever and ever] by way of emphasis.

Domazan, who, raised up on her elbow, projected her hair over her breast with a gesture, like a gilded and modest robe.

With a measured tread, making the flagstones resonate with my staff, I headed for the door. A bat cut through the air, seemingly separating the church into two. On the threshold, I had the sensation that the light of a candle moved, but I did not turn my head. I even slowed my pace slightly as I descended among the statues, striving to adopt the gait of statue in motion.

At the bottom of the slope I plunged into the firs, and then I started walking very rapidly, glad and surprised to be out of it so cheaply.

A little later, when I looked in the direction of the church, by virtue of some phenomenon that I cannot explain, its mass appeared to me as a huge black rose, a rose open in the night.

THE SPEECH OF DEAD TREES

It was not long after that happened that a great tempest blew. It came from the north, extended over the land of Comminges and drew away through the Pyrenean valleys, obedient to the destinies that regulate tempests.

After its departure I walked along the road that leads to Saint-Martory and I considered with astonishment the great distress that the vegetation had endured by virtue of the evil power of the wind. On a ridge, an entire file of firs were overlapping one another, their branches confused, like warriors abruptly struck, and who remain in the ridiculous and tragic poses that death imparts. By the roadside, an oak extended its large broken branches like stumps, and in its gesture there was a silent revolt against the injustice that had martyrized it. The supple birches that limited a field had let themselves fall in their silver robes and had not been able to get up again. In the field, all the fruit trees had a few wounds, and I saw a man who, with the aid of a pole that he had just stuck in the ground, was occupied in correcting the position of a young peach-tree.

The man ran toward me. It was Tornebut.

"I've been looking for you," he said. "I left Saint-Béat yesterday, and I won't go back again."

Tornebut had become thin. His eyes were hollow. I asked him whether the cause of that was the carpenter's soup.

"It's the harm that I've done," he replied, sadly.

"To whom have you done harm?"

He pointed toward a mountain in the direction of Saint-Béat. "To the trees that live up there."

I asked him to explain.

"I've had difficulty understanding it myself. At first I didn't listen to the interior voice. It's gradually that the verity has come to light."

"What verity?"

100

"The one that says that one ought not to kill trees. But how can one exercise the métier of carpenter without first procuring planks by the death of a tree?"

"Alas, humans often find themselves confronted by the lack of God's logic," I replied.

"It was one night that the light dawned in me, for the terrestrial night is propitious to the light of the spirit. You know that I was sleeping in the hangar in the midst of piles of freshly-cut wood. Scarcely had I lain down on my mattress than I went to sleep because of fatigue. But that night, I couldn't sleep. There were more sounds of water outside than usual and the stars were shining through the planks. Those poorly-fitted planks weren't letting through the customary frost, but the first precocious warmth of March. A languor filed the hangar. And then I perceived round, sad faces in the circles of the sawn logs, which were looking at me with a reproachful expression—not a conscious reproach, but one that must be appropriate to vegetables. What there was of the sky under the hangar caused moisture to shine that resembled tears, and by means of a special understanding I heard confused speech.

"'We live up there where the mountain streams obtain their source and the clouds come to rest. We shelter birds, insects and tinier creatures that have no names. We permit the ferns to grow and the mushrooms to swell and make their living and colored putrescence burst forth. You have stolen the gift of existence from us with your ax. You have killed us inexorably. Now our roots remain immobile under the humus in their silent eternity. Centuries of rain will flow over them, removing the terrestrial flesh to bare the naked rock. Roots do not have the possibility of complete death. Only the radicals, like a multiple network of trees, know dissolution. The subterranean mass of the tree retains the power of the eternal dolor of a mother who can no longer give birth. The witnesses of your arboreal murders are invisible, buried, devoid of bodies and faces, but they weep in the night of the earth for the death of the arborescent sons who will no longer put forth leaves in the sky,'"

Tornebut paused. Sweat was running down his forehead.

"I was mature enough to hear, and I heard, and a man who has heard such things cannot forget them. Then I got up, I fled the house where there are saws and axes and I made a vow. I shall render life to as many trees as I have caused to die. That is why I have straightened up these apricot trees and peach trees curbed by the wind, and I shall do the same for all the trees that need straightening, for the tension toward the sun produced by the upright position is indispensable to all vegetable being."

From that day on Tornebut became my companion again, and from that day on my progress over the roads became infinitely slower, because at any moment Tornebut might cry: "There's a birch that needs my care!" or "Some misfortune has overtaken that chestnut tree," or "A pole is needed here!" or "It's necessary to relieve that apple tree of that cluster of apples!" And he started running into the meadows alongside the road.

"How many trees have you truck with your ax?" I asked him once, thinking about the inconvenience of traveling as slowly and hoping for a terminus for the vow.

"I don't know, alas—but a large number."

"And how will you know when the number of trees saved equals the number of trees cut down?"

Tornebut scratched his head. He was embarrassed.

"There will doubtless be a sign. A sign made by a tree. A poplar, for instance, will incline toward me, or the flexible branch of a weeping willow on the edge of a pool will wrap around my neck."

At the time we were going along a road bordered by poplars, and to the right, a willow was dipping long almond-colored leaves into rusty water. I looked at those trees attentively, with a confused hope. The branches of the willow did not quiver. The poplars remained motionless.

"Oh, Tornebut, how rare signs are! But how empty life would be if we were not incessantly waiting for them!"

102

THE MIRACLE OF THE FIG-TREE

"I don't know why," Tornebut said to me, "but it seems to me that when the saints worked miracles, there must have been the same light in the air as there is today."

"Assuredly, it's necessary to work miracles," I relied. "Miracles are indispensable."

We were going down a hill in the Lauragais. The air had a natural color. The trees were motionless and appeared to be meditating on their arboreal destiny. Some leaves were gilded and others blue. If we raised our voices they resonated at a great distance

I was suddenly aware that the day had come. And I felt like a man who has drunk a delectable but dangerous beverage.

"Oh, Tornebut, if one does not dare, nothing ever happens. Woe to the lukewarm! It's necessary to dare! The man who dares and has faith can easily work miracles. One can work miracles with an extreme facility, for nature obeys man. If one dared, one could work miracles all the time. Jesus Christ must have worked many more than are reported, but the narrators of the gospels, timorous men, dared not record them in order not to shock vulgar reason."

Tornebut looked at me from the corner of his eye.

"I sense such a great faith within me," I went on, "that I could work a miracle, for I would be aided by favorable powers."

We had traversed a village in which the church was very small and had a provisional appearance, as if it had been placed there in order to grow more rapidly. After the last houses a small group of men and women were gathered around a fig-tree and seemed to be arguing about it.

We drew nearer, and I asked the people what was preoccupying them in regard to the fig-tree.

"Last year, and every previous year," replied a man who must have been the owner of the tree, "every time we came home from work, we had the custom of eating figs. They were big and excellent. Now, look—September is coming to an end, and the figs are dry and shrunken, more like walnuts than figs. We're wondering whether there might be some sorcery in that, for there are wicked people who cast spells on trees."

"Isn't it necessary to wait for a few days?" asked Tornebut. "Isn't it a tardy tree, like certain children who don't understand matters of education when they already have beards?"

"It's nothing of the sort," replied a fat man, smiling at such a hypothesis and raising his voice to affirm that he was an expert in the comportment of fruit trees. "Look at those figs that come away and fall if anyone touches them. They're only skin with nothing inside. The sap hasn't come out. In my opinion, it's an ill-natured tree."

"There are a few fruits here and there, though, that one could eat," said a well-groomed woman who must have been hostile to the idea that the order of nature could be troubled.

She detached a fruit, chosen with care, and gave it to a child she was holding by the hand. Doubtless the child thought he was the victim of a trick, for he pretended to weep, uttering loud cries, which is an expression of capricious anger only appropriate to children.

Completing his thought, the expert then said: "It would need a miracle for these figs to become edible.

Then I thought that it is necessary not to use cunning with the gods but to throw oneself into the water squarely. There are domains in which one ought not to maintain any means of exit, and throw caution to the wind.

"Would you like me to work that miracle?" I said, simply but with authority.

"What?" The people thought they had misunderstood.

"I'll work that miracle. I'll render that tree its habitual vitality. Those figs will immediately become full of sap, rich in flesh, delicious to taste, like their sisters, the figs of former years."

There was a murmur, and I saw an astonishment in their faces, at seeing a man they supposed to be serious and reasonable pronouncing insensate words. A young woman moved away abruptly, as if I might start dancing or making dangerous gesticulations. By contrast, an aged man who was leaning on a cane drew nearer, staring at me with an extreme curiosity with his little gray eyes, scarcely visible beneath thick eyebrows.

"He can work that miracle," said Tornebut. "He's a great man—a man who knows everything." He lowered his voice and added: "Who sometimes talks to God."

"The figs will become large all of a sudden, then?" said an incredulous thin man, with a mocking laugh.

"My God! Anything's possible—perhaps he's a saint," said an old woman, putting her hands together. Her toothless face, slightly ridiculous because of the length of her nose, took on an expression of ecstasy as she repeated: "There are saints! There are great saints! A great saint has come among us."

Those words gave me a sudden power. I felt my soul uplifted. I opened the palms of my hands as if to collect the descent of the Spirit. Everyone moved away from me with a spontaneous impulse, and I saw Tornebut, who had a finger over his lips, making a sign to the jeering man to shut up. All eyes were turned toward me. I experienced a singular communication with the people around me. I was joyful and light, and I had the sentiment that if I wanted, I could reach the nearby hill with a single bound, without any difficulty. But I did not attempt it.

"Can the Mother of the world, who is the earth and the sky, not make the wind blow at her whim and the rivers flow? Can she not do anything, since she is everything?"

I interrogated those who were close to me with my eyes, and they approved that simple verity.

"It is the divine Mother, the omnipotent Mother who provides trees with flowers, and the fruits. It is by virtue of her that we have grapes, apples and figs, is it not?"

Heads nodded to signify *yes*.

"A mother who has many children can forget one of them in the distribution of soup in the evening. What does the child do? He protests. Well, the divine Mother has forgotten a fig-tree. What is one fig-tree to her in the immense terrestrial economy? It's necessary for the fig-tree to raise its voice to protest."

I noticed that the aged man was very attentive and that the mocker had an expression of stupid astonishment that made him resemble an ox. Tornebut was praying.

I suddenly lost the faculty of being able to distinguish the people around me, and it seemed to me that I was alone on a high mountain and that invisible powers were leaning toward me.

"O Mother of the world," I cried, with a voice that I did not recognize, "I am the forgotten fig-tree. I am the tree by the side of the road, which accomplishes its duty as a tree and producer of figs faithfully. You have put me in this place for the wellbeing of weary men coming home in the evening after a day's labor. And now I cannot accomplish my mission. O Mother, listen to the fig-tree's prayer! Give me juice, give me tasty flesh, give me moistness. By your virtuous terrestrial powers, cause the liquids propitious to fruits to flow within me. O Mother, send the spirits of substance to fecundate my roots and cause thick liquids to flow in my ligneous channels that can be transformed into roseate pulp. O Mother of the world, I am the fig-tree by the side of the road, the one that is born of the soil of the Lauragais and which extends its September fruit faithfully to laborious men. I make you the offering of my branches and my leaves. Reawaken me from the slumber of desiccation. Render me the normal life of a tree."

Invoking the celestial Mother and the spirits of substance thus, I started marching around the fig-tree, identifying myself with it, and I became the tree. I expanded in foliage, I cast a shadow, and drops of gum, instead of sweat, ran down my face.

I was still at the summit of a high mountain. I gesticulated, and I said many other invocatory words. I don't know how

106

long that went on, but a moment came when the hills of Lauragais reappeared, the little village, the church that was at the beginning of its development, and the people around me. I saw then that they had different attitudes.

The majority were on their knees. I saw eyes raised to the heavens, hands joined. The skeptical individual had taken off his hat and had the pose of someone watching the Holy Sacrament go by.

"Look," I said. "The miracle is accomplished."

Without even looking at the tree, a woman started crying: "The miracle is accomplished!" She had stood up, and immediately fell back at my feet, kissing the hem of my cloak.

All sorts of cries resounded. Figs were passed from hand to hand.

"There's no doubt about it! It's a miracle!"

"Hey, look at this one! Look how big it is!"

The man who was leaning on a cane was circling around the fig-tree, looking at the figs with perplexed eyes. I heard him saying: "Not all of them, certainly, but some. There are some that are larger than they were a little while ago."

"Are you convinced now?" said a woman to the skeptic, handing him a fig. "This one is still a little dry, but look at those up above."

"Indeed, the figs higher up have become enormous."

With that, the skeptic put his hat on his head again, as if to say that the affair was concluded. That provoked further admiring exclamations.

Only the child, who had doubtless received an ill-chosen fig, recommenced uttering piercing cries.

Tornebut tugged my sleeve. "It's time to leave if we want to reach Baziège by nightfall."

Everyone surrounded us. Everyone pressed us to stay. One offered his bedroom, another his house, and a third promised us a good supper. One fat man insisted more than the others, because of an excellent pear-tree that was dead in is garden, which I could easily resuscitate.

I was almost tempted to go there, but I reflected that it is necessary not to abuse God. Tornebut was sure, without any reason, that it was necessary to sleep in Baziège.

"O my master," he said to me, when we were some distance away, "You've worked a great miracle." And he looked fixedly at his feet.

The sun had disappeared. A light breeze that was blowing sobered me up.

"Are you sure?" I asked. "They were shouting so loudly and crowding me so much that I scarcely had time to examine the fig-tree."

"It was a great miracle," Tornebut was content to repeat.

He turned round frequently and even manifested a certain anxiety. Behind us, we could still perceive the group agitating around the fig-tree, confusedly.

"What's the matter, Tornebut?"

"We'll sleep in Baziège, or even further on. What is dangerous is reflection. It sometimes happens that, when they reflect, people begin to deny even the most evident miracles."

PRAYER OUTSIDE LA DAURADE

There are two magical places in Toulouse: two places where the breath of God is exhaled. Perhaps there are more, but I don't know them.

One of them is the place where the Basilica of Saint Sernin has been erected, and the magical influence is particularly sensible around the three sepulchers for the Comtes. The other is situated outside the church of Saint-Marie la Dorée, which was once a temple of Apollo, and remains one for me. In more remote times, the Druids, who did not raise monuments, came to collect the wisdom of nature there. That is because they knew that where a river bends, the soil has a mystical property that influences the orientation of the waters. In front of the stone columns of La Daurade, the Garonne seems to make the decision to head westwards, as if it were at the point in its journey where the appeal of the distant ocean suddenly becomes perceptible to it.

Perhaps, I said to myself, if I stand outside La Daurade, with my hands together and my mind attentive, I too will hear an appeal, even though a man does not have the faculties of a river.

I waited until the nocturnal watchmen had uttered their last cry, the soldiers of the watch had made their last round, and belated thieves had gone back to the Rue de la Hache or the vicinity of Saint Nicolas. Then I slipped all the way to the Place de La Daurade, where the church stands behind its white colonnades like a genius of stone guarded by angels of marble.

The sun was about to rise, the Garonne gave the impression of running toward me and I had the revelation of a certain beauty of the world that had been fixed there for ages without number and was only visible to those who had discovered the cipher of its inanimate hieroglyphs.

"O Toulouse" I cried, "this is what I am reading for the first time in the book of stone, water and sky that you form behind the enclosure if your ramparts! Until today I have been

109

like an ignorant cleric, leaning over parchment grimoires, who knows the letter but does not know the meaning. I have been like the rustic monk who believes that he sees God in the sculpture of statues and does not know what the divine is. Glory to the towers that rise, to the streets that extended their hands to make a chain, to the welcoming porches in which the metal door-knockers shine, to the bridges curved like blows!

"I see everything that was necessary over the ages to build this city of solar bricks at the place where the river bends. How must the first man have felt who stopped his boat on the sand at the place where I am and decided to build a hut between a poplar and a wild vine-cep? O my God, how I would like to resemble that meager Tectosage, nourished on fish! Doubtless he had found that the days were too short in the Pyrenean valleys and the mountain slopes too austere. Doubtless he desired a terrain where the sunlight spread out in uninterrupted sheets. He wanted to see the appearance and death of the sun on the horizon. He plunged his oar profoundly into the rustic shore and Toulouse was born.

"O Toulouse, I can see the inclination of favorable hills and the elongation of plane trees with beautiful foliage toward your solidly-constructed gates. I can see the Druids marching with their long beards and white robes, the Roman priests with their shaven heads, the Christian saints clad in brown, the Visigoth Kings with their stitched fox-fur mantles and their octagonal bonnets. They built temples and basilicas, they launched towers like arrows. and the bricks absorbed the sunlight in the open air.

"There is the Château Narbonnais with its powerful build of a fortress. The barbicans of the ramparts spread out therefrom at intervals, in a circle, where the watchmen, in their armor, resemble metal beads along a granite necklace. Saint Sernin and La Dalbade sprang forth to the north and the east, the cloisters extended their quadrilaterals of pilasters, and the stone-carvers shaped houses with ornamented courtyards like Byzantine jewelry. But it was not as in other cities. There is an order and a beauty here that emerge from the ground, and the essence of which the Garonne perhaps brings from the Pyrenean substance where its waters are born, with the consequence that the columns of the monuments give the impression of proclaiming a message, that the simple street-corners are the announcers of a truth, that in the movement of the dwellings, the openings of portals and the gestures of turrets there is an organization whose meaning is spiritual and inclines the soul toward perfection.

"O Toulouse, you are the object of the predilection of the gods, of the benevolence of the invisible spirits that precede wandering tribes and preside over the building of cities. Magnanimous, you welcome the traveler. Pious, when all your bells sound they are audible from Bordeaux to Perpignan. Literate, you have engendered the seven poets who had the custom of sitting down on the day of the dead in a garden in Saint Étienne, from which their verses flew even further than the sound of your bells. Courageous, you carry your living strength in the fire that has coagulated the molecules of your bricks. Eternal, you combine the Occitan races in order to draw from their mixture men of great heart and beautiful structure.

"So, by the light of the rising sun, I, the humblest of your sons, beside the Garonne that passes by, I kneel down and I embrace the burned stone of La Daurade Kallichore."[9]

---

[9] In Greek mythology Kallichore was one of the nymphs who nursed Dionysus, and was sometimes considered to be a Muse.

THE VIRGIN OF MERCY

"We'll go around the old cemetery of Saint Sernin, where the tombs are so ancient that no one knows the names of the dead any longer," Tornebut said to me. "We'll go along the wall of the cloister and in the Rue des Tisserands we'll take the descending side street that goes all the way to the ramparts. It's there that it will be possible to encounter the Virgin of Mercy, provided that the night is moonless, or only illuminated by a slender crescent."

Tornebut's eyes were shining, as they did every time he talked about the Virgin of Mercy. He had mentioned her to me frequently, but I had thought that he was echoing some legend on which it was inappropriate to dwell.

"You'll see her as I've seen her," he told me. "We'll respire the air raised by her robe, which is that of spring roses. Perhaps she'll guide you toward the divine thing for which you're searching. For, in the same way that I know the location of the plane in my workshop, pick it up and apply it, supernatural creatures must have knowledge of objects that belong to the supernatural world and make the same familiar usage of them."

So, one evening, moonless but blue with stars, after we had bowed down before the three great stone sepulchers that contain the bones of Raymond Bertrand, Pons and Guillaume Taillefer, Comtes de Toulouse, we went around the old cemetery of Saint Sernin, where the nudity of steles and the inclination of lame crosses attests to the forgetfulness of the living.

After the cloister a quarter extends in which poverty and pleasure dwell together. The beggars who station themselves the city gates by day live here, and the paupers whom, because they are orphans or considered as wicked, colporteurs bring from distant towns. There is a side street especially reserved for cagots.[10] The local women come and go, appealing to passers-by with lewd gestures. Some of them, by derision and also in order to be recognized, wear the woolen hood that the Capitouls once obliged prostitutes to wear. There are taverns where there are only Moorish women and one can distinguish the music of guzlas, which rises up to accompany incomprehensible songs of mortal sadness.

A dolorous joy animated the quarter in question when we went into it. There were sounds of dancing behind the walls. On a stone Christ standing in the middle of a small square some joker had put a broad-brimmed felt had a velvet cape with a red collar, so that the Christ resembled a caricature Spaniard. A young man with a face the color of candle-wax was singing to the accompaniment of a guitar, but every time he raised his voice the sounds rang so false that those who were listening to him from windows or doorways jeered or whistled. A deformed child with an excessively large and heavy head tugged the flap of his garment but, his eyes upraised as if in ecstasy, he was following his interior song.

Suddenly, Tornebut seized my arm urgently and I saw that there was a triumphant smile on his face.

"The Virgin of Mercy!" he said. "Look! She's there."

"Where?"

He showed me, in front of us the pavement of the street, where a lantern cast a ruddy light. I made no reply, for a man who possesses imperfect senses has no need to proclaim his inferiority.

---

[10] "Cagots" were a Medieval European population analogous to the "untouchables" of India, not distinguished from the majority population by religion, ethnicity or any external feature, but nevertheless loathed, despised and cruelly persecuted throughout western France and northern Spain, for reasons that are profoundly unclear.

"Let's follow her!" he said, then. "She's raising her hand awkwardly and I can see that she has an extraordinarily tiny little finger."

We walked all the way to the ramparts, and then took back streets so narrow that two men had difficulty walking abreast.

"Look, as she passes by she's touching those who seem the most unfortunate. Their faces remain transfigured by it. A woman has just fallen to her knees."

There was, in fact, a kneeling woman, her head in her hands, but it seemed to me that she must have had that attitude for some time.

"Can you smell that subtle odor of roses, mingled with a slight aroma of violets?"

I breathed in forcefully several times but the nature of certain perfumes is to be fleeting and to dissipate rapidly.

We had come back by a long detour to the little square in which the Christ in Spanish costume stood. The singer had just concluded his song and was holding up his guitar. I overheard a few humorous exclamations here and there, provoked by the final words of the song.

"The Virgin of Mercy is now visible to everyone," murmured Tornebut, in a low voice. "Everyone receives a little of her miraculous bounty and remains comforted by it."

His hands were joined and he was staring adoringly at the place where the miraculous Virgin was. The spot was in the same direction as the singer with the waxen face.

I touched the shoulder of an old man who appeared to me to be looking in the same direction.

"Who do you see there?" I asked him.

"That's Laurent des Minimes. He comes almost every day. It's a pity that he sings so poorly."

"And there's no one else?"

"Yes, a child, his adoptive son."

"And no one else?"

The man looked at me in surprise. "You can see perfectly well that there's no one."

Tornebut took me by the sleeve and drew me into the side street that went back up toward Saint Sernin.

"Those who can see the Virgin of Mercy don't like to say that they can see her. That's well known. There are favors that cease to exist when they're expressed in language."

"Tornebut," I replied, "the favor is only real for me if I have the vulgar certainty that comes from the senses. Let's hasten our steps, if you please, in order that I can touch the robe of the Virgin of Mercy and see that minuscule little finger that you can see yourself."

"Nothing is easier," said Tornebut. "When you touch her you'll feel a slight warmth in the hand and a delicious balm in the heart."

We hastened our steps and I took deep breaths in order to perceive the perfume of roses and violets. But perhaps that slowed us down. We had not yet caught up with the Virgin of Mercy when we went around the old cemetery, and Tornebut suddenly said:

"She's just disappeared into the wall of the basilica at a place where there isn't a door. Look at the luminous trace that she's left on the bricks a little to the right of the Comtes' tombs. I can't tell whether it's white or blue, the color is so subtle."

"I can't tell either, Tornebut."

A great sadness invaded me, and it required a great effort for me not to yield to the sin of envy.

THE WIFE AND THE HOUSE

"Have you not heard laughter, Tornebut, which made you think of colliding crystals? Certain light laughter traverses walls more easily than other, heavier laughter that is devoid of wings. The laughter in question is that of my beloved wife with the long tresses the color of night. But, no matter how delightful laughter might be, it loses its value when it is repeated too frequently. Now it has just burst out again.

"In my day the shutters were closed as soon as dusk appeared. That custom must have been lost, like so many. The lamps are lit and the passers-by that we are—for, take note, we are simply passers-by—can see silhouettes going back and forth through the window-panes. How do you interpret those shutters left wide open? They're the sign of the joy that reigns in the house. They mean: *There is nothing to hide here.* Happiness fills the souls that dwell behind these walls. Those who are unhappy prefer not to be seen and remain in confrontation with the shadow that emerges from them.

"Furthermore, there has always been a joyous disposition in that house. Those two stone columns framing the threshold gave the impression of two silent friends. The windows are welcoming. The quality of the bricks is such that they store the sunlight and only let it escape slowly. I'm astonished not to have understood all the benevolent intentions of that dwelling while I was living there. If I want to be sincere I ought to admit that I never thought of anything but quitting it.

"It was my father who had bought it and he said that it was not very solid. But do houses not always last longer than men? There is a treasure hidden in the garden, my father told me. But when I asked him under which tree it was necessary to dig, in order to find it, he told me that it did not matter, that the ground was full of hidden treasures and that by digging anywhere, at random, one has every chance of discovering astonishing things. And he also told me that a spirit musician lived in the weathervane, for the weathervane sang all sorts of

116

strange tunes on windy nights. The weathervane is still there, and there, higher than the roof, are the four old trees of the garden.

"When I left I didn't even take the key to the entrance door. What use is the key to a house to which one is never going to return? I'm a passer-by looking at a house in the moonlight.

"How many joyful voices one can hear, punctuated by laughter. Doubtless my beloved wife has invited friends to a meal where delight will reign. I've just perceived the proud profile of that Seigneur de Montagnol whose origin no one knows, and who claims to have large estates in countries where no one will ever go. I thought I also recognized the pretentious Catherine de Carraton, who has the genealogies of all the royal families of Europe at her fingertips. The Bishop of Toulouse addresses her as *tu*. She's seen at every mass at Saint-Étienne. Catherine de Carraton is the greatest slut in Toulouse, and my good wife's best friend.

"They've just lit the big silver candelabras that make the mirrors resplendent. It seems to me that here's a little orchestra on the first floor. Isn't that the young Chevalier de Polastron who has just come downstairs? He's famous throughout Languedoc for the dissolution of his morals. Women question him about the manner of dyeing hair and men consult him about the color of their waistbands. And always the song of that laughter like a waterfall on gravel.

"What must Timothée think, the old servant who helped me to arrange the books and manuscripts in my library, on seeing all those people gathering in my house, to whom I once refused entry? He must be scandalized. But who knows? He likes good food and he had a long face when, for love of frugality, I only ordered him to make meager meals. I'd gladly imagine that he misses me. Surely he must miss me. But this evening his kitchen is sparkling, the spit is turning, the bottles are warming up. His face is beaming. This evening, he isn't missing me.

"By whom is one missed, Tornebut? I don't think anyone ever misses you. There are farewell gestures, moving words, simulation of dolor, but one can go to China or further, into regions from which the ships that carry you never return, without leaving any sincere regret, true, heart-rending regret. And whether you've been a good or bad husband, a good or bad father, a good or bad son, the regret is the same, or very nearly. And I might say that if one has been a bad husband, a bad father or a bad son, the regret is a little shaper. That's the way it is, Tornebut, and one can't do anything about it. And it's good that it's thus. What would my remorse be, this evening, if my house were in mourning!

"So, all's well; I'm satisfied; let's go, Tornebut. Those illuminated windows are like the gaze of the past. They appear joyful to me because they've entered the enchantment of memory. The forms of happiness are perpetually transformed. How sad it would be or me to ring the doorbell and be introduced as a stranger! How sad it would be for everyone, and what a specter at the feast I would be! Have I not deliberately chosen the role of missionary, of wandering prophet, or whatever? That role doesn't include any turning back. I'm quite content, Tornebut, with all the joy they've having without me, and perhaps because of my absence.

"The little orchestra has just struck up a dance tune. It's doubtless to give the guests an appetite. I believe you have our evening meal in that sack you're carrying on your back. We'll have it on the bank of the Garonne, by the light of the stars. It will be an excellent meal, taken on a hard stone, with a big bottle of Garonne water as a beverage. I'm enjoying it in advance! We need to go, Tornebut.

"There at the last window on the right, I've just seen my wife's face. Why is she looking into the street? Has she had a presentiment? She was, in sum, a charming wife. What a pity she always had a desire to laugh! And what a pity she never believed in anything! Faith isn't given to everyone. Faith is often a heavy burden. But then, doesn't everyone have their faults? Pull me by the arm, Tornebut. It's time to go. I'm quite content."

THE ABDUCTION OF MARIE COSE

That day, as we were approaching the Old Bridge, we saw a lot of people heading in that direction.

"Perhaps the Bishop of Saint-Bertrand de Comminges is within the walls of Toulouse," said Tornebut.

When Urbain de Saint-Gelais, Bishop of Comminges,[11] came to Toulouse, some warlike event always ensued. His great age had only increased his intolerance. A few years before, I had seen him, with the Provincial of the Minimes by his side, traversing Toulouse at the head of three hundred monks all carrying swords in their belts and arquebuses over their shoulders. He regretted the good old days when Catholics and Huguenots massacred one another ardently.

I asked a man of timid appearance—for it is always timid men who are the most obliging in informing you—what motivated the movement of the people of San Subra in the direction of the Garonne.

"The Bishop of Saint-Bertrand is in Toulouse," he replied. "He thinks that mores have relaxed. The immorality of Toulouse extends, it appears, into Comminges. He has been so successful with the members of the Parlement and the Capitouls that a torture that was only applied to blasphemers has just been reestablished for prostitutes. Those who are condemned for a bad life, before being imprisoned, will henceforth be plunged into the Garonne three times."

A fat woman with lubricious eyes stopped.

"Three times isn't enough to wash away the corruption. They ought to be left at the bottom until the river has carried away all the leprosy of their bodies."

"The time ought to be short enough for them not to perish but long enough for them to suffer," said the timid man.

---

[11] Urbain de Saint-Gelais de Lansac was Bishop of Comminges from 1580-1613.

120

He remained silent for a moment, looked at his feet, and said, slowly: "It's good to suffer. One never suffers enough."

He drew away in the direction of the bridge.

At the corner of the Rue de la Moutonnière we were preceded by a band of children who were laughing and shouting, Monks emerged from the house of Saint John. One of them was fat and jovial. He talked very loudly, and in the joy of talking he addressed himself to me."

"They're arriving just in time for sunset. The ceremony of honorable amends is very long. The old customs are the best. We need examples. What would become of us if there were no examples?"

A woman alongside us made the sign of the cross, to express the fact that she was a partisan of examples.

A tall thin, man said, gravely: "It's a girl who had led a young man astray."

"It's necessary to protect youth," added the jovial monk, laughing.

Suddenly, however, we were separated by the human masses unfurling around us like waves from al the streets ending at the Old Bridge. Then I saw that the river bank and the bridge itself were covered by an immense undulating crowd, from which all sorts of appeals and joyful cries rose up. I perceived that Tornebut had been carried away from me.

I participated in the vulgar curiosity of the people until the moment when I saw the police captain in front of me. I recognized that man, and I despised him. His name was Mauric. I knew that he was insolent and harsh with the poor, abject before the powerful. He was advancing with difficulty, parting the crowd with his arms, with a false smile on his face. Sometimes, he darted a glance behind him, at the cortege that was following him, and he seemed to be regretting not having a more numerous troop to control the unexpected crowd.

Twenty men from La Maynade were marching behind him. The sunlight was reflected from the metal of their helms and the iron of their pikes, and they were trying to make their swords resonate on the paving stones. Among them there was a bare-headed man with tousled red hair, whom everyone knew and to whom everyone as showing the finger. That was Anselme Isnard, the executioner. Next to him was his son, an equally red-haired and tousled young man, who looked like a thinner and younger copy. One of his aides was carrying a long pole on his back, around which ropes were wound and a sort of net composed of metal strips, which was fitted to a plank serving as a support.

Under a black veil thick enough that nothing could be distinguished of her features, marched the condemned woman. A chain that must have been attached to her wrist emerged from her veil and was held by a man of La Maynade, who tugged it nervously in jerks, although the entire group could only advance with extreme slowness. The black veil fell all the way to her feet, but everyone knew that she was in a chemise under the veil because she had just been, in that costume, with a candle in her hand, to beg God's pardon in the Cathedral of Saint-Étienne. The thought of that naked body under that lugubrious veil animated the crowd with an evil joy.

The man was known to everyone, for people were calling to her by name: "Marie!" Joyous pleasantries resounded on all sides relating to the torture she was about to undergo:

"Don't drink all the water in the Garonne!"

"Bring me back a fish!

And laughter went up. Alongside me, a woman was indignant because people were preventing her child from seeing, and she lifted him in her arms until he started to clap his hands.

Captain Mauric had stopped in the middle of the bridge and had reached the parapet. He leaned over the water, as if to see whether the spot was propitious. Then he stood up and I could see from afar that a frown was barring his forehead and that he was irritated by the crowd, which was hindering his movements. The crowd was, however, benevolent. It seemed to be thanking him for the spectacle that he was about to offer it. There were even cries of "Long live Mauric!"

122

I was watching that from the extremity of the bridge, where I found myself, and I turned my head to the right and left to see whether I could not escape from the spectacle. My teeth were chattering and I was experiencing a great chill in my back. If I had not been pressed from all sides, I would have sat down on the ground. I was afraid. Everything that there was around me of malevolence, and forces deprived of reason, was acting upon me, and for a moment it seemed to me that my consciousness was crushed by an evil force and that I could no longer recover myself as I had been before.

And it was then that I sensed clearly that there is sometimes an intervention in the order of things, the cause of which remains unknown but which is exterior to human beings. It was by virtue of that intervention that an eddy was abruptly produced in the depths of the crowd, and that eddy carried me from the entrance of the bridge all the way to Captain Mauric's side, as if I were the essential witness who had to watch the immersion of the girl named Marie, and found myself, for that reason, in the first rank.

And at the same time, my consciousness of the people surrounding me was enlarged. I had a singular power of reading souls. I read their absence of pity, their innate harshness, and the evil sentiments that had taken possession of them. I experienced an indescribable horror for the tall Captain Mauric, the executioner Anselme Isnard with the red hair, and their ironclad acolytes armed with pikes, like sinister marionettes of metal. I saw behind them, and higher up, in the cloud of the dream, the King's Seneschal, Jean de la Vallette-Cornusson,[12] with his arched back, his moustache and his dangling arms, and the bored expression that he always had; I saw

---

[12] Jean de La Vallette, Baron de Cornusson, was Seneschal of Toulouse in 1611 but the exact dates of his tenure are difficult to determine; an earlier Seneschal with the same surname and the forename François is recorded as having died in 1586 and there was also a previous Jean and a later François, so the post appears to have been almost hereditary.

the eight Capitouls in their loose-fitting robes with wide collars and their velvet toques, with their willful self-importance and affected majesty; I saw the members of the Parlement, with the proud President de Paulo[13] at their head, all animated by the hatred of Huguenots; I saw Antoine de Chalabre, Bishop of Toulouse, and Urbain de Saint-Gelais, Bishop of Saint-Bertrand, with their Episcopal robes, their pastoral crosiers and their enormous miters.

And from all direction the religious fraternities advanced, which were also warrior fraternities, carrying banners, crosses and sword: the Black Penitents of the Rue Peyras; the Gray Penitents of the Trinity; the Augustins and the Minimes. I saw the cells, the cloisters, the prie-Dieus where certain hermits ankylosed their knees by dint of remained kneeling down, the chapels where certain saints had been found dead on the flagstones in the midst of the ecstasy of prayer. Overhead extended the shadows of the tower of Saint Dominic and the house of the Inquisition, those of the Eagle Tower, the Château Narbonnais, La Dalbade and Saint Sernin, where phantom birds were flying. And those shadows of towers inclined, the fraternities walked in avenues of darkness, the banners flapping, the swords glinting.

That moving vision full of troops of men through which cavaliers were passing, with the constituted bodies, the guilds and their insignia, the monastic associations, were confused with the city of Toulouse, its ancient streets strewn with porticoes and turrets, its brick and slate roofs, divided by the azurean Garonne. And in the distance, beyond the misty roads, there were other cities surrounded by ramparts with other Parlements and their fraternities, and all of that was the world of men, rich, cruel, full of sap and blood, full of love and

---

[13] Like the La Vallettes, the Paulos were an important political dynasty in Toulouse, similarly linked very closely with the Order of Saint John of Jerusalem (the Knights of Malta). Several of them were presidents of the Parlement at the end of the 16th and the beginning of the 17th century.

hope, full of an appetite for justice, a justice that the priests announced from their pulpits, the symbols of which the illuminators painted on parchments, and which ended in what I saw there: a wretched woman under a black veil, who was about to be tortured in order to make the Toulousan crowd dance with joy.

I had difficulty making out the obscure form of that woman, so much more veritable than the reality was the vision that filled my eyes. I made an effort to rediscover myself in the middle of the Old Bridge. The vision retreated and dissipated. There was a great silence, an overwhelming silence. Then it seemed to me that the woman and I were alone on the earth.

Perhaps that did not last any longer than a second. Perhaps it was very long. Life had stopped. The crowd was immobile and silent. All the faces were frozen. The Garonne, between the piles of the bridge, had ceased to flow and its water had turned to marble.

And suddenly, there as a burst of laughter that resounded all way to the globe of the sun, which was about to disappear beyond the Bazacle and seemed to precipitate its descent. That burst of strange, irrational laughter had been uttered by Anselme Isnard, the executioner. Why did he laugh? That laughter had the effect on me of the laughter of evil, the evil that laughs at its triumph, and it was that which brought me back to reality at a stroke. At the same time, the crowd resumed moving, a thousand noises resounded and the Garonne began flowing again.

Anselme Isnard had doubtless laughed at what he was about to do. With an abrupt gesture he snatched away the veil that covered the condemned woman.

Scarcely had he made that gesture, scarcely had the face of an unfortunate creature with blinking eyes and a wan complexion appeared in the light than, driven by an interior force, by the certainty that I was chosen, I launched myself between them, exactly as if I were endowed with invisible wings, and I shoved the man back with such great force that he rolled as far as the parapet.

Surprise nailed everyone to the spot, and the first to make a movement to hurl himself toward me was the executioner's son. He was busy with an aide fixing the net to which they were about to attach the woman to the end of the pole that they had brought. He dropped the net, took a step forward, and was stopped dead by my gaze. I think he even recoiled, with the gesture of someone who has just felt a burn.

Cries burst forth on all sides. What did I want? Who was that person who was trying to get in the way of popular pleasure?

Captain Mauric recognized me and his face expressed amazement. For him I was a notable inhabitant of Toulouse and I read in his gaze that he attributed my action to madness.

But it was as if I were possessed by a God. An alien force inhabited me and I could only obey it. My voice resonated with an accent unknown to me when I intimated to Captain Mauric the order to release the woman who was standing close to me and before whom I was extending my arms as a sign of protection. My order was addressed simultaneously to the soldiers of the police who were surrounding me.

The God who was animating me had to know that there was nothing to hope for from those creatures with closed souls, for before they could make a gesture I addressed myself to the crowd.

I did not know what I was saying. In any case, the words were unimportant. I even believe that those I repeated were almost deprived of sense. What counted was the active projection that emerged from me. I had advanced and I had seized a tall man by the collar, into whose eyes I plunged my gaze like a sword. My exhortation was vehement and inflamed. I sensed that the power that I possessed could be compared to fire. The fire that came to my speech inflamed the beings that heard me. They were inflamed by the words *love, suffering* and *Jesus Christ* that returned incessantly and burst forth like explosions.

I noticed that the people who had invaded the bridge had particularly criminal appearances. They were not the people of Toulouse. They were the shady population of San Subra, of the Pré Montardy and the Rue de la Hache. There were prostitutes in large numbers and the men who lived with them. There were the gold-panners of the Île de Tounis, Moors of the lowest class with leaden complexions, and almost black Bohemians with their hair in braids that they caused to fall over their breasts. They had come for the joy of watching the torture of a woman. I offered them another joy: that of saving the woman in question.

Events that have not been concerted in advance happen with a rapidity that defies all anticipation. A man bent double emerged from the crowd and butted Captain Mauric in the stomach like a ram. The soldiers lowered their pikes. The crowd, gained by the fire of the deliverance, sent a wave that launched me, with all those in the front rank, against the lowered pikes.

Howls went up. There was the sound of a body bundled over the parapet that fell into the Garonne. In the tumult, the splash of the water was like the freshness of a drink in a glass. The human wave swept over and trampled the soldiers, and then came back, dragging me with it and dragging the woman in the chemise, who clung to my shoulders like a drowning woman in a tempest. To my great amazement I heard my name repeated: "Michel!" with the accent of someone who had known me for a long time.

On looking around I saw a sort of giant with thick lips and a squashed nose gesticulating and giving orders. I recognized Mérigon Combres, a popular individual in the Toulousan rabble. He was the proprietor of a celebrated tavern in the Rue des Moulins and had a liking for riots.[14] He had

---

[14] Mérigon Combres is given as the name of the proprietor of a tavern in the Rue de Moulins in an article in the *Mémoires de l'Académie des sciences, inscriptions et belles-lettres* in 1914, where Magre might have found it.

been at the head of Duranti's assassins and was reputed to procure murderers for hire.[15]

I did not have time to take stock. Arms had seized me and placed me on a platform made with a plank that formed the base of the cage that was about to be plunged into the river. At the same time, the woman, still clinging to me, was hoisted up beside me. Her chemise was ripped in two; her hair was falling over her withered shoulders. I heard her repeat my name in a low voice with an intonation to which emotion gave an amorous inflection.

Acclamations went up around us, at the same time as cries of "Death to Mauric!" "Down with Mauric!" and "Into the water!" I saw faces turned toward me with gratitude, and I heard: "He's a Bishop! Look at his crosier!" "No, he's a saint!"

I had kept my curved staff in my hand and sensed that its presence against me, contributed, with that of a half-naked sinner, to giving me the appearance of a grotesque king, the pastor of a wretched and insensate flock. I searched desperately for Tornebut, but I could not see him anywhere.

In the distance I saw men fleeing. Some let themselves fall into boats and went downstream into the falling night. Others were running with weapons. An entire band of men of evil appearance and tall stature had thrown themselves into the waste ground bordering the Garonne, in the direction of San Subra. There were huge beams piled up for some construction. The men seized them and made a barricade at the extremity of the bridge, I thought I was seeing giants accomplishing a work of evil that I had just unleashed.

Two young men who had the appearance of brothers and were dressed as butchers arrived, marching with a measured stride. They each had an arquebus on the shoulder. They knelt

---

[15] Duranti, the first President of the Parlement of Toulouse, was murdered by a mob while returning home in his coach in January 1589; this reference implies that the present novel is set in the 1590s.

down on the ground without haste and lit their wicks, as if everything had only been arranged in order to permit them to fire.

Night fell. Torches were lit here and there. The clamors that could be heard in the distance created an atmosphere of catastrophe. I made an effort to jump off the plank and lose myself in the crowd.

"No! No!" cried Mérigon Combres, who suddenly surged forth beside me. "Don't let him go away. Carry him to Saint Nicolas, He's deserved it." Turning an enormous hilarious face in my direction, he added: "You'll have the one you want. You've earned that with your courage. Marie Cose will be yours."[16] His voice swelled to a shout: "We'll marry them. We're going to marry Marie Cose to her lover."

I was unable to respond. The men who were carrying me on their shoulders launched forward at a run, shouting, through the streets of the suburb of San Subra.

A name had just traversed me more profoundly than an archer's arrows: Marie Cose! By the magic of syllables I rediscovered in the shadows of my memory the young face of someone who had been a friend of mine twenty years before, and whom I might have loved, or thought I loved. For a second, I heard her ancient laughter resonating like the voice of a mockingbird in the forest of Bouconne. But what a change! What misery of time and debauchery! If any doubt had subsisted in me it would have been dissipated by the voice of Marie Cose, a hoarse, dolorous voice, ridiculous because of the falsity of the tone.

"So you haven't forgotten me! You still love me, then!"

---

[16] Marie Cose is mentioned in the *Annals of Toulouse* as a blonde beauty of loose morals who was at the peak of her notoriety after 1600. She crops up again in the first chapter of Magre's next novel *Jean de Fodoas* (1939), in which she is considerably younger than she is here, although the chapter in question appears to be set at a similar date.

A kind of interior horror possessed me. What I had done out of pity for a human creature, out love for a suffering being, had been interpreted by the woman I had saved, and by the crowd who had helped me to save her, as an act of vulgar desire for the possession of a woman! An immense discouragement took possession of my soul. People were fighting because of me. I was being carried in triumph, with caricaturish honors, by the dregs of the Toulousan people! I felt something moist and greasy against my cheek; it was Marie Cose's hair, which she was trying to wrap around her head like a crown.

The Church of Saint Nicolas was situated in the heart of San Subra. The streets of the suburb flow around it like putrid steams. After sunset the soldiers of La Maynade never venture among the population of Bohemians, converted Moors and debauched individuals who swarmed in its leprous houses. The curé of Saint Nicolas, who was now ninety years old and was reputed to be a saint, was the only person to have any authority over that strange people, and it was said to stem from the fact that he tolerated a Christianity that was half-pagan among his parishioners.

The clergy of Toulouse had demanded a crusade against San Subra, claiming that diabolical ceremonies were celebrated in Saint Nicolas by night, but the quarter was defended by terror, for fifty years earlier it had been from there that the plague had spread that had ravaged Toulouse and a part of the Languedoc. A vast block of houses that ended in the square outside the church had been sealed with beams. The windows had been blocked. It was said that he plague-victims once imprisoned there haunted their former dwellings and could be heard walking and lamenting at night. Better-informed men thought that thieves, then very numerous, had established their lair there.

The platform on which Marie Cose and I found ourselves was abruptly set down on the steps of Saint Nicolas. There was a sound of chains, for the metal net that was attached to it was trailing on the ground behind us. I found myself upright, But Marie Cose fell on to her hands, and when she got up again she crossed them precipitately over her bare breasts, trying to veil them with the shreds of her chemise. With a disconcerting rapidity, a large circle formed around us and a clamor resounded, a clamor of joy caused by Marie Cose's nudity. Doubtless she was ashamed, for she raised a hand to her eyes. That gesture showed the chain that still held her wrist, and a further clamor, mingled with pity and indignation, rose up on all sides.

All around me I saw burlesque faces, stupefied or terrible. The events of the bridge had flown from mouth to mouth. Some were interrogating, others recounting. All of them were looking at me with admiration. A woman, almost walking on her knees, seized my garment and kissed it. A humanity never yet seen had emerged from the utmost depths of the suburb like a multitude of rats after a flood. In the same way that one wonders how animals so large and so redoubtable had been able to love in close proximity without your knowledge, I wondered how that savage, inhuman population had been able to inhabit the same city as me without my having any knowledge of its life and appearances.

I tried in vain to make myself heard. On raising my head I perceived above me the eight mummies of Saint Nicolas. On a ledge that dominated the portal, occupying the entire width of the church, they stood, grimacing, and the vague light of a torch gave them an illusion of life. It was a curiosity of the suburb that the majority of Toulousans only knew through hearsay, so much disgust did the quarter inspire. Eight mummified human forms, whose heads retained teeth and a frightful rictus, were mounted behind a grille above the porch of Saint Nicolas. No one knew the origin of those mummies. It seemed to me that they turned toward me ironically in order to testify to the nullity of what I had attempted.[17]

---

[17] Cléobule Paul's *Toulouse monumentale et pittoresque* (1840) gives the original number of the famous mummies of the Church of Saint Nicolas as twenty, although it presumably dwindled over the years.

I was no longer thinking about anything but fleeing that inferno into which I had so imprudently penetrated. I wanted to draw away straight ahead in the hope of reaching some back street, but Marie Cose was clinging desperately to my shoulder, passionately repeating promises of eternal fidelity.

At the same time, the gigantic stature of Mérigon Combres loomed up. He opened his arms wide before me and cried: "The wine's coming! Patience! We'll be able to drink as much as we want!"

And he made a semblance of moderating with a gesture my avidity to drink, assuring me that someone had gone in search of wine.

Men rolled barrels over the steps of the church and set about piercing them. My voice was lost in the midst of howls when Mérigon Combres, dominating the crowd, shouted: "We're going to celebrate the marriage!" He turned toward the mummies and added: "In the name of the eight Capitouls here present, in the name of Gonnedrille and Fillandas!" And he designated the two mummies at the extremities of the ledge.

I knew that the eight mummies had received grotesque names from the people and had been assimilated derisively to the eight Capitouls. It also came back to my memory that ceremonies were celebrated before them that caricatured everything that was sacred.

An immense clamor responded to Mérigon Combres. It seemed to me that it was followed by several distant detonations.

"Bring the light!" shouted the master of the crowd. "And tell the queen to hurry up!"

"Here she is! Long live the queen! Long live La Mérigone!"

In the street that went along the house of the plague-victims and enormous matron had just appeared, Mérigon Combres' wife, who was known as the queen of the procuresses. Her belly was covered by a church cope and she had a cardboard bishop's miter on her head, on which a death's-head had been painted between obscene emblems. Around her, a few prostitutes holding lanterns were prancing on broom-sticks, doubtless to represent witches ready to fly to the Sabbat.

"I'll crown the bride," said the queen, and headed toward Marie Cose, holding out a paper crown.

The latter must have thought that it was some trap. Doubtless she had not understood the meaning of what was happening very clearly. She uttered several heart-rending screams and threw herself at my knees, wrapping her arms around them.

The laughter had redoubled. Suddenly, however, I saw all eyes fix on the low door of a narrow house adjacent to the right side of the Church of Saint Nicolas, and there was a silence that spread through the crowd.

That door had just opened slowly. On the threshold stood a very small priest with a face covered in wrinkles and long white hair falling over his shoulders. He must have been sensitive to cold, for he had thrown a mountain-dweller's cloak over his shoulders. Behind him appeared the head of an old woman who lifted up a ruddy lantern to illuminate him. He was smiling. He seemed very benevolent. I divined that he was the old curé of Saint Nicolas.

"My little children! What is it this evening, my little children?" he murmured.

The queen's arms were immobilized. The prostitutes on broomsticks recoiled, capering, like she-devils under a rain of holy water. The crowd was open-mouthed.

But I did not have time to contemplate the serene beauty that radiated from the old man. A shout rang out: "Mérigon! They're coming!"

A man waving a stick, who had blood flowing over his face, arrived at the steps of the church and, addressing Mérigon Combres and the crowd alternately, he shouted: "They're murderers! The Capitoul of La Daurade came with two culverins and arquebusiers and he's swept the bridge. They're going to try to surround the church."

133

Mérigon Combres, plunging his head into his shoulders, took few steps forward, opened his arms and said: "I'll do to the Capitoul of La Daurade what I did to the Capitoul Jean Madron. I'll break his nose."

In fact, fifteen years before, in the course of a riot, he had broken Jean Madron's nose. Arquebus shots resounded near the square.

"Put the lights out!" someone shouted.

At a stroke, all the lanterns were extinguished. There were moans and curses, and the crowd undulated to the sound of weapons.

A powerful hand seized me and drew me away, forcing me to run in the dark. I recognized Tornebut when he said: "Turn right. We'll hide in my house."

I only turned round once, and in the distance, like a delicate illumination, under the eight sinister mummies of Saint Nicolas, among the shadows streaked by gunshots, I perceived the smiling old priest, making calming gestures with his trembling hands to his little children.

ON THE ROAD TO PAMIERS

"A check ought to fortify resolution," I said to Tornebut, "if one has a well-tempered soul. I don't despair of enabling the salvation of humankind. I shall discover the Grail and I shall transform hearts, as an alchemist transforms lead into gold."

Tornebut, who turned round anxiously, replied: "If only we could transform those riders that I can see on the horizon into peaceful peasants returning from work! They look to me like police sent by the Capitouls to pursue us."

We had arrived at a crossroads. Sheaves of straw were accumulated on the edge of a field. There was a spring that was pouring water into a hollow tree-trunk. In the distance I could see the first houses of Pamiers, through which the Ariège passes and over which the Pyrenees cast shadows. The countryside had been gripped by one of the powers of silence that descend a little before dusk and seem to announce it.

"Those horsemen are still too far away to have seen us," said Tornebut then. "Let's lie down among the sheaves and let them pass."

That was what we did. But we had not foreseen the attraction that a spring can exercise on weary horsemen. The cavaliers—there were five—dismounted and sat down not far from us while their horses drank. One of them, whose jovial face I recognized, soon got up in order to spread water over his sweaty face. At the same time, he continued a conversation with his companions already commenced on the road.

"His wife," he said, "has taken advantage of the opportunity to go away with the Chevalier de Polastron."

"No one can hold it against her," replied the man who was closest to me. "When one is young and pretty one doesn't like to see an aging whore like that Marie Cose preferred."

"He hasn't been in his right mind for a long time," said another. "I have relatives in Avignonnet—well, I know that he amused himself out there taking down hanged men and giving them a sepulcher."

"But why did he do that?"

"Madness."

"The son of a Capitoul of a quarter of Peyrou!"

The men exchanged other remarks on other subjects. In the end, they left.

When the sound of the horses had died away in the direction of Pamiers, I parted the sheaves that were covering me.

"Did you hear, Tornebut, what that policeman said about me?"

My head was so deep under the straw that I couldn't make out their words," said Tornebut, who, to my knowledge, had keen hearing, "but I've always heard tell the policemen are men of little faith, and scarcely worthy of confidence."

We took a little path that led us away from Pamiers, but ought to bring us back by a detour in the direction of the mountains.

As we were walking in silence I asked my companion: "Do you know a man called the Chevalier de Polastron?"

"There were Polastrons in the Rue d'Astorg, it seems to me." And Tornebut made a gesture meaning that the family in question ought to be expelled from the conversation.

But I went on, obstinately: "The Polastrons all have one particularity. The form of their face, and especially that of their globular eyes, links them to the species of frogs."

Tornebut started to laugh, but much more loudly than the comicality of that comparison warranted.

At that moment, on the edge of a pool, frogs began to croak, Tornebut laughed more loudly and I was conscious of the futile paltriness of my words, for the song of beasts is a light in the soul.

THE VILLAGE OF CAMORS

Beyond Lavelanet in the Ariège there is a small valley with a village named Camors. There, since the most ancient times, men have been more unfortunate than elsewhere, and the church they built as testimony to their woes as been called Notre-Dame des Misères.

In the valley of Camors the land, by virtue of a secret malice, hardly produced anything but thorny plants or ferns, which have no edible fruits. There was a stream that ran among stones, but its water was sometimes red-tinted and had a singular taste, as if some mountain spirit had poured some poison into it. The children were almost all born with a goiter and strangers with slim necks who were unfortunate enough to come to live in Camors became goitrous after a short time. An evil wind, always cold, blew through the valley. The animals in the farmyards died of unknown maladies. The howling of dogs by night was desperate and there was even something plaintive in the song of crickets in the valley of Camors.

Now, I had learned that the curé of the village was named Poitevin, and was the son of Poitevins who had lived there for as long as it as possible to go back through the tenebrous paths of genealogy. Poitevin! One of the four heroic men of the night of Montségur.

We were traveling in the rain and I was not entirely sure that we were on the right road. We encountered a woodcutter and I asked him whether Camors was far away.

He responded with surprise. "Very far," he said. "When you reach that clump of trees, you'll see Camors."

Now, the clump of trees was not far away. We continued to follow the zigzags of the rising path, which ended in a few firs that seemed to be having great difficulty sustaining their branches. When we arrived at those firs, we saw before us an inexpressibly sad valley, in the depths of which there was a lake. The waters of the lake were troubled, and in the middle protruded a steeple. Here and there the crowns of a few trees rose up, and on the steeps slopes cut by the still water paths were visible that must have ended at the thresholds of immersed houses. The village of Camors was now replaced by a lake. I noticed that two white birds, after having traced several circles in the air above the water, settled familiarly on the vestige of the steeple, as if it were their dwelling.

As I remained perplexed by the unexpected spectacle that I had before me, I saw a horseman riding along a circular path that overlooked the valley, and was immediately struck by the fashion in which he was examining me. He was wearing a monk's robe and had an unusually long sword at his side. Contrary to the custom of monks who, when they are armed, wear their arms under heir robe, he wore his sword on top, ostentatiously. He was also remarkable by virtue of the length of his spurs. Drops of rain were shining in his black beard and his piercing eyes were fixed with curiosity on my garments and Tornebut's.

At my gesture he pulled the reins of his horse and I interrogated him about the destiny of Camors.

"Apparently, nothing happened that was not perfectly natural. The most marvelous events are sometimes disguised beneath normal appearances. The waters, by their subterranean movements, caused the displacement of a lake that was located in a higher valley than that of Camors. The village of Camors was immersed by virtue of causes and effects related to the elements. It was a matter of the play of superimposed lakes, the man will say who studies water and the earth. And yet I, who was the friend and confidant of Julien Poitevin, know that the drama happened in the interior of his soul. It was him who summoned the waters, and the waters came in order to swallow him."

"Julien Poitevin was the curé of Camors?" I asked.

"For years. I was raised in the same convent as him. He was a saint. He was a saint for a long time. Until the day when an idea took possession of him. What idea? I never knew. He had a secret but he did not reveal it. What mysterious road can the soul of a saint follow to reach the realm of evil? Julien

Poitevin had heard tell of the power of misfortune that the village of Camors harbored. He wanted to defend its inhabitants against the destiny that afflicted them. He had no difficulty obtaining the position of curé of Camors. He did not struggle for long. He was very quickly seized by the vertigo of misfortune. There is a relationship that it is difficult to distinguish between the disease of the soul and the power of proofs.

"The last time I came to see him. I understood that he was doomed. And yet he prayed incessantly. But he no longer addressed himself to God. They will tell you that in Lavelanet. He went to lie down in the evening on a dolmen that is over there, on the other side of the lake, at the place where you can see a path plunging into the water. He appealed to the Poudoueros, the witches who live in the brushwood. He was always wrapped in a kind of red shawl, because he had acquired a goiter. It was the fault of the water. Above all, don't drink it. At first he was ashamed of it. Later, he allowed it to be seen and drew vanity from it. He told me that the goiter was the sign of fraternity with the mountain.

"He ceased to say mass. He confided to me that he said another, but in the midst of the rocks. He wanted me to company him by night when he went into the wild places. 'I'll introduce you to Bassa Jaon,' he said to me. That was a man returned to savagery who lived on the heights.[18]

"One evening I went with him as far as the edge of these forests, very high. He showed me the silhouette of a man larger than natural. 'There he is—he's waiting for me," he murmured.

"I fled, but I heard the curé of Camors behind me howling like a beast. Well, it was him who summoned the waters.

---

[18] Several nineteenth century books on the folklore of the Basque country and the Pyrenees refer to a monster named the Bassa-Jaon, and many of the same sources also refer to the witches known as Poudoueros is a proximal passage, presumably having copied the dare from one to another.

They came. It was not a punishment of Heaven, as one might think, but the response to a prayer, perhaps an order."

The monk stopped and considered the lake in front of us pensively.

"Do not those white birds above the steeple signify that the spirit escapes forces from below?" I asked him.

But he had raised his head, like someone suddenly seized by other preoccupations. He put out his hand and palpated the cloth of my garment. "It's good quality," he said.

He seemed to hesitate, and then shrugged his shoulders slightly and released the bridle of his horse.

"May I ask you to what order you belong" I said.

"I'm a Capuchin. I'm a mendicant now, but on my own account." And he raised his head proudly, agitating his beard.

"I've never seen a mendicant on horseback."

"That's to ask for alms more frequently."

"Nor one with such spurs."

"That's to flee more rapidly, when it's necessary to flee."

"Nor one with such a long sword."

"That's in order to chastise uncharitable men."

I wondered whether he was about to include me in that category, but he drew away, making a vague salute.

THE CHAIR WITH YELLOW PORTERS

Time had passed. There were other Capitouls in Toulouse. I had doubtless been forgotten. Then too, the city with a hundred churches exercises an attraction that it is very difficult to vanquish.

"It's Mardi Gras and no one will be thinking about us," said Tornebut.

It was a mild afternoon. Sitting by the roadside, after having taken the nourishment that Tornebut's satchel contained, we were getting ready to set off again. The towers of the city were visible in the distance. We were struck by the sound of voices and we saw a strange cortege coming along the road we had just followed.

It was primarily composed of women. Most of them were traveling on foot, with difficulty. Some were mounted on mules or donkeys. The bright colors of their garments were almost blinding. An individual with a large hat, clad in black, was marching at the head and drawing dolorous sounds from an Arab guzla. A dwarf with white hair leaning on a staff sometimes raised his arms and seemed to be giving encouragement to others.

When the group had drawn level with me it stopped spontaneously. I distinguished that all the female travelers belonged to a well-defined category, that of prostitutes.

Cries and moans resounded. Each of them dropped the baggage she was carrying. I saw traces of fatigue and woe on faces with faded make-up. But I did not have to wonder what catastrophe had struck those creatures and thrown them together on the road. I learned immediately by virtue of maledictions and complaints. The aged white-haired dwarf explained to me volubly.

The consuls of Pamiers, Huguenots of great austerity, had made the decision three days ago to expel all the prostitutes from their city. Doubtless they had wanted to avoid the licentious scenes produced the previous year during the carnival. But those consuls with hearts of stone, who were secretly more depraved than the others—the dwarf could affirm that personally—had only given the unfortunate women a few hours to gather their clothes and cross the limit of the ramparts. The name of Raymond Pellipar recurred incessantly in the maledictions that rose up against the consuls. It was him who, in his youth, had roused the inhabitants of Pamiers and organized the pillage of the Jesuits' house. Now he was told he was expelling defenseless women! And did I not think that in going to find the Jesuits of Toulouse and saying to them: "Here are the new victims of Raymond Pellipar!" they would not stimulate armed men who would go to lay siege of Pamiers and return the men to their houses?

No, in truth, I did not think so. The Jesuits of Toulouse scarcely occupied themselves with the fate of women. They were no longer thinking of reentering their destroyed college in Pamiers, in spite of a provisional peace between Catholics and Huguenots established by a recent royal edict.[19]

The dwarf knew about that edict and shouted to the ignorant women to shut up.

I even bent down to whisper in the ear of the little man, who appeared sensate to me, a doubt regarding the welcome that would be given to the prostitutes of Pamiers by the guards at the gates of Toulouse. Access to the city was forbidden to strangers—I dared not say to beggars and people of low life.

I had spoken too loudly. I was overheard by the nearest women. Clamors of despair and revolt burst forth.

So they were going to be chased away everywhere! There was no place for them on earth! Was Toulouse not a Catholic city, then? And I understood that there was a bizarre association in their minds between the Catholic religion and their profession. They had put all their hope in Toulouse. If they could not get into it, they were doomed to die.

---

[19] The reference is to the Edict of Nantes, signed by Henri IV in 1598, so this part of the story is presumably set in the early 1600s.

A tall prostitute dressed in red, with hair almost the same color as her robe, started gesticulating in front of me.

"I'm Bonice the Provençale, Everyone knows me in Toulouse. You've heard mention of Cornusson, the former King's Seneschal. He'll do anything I want. As soon as he sees me, he'll install me in a palace."

An aged woman enveloped in a maroon capeline and leaning on a staff approached me and pushed me a little in order to speak to me apart, as two friends do in order to reach an understanding, by the habitude of the same concerns. She was a brothel-keeper.

"My sister Honorine Rouziès has a house in the Rue de la Hache. She'll take in at least four of these poor women. Isn't that great pity? And note that she's asking for the oldest, those who'll have the most difficulty in living. Get me into Toulouse with those four you can see over there and I'll give you twenty-five écus."

She even made the gesture f taking that sum out of her garments. I noticed among the women she pointed out to me a calm little old woman who was carrying a basked covered by a cloth preciously under her arm.

Tornebut shook his head. The guards at the gates of Toulouse had been more severe in recent years. I remembered that not long ago, for fear of the plague, the mendicants of the Lauragais and the region of Narbonne had been left to die outside the ramparts. It was summer and those unburied cadavers had nearly provoked the plague, the fear of which had caused their deaths. The violence of brigands who roamed the region or a sudden attack by Huguenots were also feared. It was true that the recent peace ought to have relaxed the surveillance, but I did not know to what extent.

Everyone formed a circle around me. I was designated as a savior. I saw women precipitately arranging the pleats of their shawl. Others were directing enticing gazes at me. A brunette with large sad eyes, whose face was partly hidden by a mantilla and who had remained apart, mounted on a mule, dismounted in order to approach me.

I assumed that the guzla player was not in possession of all his reason, for he continued playing in spite of the gravity of the deliberation, and his thin legs sometimes sketched a highly unusual dance step. The dwarf touched a finger to his forehead, making me a sign to excuse him.

"It's the nights of the red lantern that have caused him to lose his mind,"

"Perhaps," I said to Tornebut, "it's still Antoine de Peyrolade who's in command at the Porte Saint-Étienne. By representing the fate of these creatures to him, it's possible that he'll let them into Toulouse."

I made a sign inviting the troop to follow me and I took a little path that led around the ramparts and led to the Porte Saint-Étienne. The dwarf had set himself to my right. The guzla player took up a position to my left and sometimes interrupted his tune to hop in a strange fashion. The women followed, as well as a few men of criminal appearance.

We were not very far from the Porte Saint-Étienne when we found ourselves face to face with another troop of creatures no less singular, who emerged from another path. They were heading for the Porte Saint-Étienne too. I recognized by their costume that they were Moors.

Recently expelled from Spain, a large number had spread into France. The majority had been directed through Provence and embarked for Morocco, but small groups had escaped the surveillance and tried to live by appealing to the harsh charity of men. They were chased away by throwing stones and sometimes welcomed in order to rob them, for the rumor had gone around that many were hiding Spanish doubloons in their belts.

Those we had just encountered were led by a tall man so thin that he looked like a skeleton. He was carrying an enormous book under his arm, and a young woman who must have been his daughter was caring other books tied together with string.

He approached me, and it seemed to me that his face lit up at the sight of me. He touched me rapidly at the location the heart with the tip of his finger. I thought at first that he wanted to strike me, but I had enough self-control not to budge. He started speaking with an extreme rapidity, but in a language that I did not understand. From time to time he pointed to his book.

Fortunately, one of the women from Pamiers, who was of Moorish origin, approached us and translated what he had said. He had recognized me as a brother and he was counting on the bond that united us to get him and the Moors who were accompanying him into Toulouse. He intended to give public lectures in the Arabic language, not doubting, in view of the reputation of Toulouse, that all the students understood that language. He had attempted to pass through a gate near a large château but the soldiers had sent him away.

I thought that if he and his companions had not been imprisoned at the gate of the Château Narbonnais, where the terrible Astorg was in command, he owed it to his lucky star, which had brought him to Toulouse on the day of Mardi Gras.

I cast a glance over the individuals in wretched multicolored costumes who were surrounding me and I wondered by what strange destiny they had placed a very imprudent confidence in me. But I could not retreat. Internally, I invoked the law that moves events, praying that it might deflect its efforts in a favorable direction. Thinking of Antoine de Peyrolade, I put the jovial expression on my face appropriate to meeting an old friend that one has not seen for a long time, and I walked with a firm stride toward the Porte Saint-Étienne.

It was closed, but the little door alongside it was open, and it was with great satisfaction that I saw Antoine de Peyrolade sitting on the little bench carved into the stone of the rampart. His belt was unfastened, his rubicund face shiny, and he gave the impression of being placed behind his belly, as if it were not part of him.

I did not have to pronounce the phrases I had prepared. Antoine de Peyrolade's shining little eyes passed by turns over the Moors and the women of Pamiers; but the surprise immediately disappeared from his face. He had understood. I never found out exactly what he thought. Did he think it was a carnivalesque joke that I wanted to play on the inhabitants of Toulouse, which had been prepared outside the city boundary in order to cause a greater effect of surprise? The bells could be heard ringing for the mass that the Archbishop celebrated on Mardi Gras in the Cathedral of Saint-Étienne for the students and the trade guilds in fancy dress. Doubtless he thought that we were going there. He could not resist the pleasure of playing a role in that marvelous farce, which must have been prepared with so much care.

"Open the main gate!" he shouted to the men on guard in a resounding voice.

I hastened to wink in his direction in a comical fashion.

I would have liked to make a sign to all those who were following me to put a joyful expression on their faces. On the contrary, in order to inspire pity, they had aggravated the sadness of their demeanor, but the jovial Peyrolade must have thought that that was part of their role-playing.

"You're lucky to have been able to procure this one," he said, putting his hand on the dwarf's shoulder.

Fortunately, the cunning old man had understood, and grimaced, while gesticulating. He even held on to the guzla player and danced with him.

Antoine de Peyrolade guffawed. "The Moorish skeleton with the book is superb!" he said.

Everyone made haste. The Toulousan air was filled with the music of bells. The sun, veiled momentarily behind a cloud, illuminated the scene. I noticed that an entire flock of pigeons lined up on the ramparts took off, without any apparent reason, with a great flapping of wings.

And it was then, at that very moment, that I noticed, some distance away on the road we had followed, a sedan chair with yellow-clad porters coming in the direction of the Porte Saint-Étienne. I say "some distance away," but I had miscalculated; it must have been very close when I saw it for the first time, for only a few seconds had gone by, and I had scarcely turned my head, when the porters of the chair were already among the last of the women of Pamiers, who were hastening to enter the promised city.

It was, in truth, an extravagant chair, with porters such as I had never seen, narrower and, in particular, taller that the usual format, the wood of which was an impressive yellow color, a yellow almost unknown, whose hue evoked confused images of despair. Perhaps—I am not certain—the curtains were black. And the porters, the two porters, with waxy faces under yellow tricorns—the same yellow as the chair—did not resemble the usual porters of the Toulousan fraternity of porters. I cannot say how they differed: perhaps a bleak impassivity, the automatism of their gestures, something empty and fixed in the gaze.

And as I gazed at that enigmatic chair, stupefied, one of those curtains, yellow or black, lifted, and for a second I saw a woman's face, a grimacing face, spectral and yet spit by a mortuary smile with the teeth of a cadaver. At the same time, an ivory hand, which I would have sworn was dead if it had not been agitated toward me, made a rapid gesture of thanks: a slightly disdainful gesture, such as a queen might have made. Then the curtain fell back.

Everyone had moved aside. The two porters started running briskly. I saw that the laughter had frozen on the face of Antoine de Peyrolade. He seized me by the arm.

"That yellow! Did you recognize the shade of that yellow?"

"No, but...."

"It's the yellow of the uniform that the Captain of Health wears, and those who are responsible for collecting the dead. For twenty-five years, since the time of the great plague, it's a yellow that no one has dared to wear, in order not to attract misfortune."[20]

---

[20] This chapter and those following probably originated as a separate story set in a different period, as the reference to the "great plague" seems most likely to refer to the plague of

THE MASQUES OF SAINT-ÉTIENNE

I advanced toward the Place Saint-Étienne, crushed by the weight of my good dead. None of those I had enabled to enter the walls of Toulouse wanted to quit me, and they were all marching behind me.

A large crowd was gathered in the Place Saint-Étienne, but there was a large empty space in the middle, in front of the cathedral. It was into that space that I emerged, pushed by those who were coming behind me, carried away by the confused hope of liberating myself by virtue of walking rapidly.

I was gripped by vertigo. To the right of the cathedral stood the sixty members of the Parlement, whom I scarcely recognized, so enormous and geometrical did their square bonnets seem. To the left, the King's Seneschal was leaning solemnly on a cane with a gold pommel, with his counselors, his officers, his squires and the eight Capitouls with the strangely bright red sashes designating their rank. A little further away were grouped representatives of all the religious orders and the various monasteries, with their banners, their crosses, reliquaries, caskets containing the bones of saints. I recognized the Chapter of Saint Saturnin, at of La Daurade, the Blue Penitents, and an Order whose name I did not know, whose members bore silver Holy Spirits on their breasts and raised white sticks in their right hands. On all sides, I saw the glint of crosses, reliquaries and golden halberds. Twelve men in violet uniforms were raising enormous trumpets toward the heavens.

And not until I was in the center of the square did I become aware of my imprudence. Too late! An immense clamor resounded. And I saw with amazement the group of members of the Parlement break up, and the majority launch themselves

---

1629, which was followed by a serious recurrence in 1652, although lesser outbreaks were not uncommon before then..

toward me. The King's Seneschal started a grotesque dance, which the Capitouls imitated. At the same time, the twelve trumpeters launched a resounding fanfare into the sky.

It was only then that I perceived the disproportion of the trumpets, the excessively dazzling character of the reliquaries, and distinguished the comical character of the silver Holy Spirits and death's-heads on the breasts of the monks. I saw that the President of the Parlement had stilts under his rope in order to appear taller, that the Abbot of Saint Sernin was wearing a false nose that he agitated with a string, and that the Seneschal's moustache wad made of stuffed snakeskin.

And I also saw in another part of the square, an Emperor Charlemagne with a beard so long that two pages were required to sustain it, and a Chevalier Roland brandishing a cardboard sword as large as him. Alongside him there were allegorical characters, gods of mythology, and the entire dynasty of the Kings of Spain, represented by the fraternity of Spanish students, whose provost I recognized, an ignorant old student celebrated in Toulouse. A few gods and a few kings were running in my direction.

But it was not me who had caused the agitation of the population of masques. The young brunette mounted on her mule had taken off her mantilla; her sadness had disappeared; she paraded an amused gaze over the crowd and gave the impression of a queen accompanied by a vulgar court avid for pleasure. The women of Pamiers around her had abruptly changed their appearance. I saw one of them pouring the contents of a bottle of perfume hidden in her sleeve for some opportunity of seduction over her poorly-tressed cranium. Several mirrors were shining here and there. Hirsute tresses had become shiny and harmoniously-parted tresses in a matter of seconds. Hope animated gazes. A professional joy swelled breasts and stretched torsos. The guzla player made several pirouettes. Only the old lady with the basket had a mysteriously celestial expression on her face.

149

The greatest disorder was unleashed. I would have been knocked to the ground but for Tornebut, who sustained me in his arms.

"It's me, Olympian Jupiter, who makes you a present of these unknown women," cried the individual wearing the costume of the king of the gods in a resounding voice, removing his beard.

He was standing up on his throne. The crowd doubtless recognized a person popular in Toulouse, for an exclamation rose toward him. He replaced the hooks of his beard over his ears, and loud laugher circulated in the Place Saint-Étienne.

Meanwhile, there was a melee around me. The women uttered screams, simulating resistance. The young queen, laughing provocatively, had made her mule rear up, and no one succeeded in reaching her. Students with turbans in the costumes of princes of Granada mingled with the real Moors, whom they seemed to find less well disguised than themselves. The provosts of the students, carrying short sticks, with which they delivered little blows here and there, tried in vain to reestablish order.

"We've done all we could for those whom Providence has sent us," I said to Tornebut. "Let's take the opportunity to get away from them."

We cleaved a path through the crowd, not without difficulty, traversed the square, and ran into the Rue de la Croix Baragon.

I cannot swear to it, but I believe that in front of us, at a certain distance, at the place where the Rue de la Croix Baragon is intersected by the Rue Tolosane, the chair with the yellow porters was gliding rapidly and silently, almost without touching the ground, and it disappeared.

But footfalls resounded behind us. Doubtless, in having the Porte Saint-Étienne opened, I had inspired an elevated idea of my power. The man with the book and his companions had not wanted to quit me. It was the same for the guzla player and a few women deprived of all attraction, whom the masques had allowed to depart.

150

I hastened my steps; they did the same. The streets were full of people but I saw that I could not hope to lose them. In the Rue Saint-Rome I appealed to a few inhabitants and exhorted them to charity. Could they not receive poor folk in their houses? But I only provoked indignation. Those "poor folk" were nothing but pagans and loose women. They had severe orders from the Capitouls relative to both. I was lucky that it was a feast day!

We wandered through the streets for a long time. I sensed that my companions were vanquished by fatigue after long marches. I was no longer thinking about quitting them. I felt sorry for them. I even sustained the bearer of the book with my arm. All doors were closed before us. In the Rue du Taur there was almost violence; people came out with sticks. A matron recognized me and allowed an insulting fury burst forth.

"Don't you know that I have two daughters! And you want me to take *that* into my house!" She pointed scornfully at the wretched creatures from Pamiers who, exhausted, had let themselves fall along the wall.

The man's husband appeared at the window. He had a caustic wit. "You've changed profession, I see—the old one was more honorable."

"Why doesn't he take them home himself?" said a neighbor "He had a fine house in Arnaud Bernard."

That was an idea. I remembered that my wife had left with the Chevalier de Polaston.

"Come," I said. "You're at the end of your troubles."

Dusk was falling when we reached the Porte Arnaud Bernard, not far from which my house was situated. As luck would have it, Timothée was in the small house adjacent to my garden, where he lived.

"There's not much left," he said, "but there's the furniture."

All the rooms were rapidly occupied. There was an incident regarding the one on the ground floor, the windows of which overlooked the street. It must have appeared to the women to be more comfortable than the others, and they disputed its possession."

"We'll go spend the night in your house," I said to Tornebut.

As we drew away I cast a glance backwards. Timothée had just lit a lantern. In the frame of a window on the first floor I perceived the old Moor with the book, asleep on a chair. Somewhere, the guzla player was still playing, and perhaps dancing. A woman was already combing her hair on the ground floor, and already watching the street while she combed.

It was necessary to get back to Saint Cyprien. Tornebut and I were very weary. Along the Garonne, in the direction of Tounis, I saw the chair with yellow porters still gliding, and when it went past the lantern of the Old Bridge, it suddenly cast an immense shadow, a thin shadow that gave the impression of cutting the city in two, as if with a sword of darkness.

THE PLAGUE IN TOULOUSE

"The plague is in Toulouse," said a brutal man to the old Comtesse Adelaïde de Montpezat, a benefactress of the city celebrated for her tall stature and courageous qualities.

"You're lying," she replied, with her habitual energy.

She stood up and fell down dead. Fear delivers death with more certainty than malady. For years it was forbidden in many Toulousan milieux to pronounce the word "plague," and when it broke out it was agreed among enlightened individuals that, in order to reassure the people, everyone would deny that it was the plague. The enlightened individuals would spread out thought the city, saying and swearing that it was not the plague and that there was no need to be afraid, and thus they would inform everyone who did not know that it was established in Toulouse and they would spread fear as one spreads fire with a torch.

It was at that precise moment that I had just been afflicted by melancholy. That melancholy had descended upon me like a black bird on a field of wheat. I had been possessed by it without reason, and it was doubtless that to which I owed being protected from the plague, for someone who is completely filled by sadness or joy is like a vase that no longer has the slightest room for a germ of disease.

There was no house attained by the contagion into which I did not go: I saw and cared for almost all the sick of Toulouse. The greater the evil was, the more I had the sentiment that it was the result of a necessary force, against the expansion of which I was perhaps wrong to struggle. Suffering and death were reactions of the inferior domain, useful to the activity of souls. I did my best to combat them, but I was not sure of being right and not harming the divine order, for the sole efficacious action for the good of one's fellows is one that is exercised in the spiritual domain.

How had the plague entered Toulouse? people asked one another—and everyone secretly thought of the fate of Jeanne de Saint-Pé, who, a century before, had been condemned to be burned by the Parlement because someone had accused her, without any evidence, of being a carrier of putrid miasmas.

There was a solemn procession of Cordeliers along the ramparts, and in particular in the vicinity of The Porte Montolieu, at the place where the mendicants from the direction of Narbonne, whom fear had denied entry to Toulouse, had died miserably. A visionary Cordelier had seen at the time the irritated souls of those mendicants floating around the pitiless city. He had even conversed with the souls, who had assured him that punishment would not be long delayed. Ever since then, the Order of Cordeliers, which had faith in that saintly man, had lived in the expectation of great misfortunes.

The evil raged above all in the brothels of the Rue de la Hache and on the Île de Tounis. The Capitoul of Saint-Barthélemy, who had a Cordelier for a confessor, dreaded that the irritated souls of the mendicant of the Lauragais might strike his quarter, which was contiguous with the afflicted quarter. He recruited archers who had the mission of launching arrows into the sky. The Cordelier advised him to do that, assuring him that the souls would not, of course, be transpierced, since they were immaterial, but that the arrows, by virtue of their unusual presence, might inconvenience them and incite them to withdraw. In falling back the arrows wounded a few inhabitants, and it required the insistence of the Capitouls, united in council, to oblige their colleague to interrupt that means of protection.

Many people said that it was not without reason that the plague had first appeared in the Rue de la Hache. What was the disease, after all, but a manifestation of the internal putrescence of creatures? The black buboes that burst forth on bodies had a relationship with the debauchery of life, corrupting the blood and the soul. Too much indulgence had been shown to the prostitutes. The punishment of the whip had been abolished for women who went out in excessively luxurious robes. The women expelled from Pamiers by the Huguenot consuls had been allowed to enter, without anyone knowing who was responsible. Had no one heard it said that there was plague in Pamiers?

I sometimes asked myself questions on that subject. Had I not unwittingly been one of the instruments of the fatality? Had not a contaminated creature slipped in among those for whom I had had the Porte Saint-Étienne opened? And what of the strange Sedan chair that I had seen on that day and had never encountered again? There was a mystery there that I never succeeded in clarifying.

I am obliged to say that almost all the women from Pamiers were afflicted from the start. It was the Rue de la Hache and its taverns for soldiers that had sheltered them. A guard had been placed on the bridge leading to the Île de Tounis and the two extremities of the Rue de la Hache had been closed with chains. There were special men, more courageous or less sensible that the rest, who occupied themselves with the plague. They were known as the Fayssiers[21] and they were clad, I don't know why, like the Captain of Health, in a lugubrious yellow uniform with a cap of the same color and a red Saint Sebastian embroidered on the breast.

Nicolas de Tolentin, the Captain of Health, was an enigmatic man. He had a total absence of pity; I never saw him pray next to a dead man, and yet he fulfilled his redoubtable task almost gratuitously. He scarcely slept, penetrated into houses by force, and helped to transport the sick to the hospital of Saint Cyprien personally. I asked him once what the secret motive was that drove him to such a great devotion, and he replied: "I like death."

Honorine Rouziès kept the largest brothel in Toulouse at the sign of the Flower-Basket in the Rue de la Hache. She had welcomed her sister Marianne and the four women with whom the latter had occupied a more modest house in Pamiers. I went to the Flower-Basket every day. I was more specifically

---

[21] A French dictionary of the Occitan language gives the French equivalent of *fayssier* as *portefaix* [street-porter].

charged with the Rue de la Hache, the other physicians occupying themselves with the Île de Tounis, the Rue des Paradoux and a few convents where the plague had appeared without any apparent reason.

I had noticed the remedies that the physicians applied, as well as those invented by charlatans, precipitated the malady and caused death. So far as I knew, the plague could only be cured by an abrupt development of an elevated virtue in the soul of the invalid. But the bursting of purulent buboes in the groin or the armpits inclined the individual struck by such a frightful evil more to depression or to blasphemy. I did my best to resolve that difficulty. But it sometimes happened that if the love of God, the detachment from property, suddenly took possession of a sick person the malady was cured in a short time, as if the soul had sent a luminous projection over the misery of the body and had thus transformed it.

Several women in the Flower-Basket had died. Two had been recently afflicted, and Marianne Rouziès had just gone to bed saying that she had sharp pains in the groin. Despair inhabited the house.

One morning, as I arrived at the entrance to the Rue de la Hache, I saw Honorine Rouziès, who was coming to fetch the vegetables that the merchants left at the end of the street for the inhabitants. There was something brisk and almost joyful in her step.

"Are the patients improving?" I asked.

"They're getting worse."

"So?"

"Marie Seli has had a dream."

Marie Seli was the aged woman whom I had noticed among the companions of Marianne Rouziès because of the basket she had under her arm and her tranquil face. The night before, Honorine told me, she had not gone to bed. She had been found on her knees at dawn. She had gone to sleep while praying and it was in that attitude that she had had the dream.

The dream had been preceded by the words of a voice, which had said distinctly: "Marie Seli, get up. Go to the

Church of Saint Sernin and pray to Jesus Christ and Saint Saturnin beside the underground lake."

From the rest of the dream, the account of which remained vague, it resulted that the plague would cease if Mare Seli prayed to Jesus Christ and Saint Saturnin, as had been prescribed.

The vagueness of the account should have made me think that there was something else in the story reported by Honorine Rouziès, but I only occupied myself with the voice that had resounded, and I made her repeat the exact words heard by Marie Seli ten times. For that voice seemed to be similar to the one that had once called to me and had launched me on the quest for the Holy Grail.

I noticed, while begging the pardon of the invisible powers internally, that the vocabulary of the supernatural voice was limited. There was the same formula that had been employed for me: "Michel de Bramevaque, get up." In both cases there had been an imperative invitation to change attitude, to get up, and to fulfill a difficult mission.

I went to the Flower-Basket and I saw Marie Seli, but there was little to be extracted from her. Until then she had impressed me with her calmness and perfect serenity. I was surprised to find her in an even greater calm, a state close to religious ecstasy. She emerged from it with difficulty and that was to question me about the singularity of the words she had heard and the difficulty of obeying the order given. Where could an underground lake be found? What was that miraculous lake, and how could it be reached?

Then the memory of an ancient legend came back to me. The Church of Saint Sernin had been built, long ago, on the site of a sacred lake. It was on that lake that the power of ancient gods had once been manifest. The Druids came there to practice certain rites relative to the water. It was into that lake that the Gauls vanquished at Delphi had thrown the gold bought back from heir distant expedition. Bishop Sylvius had drained it when he laid the foundations of the great Basilica of

Saint Sernin.[22] In order to do that he had dug wells into which the waters had been swallowed up, then forming a lake around which were the foundations of the basilica. Arrosus, Bishop of Toulouse in the eighth century, had hollowed out a stairway down to that lake.[23] He was occupied with magic and he claimed that there were hostile forces underground that it was necessary to combat. He was found dead at the foot of that stairway, so his successor, Murcio, had walled up the entrance. It opened of its own accord in the next century, the chronicle said. It was no longer touched, but the tradition remained among the Abbots of Saint Saturnin of not authorizing the decent of that stairway, and even of denying its existence.

It was certainly beside that mysterious subterranean lake that Marie Seli had been enjoined to go to pray.

---

[22] Saint Sylvius of Toulouse was the Bishop of the city in the later part of the fourth century.

[23] The lake and the stairway are fictitious but "Arrosus" is presumably based on Arricius, who was known to be the Bishop of Toulouse during the latter part of the eight century because of the preservation of his epitaph, now in the museum of Foix. His successor, who replaced him in 785, was Mancion, presumably Magre's "Murcio."

THE LAKE OF SAINT SERNIN

I had previously given my cares on several occasions to monks in the monastery of Saint Sernin. I knew the Abbot of the Chapter, a fat and terrible man, always at odds with everybody. He suffered from his obesity, caused by the excess of nourishment, and he suffered from it all the more because he had an ascetic ideal within him that was never satisfied. He had asked me for a means to get thin while continuing to eat abundantly. He considered me to be a secret heretic, suspected me of magic, and had made that request while winking at me, meaning that he would submit, if necessary to some procedure of sorcery. I had not been able to satisfy him; he was still obese, and he had not forgiven me.

The Abbot of the abbatial Chapter of Saint Sernin was one of the most powerful men in Toulouse and one could not see him easily. He was always surrounded by a court of monks, with whom he indulged in interminable meals.

I went to his house near Saint Sernin and was able to have myself announced and introduced at the moment when he was finishing his meal. But I only got as far as the door of the dining room. I heard a rumor when my name as pronounced, as well as the words *plague* and *contagion*, repeated several times. The powerful voice of Abbot Bernard rose behind the door, left ajar.

I saw plague victims every day and the most elementary prudence counseled not approaching me. He congratulated me for my courage. What did I want? He asked me to be brief. It was very difficult for me to explain through a door, but I tried.

"Abbreviate," cried the Abbot's voice.

When I mentioned the dream I heard him laugh and he said to a canon, in a low voice: "He's come to tell us about a prostitute's dream." But when I mentioned the words *subterranean lake* there were a few seconds of silence; then the Abbot's laughter resounded, but in a more exaggerated fashion than the comical character of the lake warranted.

"There is no lake," he said to me through the crack in the almost-closed doorway. "Think about it. How could a monument like Saint Sernin repose on a lake? It's a story good for the house of the Flower-Basket. *Au revoir.* I have very aged canons with me for whom the slightest influence of contagion might be very harmful."

And he closed the door.

I knew to whom the guard of Saint Sernin was confided during the night. A watchman who slept by day marched incessantly through the circular chapels of the Basilica and past the entrance to the crypts where the relics were and the immense treasures of the church. He was a layman, a former soldier in the force of age who mounted guard with his naked sword in his hand. Antarès Libona was reputed to be a rigorously honest man.

He was a killer of Huguenots. Thirty years before, he had made himself illustrious during the defense of Saint Sernin during the six days when the *religionnaires*, masters of Toulouse, had tried to destroy the basilica.[24] It was even said that he had brought back several heads, cut off by his hand in the grounds of the monastery. Since then he had been unable to embrace and other profession than that of defender of Saint Sernin, even when the greatest security reigned.

I shall not report at length the conversation I had with Antarès Libona. He had the same laugh as Abbot Bernard when I mentioned the subterranean lake. But the incorruptibility of the soul is in narrow proportion to the magnitude of the offer that is made. As I spoke to Antarès the lake became more and more real to him and its existence, which I doubted, was confirmed. There was a lake and he had the key to the staircase that led to it. If I had not judged the order of the motive that impelled me to be sublime, I would never have been able

---

[24] Clément Compayré's *Études historiques* (1841) dates the Protestant *religionnaires*' assault on Saint-Sernin as 1575, which implies a date for the events of the present chapter s 1605 or thereabouts.

to tempt Antarès Libona. My offer was, however, accepted all the more rapidly than I would have believed, and with a visible joy.

I had left in the cellar of my house a large sum in gold in anticipation of an event of this sort. There are problems that that can only be resolved by that essentially corrupting metal. I went to dig up that gold and I took the agreed sum to the guardian of Saint Sernin. I shall not write the figure because it is a bad thing to fix in any manner whatsoever the price by which a man can be deflected from his duty. It was agreed that Antarès Libona would let us into Saint Sernin three hours after midnight through the door of the seven deadly sins, because everyone was sleep at that belated hour.

Habituated to seeing me resolve the problems of their life, the Rouziès sisters were scarcely astonished by the success of my efforts. It was still necessary to get Marie Seli out of the Rue de la Hache in spite of the guards posted at the two extremities of the street, but I was too well known to them for there to be the slightest difficulty.

It was agreed that Marie Seli, since she could escape the Hell of the Rue de la Hache, would not return there. She was dressed in new linen and her robe was washed and then dried in front of a large fire, lit expressly for that purpose. That was not so much in order that she would not transport contagion of the plague elsewhere as to enable her to present herself with pure vestments in the mysterious sanctuary to which she was going in response to an order no less mysterious.

And I thought within myself: *In truth, perhaps I was wrong not to go and live in Pamiers. People kill more willingly there for questions of religion, but there is no other city in France and even on earth, where there are such brothel-keepers, and a prostitute similar to Marie Seli.*

The announcer of the nocturnal hours had just cried three hours after midnight. He drew away along the Rue du Taur. Marie Seli and I were motionless outside the door of the seven deadly sins.

The latter had not pronounced a word since our departure from the Rue de la Hache. She walked at a modest and tranquil pace, animated by an interior certainty. She had her basket under her arm.

"A little linen and a few provisions," she had murmured as we departed. She would go back on foot, in short stages, to her natal village at the foot of the Pyrenees.

The door of Saint Sernin was ajar, and I saw the tall figure of Antarès Libona.

"Is this the lady who has to say her prayer beside the lake?" he asked.

"This is her."

The church was illuminated by candles in the chapels and in front of certain tombs. It seemed immense, and made me think—I don't know why—of a deserted Purgatory. Antarès only spoke in a whisper and was troubled by the unusual character of his action.

"No one has ever come here at night," he said.

First, he took us down into the crypts.

He had given each of us a lighted candle. There was an odor of dead stone and decomposed incense. I thought about the incalculable treasures heaped up in the crypts for centuries. On a massive gold plaque there was a fragment of white silk that betrayed the contours of a human skull. It was the skull of Saint Saturnin, which was placed in the choir for important feast days. A little further on I recognized the crucifix of Dominic, with which he had exalted the souls of the crusaders to massacre the Albigensian saints. And further on, there were the gold and silver chasubles that went back to the origins of Christianity, precious caskets in which jewels were heaped, donations made by repentant sinners thinking to redeem their sins by depositing a precious stone in a crypt; and all sorts of miscellaneous objects—crosses, miters and pieces of armor—that had belonged to saints dead for centuries.

A narrow door, masked by a heap of chasubles, opened with difficulty, and immediately, a powerful, icy, terrible breath emerged from an unknown depth and blew out our candles. It was necessary to relight them.

It's only the first breath," stammered the guardian. "I've heard it said that it was the respiration of the dead. For there are dead men here. The last one was deposited five years ago."

"What dead men?" I asked.

"It's necessary to warn you so that you won't be afraid. Almost at the bottom of the stairway, before reaching the lake, there's a room, a narrow and long room. The soil has the property of conserving the dead. There's a privilege for the cenobites of the monastery, those who never emerge from their cells and never speak to anyone. They have the right, if they request it, to be deposited there in order that their form in conserved. For there are some who believe that they will thus be advantaged for the moment of the resurrection of bodies, and will be entirely ready when the trumpet sounds.

He was about to precede us, but he changed his mind.

"I'll wait for you here. The stairway is long; you only have to go down it. The dead are to the right, but it's better not to look at them."

I preceded Marie Seli, whose features reflected the greatest calm, and we went down. The steps were worn although few human feet had trodden them. Time labors all matter and destroys its principles, even in the mute immobility of darkness. The air was dense and oppressive, and yet there was a slow circulation whose origin was unknown. I forgot to count the steps, but the descent was so long that I estimated the depth to be equal to the height of the steeple.

I leaned against the right-hand wall, the power of which was reassuring. Suddenly, my hand felt a void. I advanced the candle that I was holding in my left hand and, like a revelation of the repose and silence of the life beyond the tomb, the dead appeared to me. They were neither disquieting nor frightening. They were human trees that had dried out. They were sad mummies. There were a dozen, neatly aligned, with hands crossed over the breast, with only one exception, who must only have possessed one arm and whose unique hand was very large, with fingernails so long that one was obliged to think that they had grown after death by virtue of a fairly frequent but impressive phenomenon.

The alignment of the defunct cenobites had something reassuring about it, however, for one thought that they were still such as they had been placed after their death and had not got up after the departure of the living in order to stretch their bones, climb the staircase and exchange spectral regrets. An inexplicable perfume rose from that funereal room, not at all horrible, as pure as the essence of the eternal substance.

"They're dead," said Marie Seli, simply. And she raised her voice slightly to say: "I can see the water."

The motionless water did, indeed, extend a few steps lower down.

It was a surface devoid of reflections, a somber blue that made one think of a sapphire whose interior spirit is dead. And yet it was not death that rose from that redoubtable and mute water. The candle that I held over it revealed to me the oval of a supernatural mirror, infinite and of a depth that must be unknown, suggestive of a corridor of water descending all the way to the center of the planet.

And over that immeasurable depth was designed for me, for a second, the contour of a face, which immediately disappeared: a face larger than natural, and which no words can describe. An enigma on immobile waters...a smile of apparition...a gaze devoid of joy and sadness, beneath unblinking eyelids....

Might a soul belonging to a hierarchy superior to that of humans have its dwelling there in the inviolate darkness, under the accumulation of the Byzantine structures of the ancient basilica? Perhaps, in a remote epoch, the mysterious essence that is the soul of a city, the soul of Toulouse, had built its dwelling with the subterranean stones, tinted with the glimmer of niter and saltpeter, and the blue water deprived of solar renewal, the water that descended endlessly into the body of the physical world like an immortal blade.

The reflections of the candlelight were repelled, rejected, as if that water of subterrestrial essence could not be traversed by a light of human origin. I saw that between the smooth walls and the dead tin of the water there was scarcely a little gray sand, just enough for the passage of a courageous man who would not have felt the inverse vertigo of a hermetic surface under an inexorably low vault.

And I then experienced an irrational attraction. It seemed to me that I found myself before an enigmatic door, simultaneously the receptacle of a superior existence and a tenebrous horror. I was on the edge of a nameless realm, a beyond of which no dream can give the image, where there is no cypress, or stele, or sepulcher, or any known form of death, but which contains the key to infinite metamorphoses. And I took a step forward, moved by the powerful temptation of those inexplicable figures, those formless beauties, which I had before me, and which I divined behind the waters, superior to humans and belonging to another world.

A gesture from Marie Seli retained me. She was standing up straight, her basket in one hand, her candle in the other, not at all troubled. She had come to say a prayer on the edge of the lake. She was waiting to be alone in order to fall to her knees.

I hesitated. Then I went back up two or three steps. "I'll wait for you at the top of the staircase," I said.

She nodded her head and as I climbed the stairs I saw her bend down in order to stick her candle into a crack in the last step.

I did not have to wait very long. Her prayer must have been very short. After a few minutes she came back up, with the same tranquil expression on her face.

The guardian closed the door carefully behind us. He looked in all directions anxiously, and yet he repeated: "There's nothing to fear. No one has ever come during the night."

At the moment when the last syllable of that sentence resonated, and as we emerged from the crypt, we saw a monk who was standing up, his shoulder leaning slightly on a pillar.

He had a face of stone and his eyes were fixed intensely on mine.

I turned to Antarès Libona. He had seen the monk too, and he murmured: "Oh my God! It's the first time! A member of the Chapter."

He pushed us toward the door.

The Place Saint-Sernin was deserted. I asked Marie Seli where she was going and she replied that she intended to return to her village. She made a vague gesture that signified that neither that, nor anything else, was of much importance now, and she drew away at a measured pace along the Rue du Taur.

THE EMERALD CUP

It is certain that, if the plague was not stopped as if by a divine order, it began to decrease from that day on. It decreased abnormally rapidly, but not sufficiently for a miraculous action to be distinguished with certainty. Nature is faithful to her method. Even when a supernatural revolution occurs, it is always possible to attribute it to the normal rhythm of a law.

Marianne Rouziès approached death without dread and without astonishment. She was not one of those that the miraculous prayer was intended to save. Afflicted before the voice had addressed its order to Marie Seli, she found her regular death. To my great astonishment, she did not confess when the curé of La Dalbade came with the sacraments. The church forbidding her, because of her profession, the public masses and ceremonies of the religion, she had ended up rejecting the religion that rejected her.

I passed the priest as he was leaving.

"My sister is waiting for you," Honorine Rouziès told me. "She needs to speak to you."

Marianne Rouziès was lying in a little mansard room at the top of the house. Her hard face did not soften when I appeared. She started to speak immediately, like someone who fears dying without being able to do so.

"I thought that you ought to know everything, since it's thanks to you that everything has happened. I wondered why you weren't more astonished that Marie Seli became a kind of saint. There are no saints in houses like this, nothing but wretched girls condemned to the whip if they go into the streets, and who are marked with red-hot irons in some cities. There are priests that refuse them absolution and some who condemn them to death if they cross the threshold of a church. There are no saints, only the accursed, creatures of Hell, who are condemned to eternal damnation because they give pleasure to men. I can tell you that because I no longer fear anything.

"I've always thought that there was no God. He wouldn't let injustice triumph if there were one. And now I'm wondering what there is. There's no God, but there are mysterious things. Listen....

"The house that I kept in Pamiers had been kept by my mother, and before that by my grandmother. And neither of them, I know, believed in God, because of the evil they had seen. The house was called the Red Lantern: a house like all those seen in the cities. I even believe that my grandmother, in the old days, expelled women who had a religion, saying that they were allied with those who are evil, those who condemn women to tortures. And this is what happened to my grandmother.

"One night, a man with a horse knocked on the door. It was late. One no longer had the right to open up after midnight, but she opened up, out of pity, because the man said that he was exhausted. He was a knight, with a long beard and a cross on his breast. He was very handsome, it seems.

"'You opened up to me because I'm a Hospitaller,' he said, and emitted a loud burst of laughter.

"My grandmother realized that he was mad. How can one not welcome a madman who knocks on your door by night? He said that he had spent three days without quitting his horse, without eating or drinking. And he was so fatigued that he died."

"You say that he was a Knight Hospitaller?" I asked.

"He must have been. But as he was about to die, in order to thank my grandmother, he made her a gift. He gave her an object of great value he said, which he carried on his breast."

"Do you know the name of that knight?" I asked then. "Did he not say that his name was Antoine de Cassagnavère?"

"I don't know. My grandmother thought that the object, which had the form of a cup, was an enormous emerald and could be sold very dear. She thought at first of washing the cup, because there was something at the bottom that resembled dried blood. As she was about to pick it up in the room where she had left it, because the room was dark, she perceived that the cup was emitting a glow, and that by looking at that glow one felt a certain peace of soul."

My heart was hammering forcefully in my breast. Marianne Rouziès' features had lost a little of their hardness. She paused for a moment.

"And then?"

"She didn't wash the cup and she placed it under a cloth in a little room where no one ever went, a little mansard room at the top of the house, rather like this one. She got rid of everything. In that room there was no longer anything but the cup, placed on a little table, and from time to time, all alone, she went to look at it. And this happened. One day, a woman went into that room. The curtains over the widow were drawn, it was dark, and she saw the cup with its dried blood, which was radiant. For it was from the blood, above all, that the light escaped.

"The woman went back downstairs and couldn't stop weeping, and then spent days praying. She no longer wanted to exercise her profession, and in the end she left, and entered, it's said, a convent of penitents. My grandmother guarded the key to the room carefully, but there was always, from time to time, a woman who managed to see the cup, and who had remorse for her life, started praying, and became a saint."

"But the cup—what became of the cup?"

"Wait. My grandmother bequeathed it to my mother, and nothing changed in her life. There were women who, in consequence of some circumstance or other, saw that astonishing light, and began to pray to God from that moment on. But when my mother died, it was to me that the heritage came."

"So, what has become of the cup? What have you done with it?"

"Wait. I didn't want to change anything of what my grandmother and then my mother had done. I left the cup in its place. But I never looked at it. I put a thick veil over it. I've never seen it. I didn't want to pray to God. I didn't want to associate myself with the evil, those who oppress without pity, who build great stone cathedrals in which there's no place for certain women, those who are the most unfortunate."

"But then, when you left Pamiers…?"

"The consuls only gave us a few hours. It was almost as if they were sending us to death. I said to Marie Seli, giving her the key of the little room at the top of the house, to take what she found there under a cloth. I had other things to think about. We left. Marie Seli told me that she had put the cup in her basket. Afterwards, I heard her say: 'I can't explain what's just happened to me. I've become someone else. I've rediscovered in an old cup all the prayers that I'd forgotten. But those aren't appropriate. I've composed one while walking.'

"Marie Seli had composed a prayer! You can't imagine what she was before, and what the idea of such a creature composing a prayer represented. My mother had taken her in out of pity. She was a peasant from a village lost in the Pyrenees, called Cazaril, I believe. After leaving Pamiers we slept in Venerque in a barn. I woke up in the middle of the night I saw Marie Seli on her knees, facing the wall. She was praying before her basket!"

"But afterwards, what became of the cup?"

"Everything thereafter depended on you. It was you who did everything. I should have told you the truth sooner. But I had seen so much evil unleashed as soon as something valuable was at stake! I remembered my grandmother's prudence. I, who don't believe in God, thought that things had to happen as they had been prescribed, I don't know by whom. Marie Seli heard a voice that enjoined her to go and pray beside a lake. Can you tell me to whom that voice belonged?"

She interrogated me with her eyes.

I stammered: "There are invisible powers that are not God but are above men, and which sometimes—very rarely—intervene."

Marianne Rouziès laughed bitterly. "Yes, very rarely!"

She went on. "Having heard the voice, Marie Seli came to me to report what it had said. I made no reply and I showed her he swellings that I had in the groin, which were beginning to hurt. She exclaimed: 'It's better to die! It's a great joy!' and she resumed praying. Then she saw herself in a dream. She was on the edge of very deep water, so deep that she had never contemplated its like. She opened her basket and she threw into that water the emerald cup with its radiant blood. Then she leaned over the lake and she saw a great light, which accompanied her thereafter until she died."

All I murmured was: "I understand." And I went away. Above all, I had a need to understand.

ISAAC ANDRÉA

I went to find, on the road to Seysses, the only sensate man in the city, and, without confiding to him a secret that was not mine, I questioned him about the mysterious voices that call to humans in the night and the quest for the Grail.

Isaac Andréa spoke while looking into himself, and because of that his words acquired a great force, as if he were expressing words engraved on spiritual marble, perceptible for his eyes alone.

"Why are the voices not more explicit, and why are there incoherencies in their indications, you ask? But if you touch an ant-hill with a stick, do you spend your life examining whether your action has done justice or injustice among those tiny people? Beings belonging to hierarchies superior to us have an accessory interest in humans. They give an indication revealing a verity and they pass on. They are subject to error, like us. They are not impassioned by our mediocre interests. They are susceptible of deceiving us without meaning to.

"Then too, the law, the order or things, God—what does it matter what name we give to the power of powers?—has determined that the worlds are rigorously separated. Communications from one world to another are very difficult. After twenty years of prayer, a saint sometimes obtains a syllable, and a young woman who has no soul, like Lucida de Domazan, brings beings of the beyond around her, perhaps because terrestrial beauty has a correspondence in the other worlds. All is mystery around us and the voices heard only aggravate that mystery. Perhaps it would be better not to listen to them.

"And you also ask me whether I believe that the blood of Jesus Christ can act upon human beings after centuries? Yes, there are talismans, powers that are stored in objects, forces that radiate and sometimes burn souls. But where is the blood of Jesus Christ? Where are its miraculous particles? Where is the ineffable essence that rises from its vapor? Do you not know that the evil genius of human beings makes them accomplish thefts and forgeries, inspires diabolical cunning in them as soon as a motive of an admirable order is in play? Wealth, the attraction of gold, does not provoke as many crimes as the hope of soiling that which is divine.

"The Crusaders have already found the cup of Joseph of Arimathea, full of the blood of Jesus Christ, in the Orient. It can be seen in a church in Genoa. But it is a false cup, a false emerald, a false blood. A long time ago, a vulgar imitation was substituted for that cup. Do you know that there are a great many churches in the Occident that posses among their relics a cup, a vase or a tube containing the precious blood— so many churches that if one gathered all their relics together…but it's better not to think about that.

"There is also the blood of Jesus Christ on the shrouds in which he was wrapped—and there are several shrouds. In a chapel behind Saint Sernin a few years ago there was a holy shroud that had been transported from the Périgord for fear of pillage, the Holy Shroud of Cadouin. It was in a box to which six locks had been fitted, whose six keys were confided to six honest individuals, Capitouls, notaries and ecclesiastics. Well, the Holy Shroud was stolen anyway.[25]

"The purified bodies of great souls retain a power. It impels those who approach them to purify themselves, to detach themselves, to advance toward God. Sometimes, it is sufficient for a creature to approach a fragment of bone to be transformed internally. I cannot explain the reason to you. There are so many things that happen in the invisible that we do not know. But that is why so many men are avid to acquire the remains of those who have led a perfect life.

---

[25] The Holy Shroud of Cadouin, brought back from the first Crusade by Adhémar de Monteil, was sent to the parish church of Cadouin when its authenticity was questioned, and subsequently transferred to the Abbey, which then became a significant place of pilgrimage. It was removed to Toulouse between 1392 and 1455 before being returned to Cadouin. Carbon dating eventually proved its inauthenticity.

"Have you asked yourself why the Church, in the time of the Albigensians, instituted so many condemnations to death? Those deaths were always the Perfecti. The Church had been conquered by the powers of evil. It had the cadavers of those saints disinterred in order to annihilate their substance, because it knew that a radiant force remained in that matter. The dust of those corpses flew away in the pyres. But there are, outside the holy ground in which the Christian dead are interred, solitary tombs of Albigensian Perfecti who escaped the pursuits of the Inquisitors. Those tombs are located on the edges of certain villages, near remote springs, or in grottoes on the side of a mountain. There are still men who, on certain days that are not Christian feast days, by virtue of a tradition transmitted from father to son, go to those locations devoid of crosses, without knowing why, to say wordless prayers; and they almost always perceive that that, merely by approaching those places, they are more fraternal with one another.

"Yes, the Grail really is in Toulousan soil, but not in the unique form that you think, made of an emerald cup and the blood of Jesus Christ. Many Christs came three centuries ago to inform humans of the road to salvation. They were the Albigensian Perfecti, the brothers of Jesus Christ. They were not recognized, and they were put to death. And if a thousand came, it would be the same. Perhaps it is written that humans ought not to be saved by other humans, but only by themselves."

Thus spoke Isaac Andréa, the most knowledgeable man in Toulouse, who had the wisdom to hide his knowledge, and whose benevolence could only be perceived by surprise.

And he added: "Go—it is necessary to seek in order to find. But when one has searched assiduously for something, it sometimes happens that one finds something else, and is content. When you are weary of searching, remember that there is a house here from which one can perceive the towers of Toulouse on one side, and the blue of the Garonne on the other, a little cloister with crypts and an amicable old man."

THE LINDEN OF LARDENNE

"O my master, there has been a sign for me," Tornebut told me when I was about to ask him whether he was going to depart with me again by the road to the Pyrenees.

"And what was that sign?"

"The great linden tree that is on the Lardenne road beyond the Porte de Muret spoke to me in the linden language."

"Are you sure? What did it say?"

"As I was passing along the road and I approached the tree, all its branches began to move in a sudden fashion and I understood that they were speaking an addressing themselves to me."

"But wasn't the wind blowing strongly?"

"Eh! How can one pay any heed to the wind when a linden tree is talking to you on the road and making you a plea? What does the wind matter anyway? The linden said this to me: 'I am going to die if you don't come to my aid. My death is near, my death is near! Save me, save, me, you who are passing by!' It said very simple things to me, either in order to be better understood or because a tree can't make speeches like a human.

"I looked at the old linden and I understood that it would soon die if I didn't bring it rapid aid. Firstly, there were many low branches that it was necessary to prune, for the older a tree gets, the more it needs its strength for the part that it extends toward the sky. Secondly, there were many vegetal parasites that had profited from its shade and stealing the substance of soil that belonged to it as legitimate property by virtue of more than a century of presence. It was necessary to get rid of those parasites.

"But that is nothing. A linden needs dry clayey soil and has a horror of perpetual damp. Now, the Garonne flooded a little while ago and after a few movements of earth, a marsh has formed in the field adjacent to the road, under which the linden extends its roots. That field doesn't belong to anyone, and the marsh will stagnate until celestial heat has caused the water to evaporate. By then, though, the linden will be dead. And that's why it has appealed to me for help.

"I saw that by digging a ditch, the water of the marsh could be diverted elsewhere and the ground into which the linden extends its roots will become dry and benevolent again. It's necessary for me to dig that channel.

"I won't mention a population of aphids, millions of aphids that have attacked its leaves, and which I intend to exterminate with a certain oil I know. Nor will I mention an entire population of tenacious, voracious and agile ants that live in the cavities of its trunk, hollowing out corridors, rooms and communication tunnels there, and various populations of furry, horned and hairy caterpillars, and other insects with beaks, tubes, drills, saws and siphons that do their best to pierce its bark and nourish themselves on its sap, which I shall kill with the same oil.

"For the death of that fecund, ancient and venerable linden would be a great calamity. Lindens are rare in this region, perhaps because of the water of the Garonne, which spread over the land every spring and corrupts the roots of lindens. People come from Saint-Simon, Portet and even Montgiscard to extract its precious sap—not to mention the people of Toulouse. Note that the incisions they make in the fat of the wood are harmful if they are too deep, made by virtue of ignorance of the life of trees, and someone needs to put a stop to it. For astonishing remedies can be made with that sap. It cures epileptics. One can also obtain a fermented beverage from it, delightfully sweet, which produces pleasant dreams.

"The leaves that fall are much prized by small creatures, and unfortunately, the people who collect them for their poultry yards, if they don't find a sufficient quantity on the ground, unscrupulously cut living foliage. It's necessary to put a stop to that too. As it's notorious among painters and those who make drawings that linden branches can advantageously replace charcoal, they sometimes come to cut the young branches; they come in bands of at least fifty, with models who sing and billhooks attached to long poles. They cut all the young branches and they leave the tree deprived of its youth, of the youth of the year, of its old youth drawn with difficulty from the marshy soil. It's necessary to put a stop to that too.

"And as one can also cut the flowers to make a marvelous beverage that procures sleep for some and a mild excitement for others, in accordance with the cooking, thanks to a richness that only belongs to the linden, all that remains when autumn comes is a poor deprived trunk on the Lardenne road, which only has a marsh for alimentation. The linden appealed to me because it knew, in its arboreal soul, that I had a debt to pay. I shall pay my debt to the linden."

Tornebut was about to leave, with a spade on his shoulder, for the Lardenne road.

"How fortunate you are to have had a sign," I said. "Signs are rare. The words of the gods are uncertain. How I envy you for devoting yourself to a tree, an object of precise and certain consecration, limited in space: an ideal that you can see, touch and respire; a living ideal!"

THE FOREST OF CRABIOULES

The village of Cazaril is situated on the side of a mountain above Luchon, and there is not even a road that leads there—nothing but a path impracticable in winter. The Bramevaque estate is a little further on, in a valley more profoundly hollowed out in the mountains.

"A woman named Marie Seli? Yes, she's the one that left the area thirty years ago. She came back. She had a basket under her arm. She said that she wasn't worthy to enter the church. She knelt down under the porch and was found dead the next day. There was nothing in her basket. Someone claimed to have seen a glow around her head."

The peasants had gathered around me. But they could not tell me anything more. In order to know whether the Grail was in the subterranean lake of Saint Sernin or whether it was still necessary for me to search for it in the Toulousan region, as the voice had prescribed for me, I no longer had anything to rely on except my interior verity. And now, I even doubted the origin of the voice. I had no more certainty. I doubted everything.

Then I remembered a very profound forest into which only a few woodcutters had scarcely penetrated, a forest that was a little further on than the stones of my former dwelling; and I thought that I might see more clearly beneath a thick vault of trees where there was no light. So I went to join the road to Saint-Aventin.

"Bonjour, Michel de Bramevaque. Where are you going, then, with your staff in the form of a crosier? I thought your flocks were dead and your château in ruins?"

"Bonjour, Seigneur de Cazaril. I'm going further than the ruins of my château, into the wild forest of Crabioules, to try to find the great lost flock of my dreams."

"Aha! Dreams! You haven't changed, Michel de Bramevaque. Perhaps we'll encounter one another in the forest of Crabioules, for I intend to go hunting bears there."

"No one changes, Seigneur de Cazaril. One pursues dreams and the other bears."

By dint of living alone in his little stone tower in the company of uneducated peasants, the Seigneur de Cazaril had lost his reason somewhat. It was claimed that a bear had once devoured his fiancée. Since then he pursued those animals in the mountains and tried to capture them. He crucified them on trees, between their cubs, when he could. Then he approached them, presented them with bile on a sponge and killed them with a thrust of a spear. It was a sacrilegious and insensate parody. But he was a good Christian and took communion every Sunday. Then again, that happened high up, among the desert rocks, and it was difficult to have any proof of it.

"Bonjour, Michel de Bramevaque. Where are you going, then, with your staff in the form of a crosier? The wolves have been prowling around your château for a long time, and it appears that a fir tree already thirty years old has emerged from your well like a great hairy genie and blocked the entrance completely."

"Bonjour, Dame de Moustajon. I'm not going to drink the water from my well. I'm going further, into the wild forest of Crabioules in order to learn the science of solitude there and listen to the gods speak, for they speak more willingly in inaccessible woods when the nights are pure and the moon is shining."

"There is only one God, Michel de Bramevaque, who does not speak to heretics. Come with me to the Château de Moustajon. I'll gladly give you hospitality. But in the evening, before going to sleep, I'll teach you the catechism again."

The Dame de Moustajon smiled, an engaging smile that became a grimace because of a few teeth she lacked. The Moustajon abode was perched high in the rocks, but the dame came down every day to pray to Saint-Avenin, to converse with women and met some young man. She made a sign to a laborer valet to bring a mule for me, because the slope was steep all the way to Moustajon.

But I shook my head.

"I'll soon have the visit of the Domazans of Toulouse, with the beautiful Lucida, and Domitien de Barousse, who has become such a holy man."

"Thank you very much. Dame de Moustajon, but I prefer solitary meditation in the forest of Crabioules."

As I moved away she ran after me. "I know why you've chosen that forest. One has strange encounters there. But perhaps we'll see one another again. I can admit to you that I sometimes go there in secret—it's because of my hair."

She lifted up the net that covered her thick hair, and I saw that it was completely white.

"I have a few silver threads appearing here and there. When one dips one's hair into a certain spring in Crabioules, it becomes as black as night again, thanks to the virtue of the water. I'll take you to that spring, for you seem to have need of it."

"Au revoir, Dame de Moustajon. I prefer white hair to black—as for souls."

A little before the forest of Crabioules I encountered a woodcutter.

"There are great dangers, Seigneur de Bramevaque, and great mysteries in that forest. But if you take the path by which the wood was once slid out, you'll find a clearing with an abandoned cabin dominated by a high rock. We constructed it long ago, but we no longer go there since big Anselme died there without anyone knowing why."

It was agreed that the woodcutter, from the village of Oo, would bring me my week's nourishment every Sunday.

A man traversing a forest easily believes that it is silent and uninhabited. When he settles down to live there, he perceives that it is full of noises and languages and that it shelters beings of all shapes and sizes.

I recovered the faculty of my childhood that permitted me to understand the language of birds. I also distinguished the meaning of the calls of the grouse in thickets strewn with wild carnations, the grunts of wild boars, the low barking of foxes and the slight scratches that lizards make on rocks in order to say things related to the life of flies.

I strove to recognize the different sounds that the various species of trees make. The poplars did not speak like ash-trees. There was a tenderness in the language of birches that was reminiscent of the conversations of young women. The fir trees sang religious homilies; they were the vegetal priests of the mountain. The acacias had the speech of warriors. But all the voices were drowned out when the oaks agitated their branches. They were the patriarchs of the territory, the true masters of the stony soil, and through their branches they enabled a wisdom of the commencement of the world to speak.

In plunging into the wildest parts of the forest I discovered a mysterious center of trees, a council of millenarian trunks, hollow and ravaged, which, over time, had taken on faces of a sort, on the human model. Those gray faces were disposed in a circle around a clearing. But the bodies, unlike those of the human species, developed above the heads, their leafy feet turned toward the sky. The faces and the bodies were covered with deformities: polyps, goiters and other parasitic excrescences. The frontal bones were monstrous, the enormous mouths formed by a crevice. Those ligneous wounds and wooden tumors were royal signs, the emblems of time and power. And those inverted kings considered me silently.

In interrogated hem in a loud voice, even shouting, with the hope that there was a force in the resonance of words capable of attaining their profound source of comprehension; but it was in vain. A blue-tit uttered a cry devoid of meaning. High in the sky, there was an eagle that was tracing circles, but they were not the signs of any symbolic geometry.

I climbed the walls of Crabioules and reached stony plateaux on which nothing grew but arnica and blue thistles. At a rocky intersection I suddenly found myself confronted by thee crudely carved crosses. The remains of a bear were attached to the middle one. Wild animals had devoured its flesh and the white skull was visible under vestiges of skin. That cranium was turned toward the sky and, I don't know why, it expressed a great force of silence, the silence of resigned nature.

At night, however, when I had closed the shaky door of my cabin and I tried to go to sleep on the bed of ferns that I had prepared for myself, I heard, without any doubt about it, voices speaking, unimaginable voices conversing around me, as if of fantastic passers-by in the midst of the trees and the darkness.

To whom did those voices belong?

I knew that, by virtue of retrograde forces, and the excess of passions never mastered, there were beings who had allowed evil to dominate them. Legend said that that area of the mountains was inhabited by an old man named Bassa Jaon. It was him who had driven the holy man of Camors mad. The immeasurable love of life and the inferior joys of the body had permitted him temporarily to vanquish the limits of death. A date was assigned to his birth, and it was the year one thousand. He stole shepherdesses who took their flocks too far into the mountains and took them into the caves that are above the sacred lake of Mount Sacroux.

For there were lakes whose crystal water had never been seen by anyone, lakes forever imprisoned beneath a hermetic lid of ice. And sometimes that ice cracked, and from the depths of the waters the green goddess Mathagarri emerged. She too had lost her soul up there in the abode of stones, and she went to find Bassa Jaon. Then, the wind blew, and their cries were heard far away in the valleys. They lamented together because they knew that a day would come when an inexorable law would change both of them into motionless tones, incapable of knowing enjoyment.

But everyone has the gods they deserve. I gazed ardently into the darkness, knowing that the mountain could send to me the person who permits a man to purify himself, to elevate himself in the scale of beings. It is sufficient to have met her gaze once. That is Ilixone, the last Cantabrian goddess, who has taken refuge in the high crags of the Pyrenees, and who sleeps in the hollows of glaciers.[26] She walks between a white chamois and a white otter, she wears a swanskin cloak over her shoulder, and her feet are so white that they are confounded with the snow.

That Sunday, Placide Escoube, the woodcutter from the village of Oo, arrived much later than usual.

He had grave things to tell me, he said. He had learned them in Saint-Aventin, where there was a market that brought together the inhabitants of the Val d'Asotos, those of the valley of the Oueil and even those of Luchon and the borders of La Pique. The old curé of Saint-Aventin had preached against a heretic.

That heretic came from Toulouse. He abused the peasants by means of false miracles, and took down the cadavers of condemned men from the gallows by night, doubtless to make magical use of them. He had attempted to rouse the dregs of the people against the Capitouls and, driven by a perverse desire for pollution and profanation, he had introduced a prostitute into a secret place in Saint Sernin. He had converted his own dwelling into a house of debauchery. Now he was maintaining commerce in the forest of Crabioules with the old gods of paganism. He had attempted to draw with him the virtuous Dame de Moustajon. The testimony of that pious individual, who had made it on oath before the ecclesiastical authorities, could not be revoked. She had rendered justice at

---

[26] Ilixone was the original name of the town nowadays known as Luchon; it is interpreted by some antiquarians as the name of a river goddess. The previously-mentioned Mathagarri is untraceable in a Pyrenean context.

the same time to a calumny concerning the venerable Seigneur de Cazaril. It was the same heretic who crucified bears in the mountains in order to make a caricature of the Passion and to degrade the divinity of Jesus before the eagles of the summits.

And that heretic was me.

The curé of Saint-Aventin had announced that an extraordinary punishment was going to strike the impious individual whose name he dared not pronounce. And Placide Escoube had immediately enquired, on leaving the church, what that punishment might be. And this is what he had also learned.

For some time there had been an ecclesiastic in the area who was investigating the vestiges of ancient heresies. He had the title of apostolic legate and was a former Inquisitor of the Lauragais. He was only responsible to the Pope and his authority extended over the entire Church. His name was Alphonse Urraque, and the Dame de Moustajon, after the Friday mass at Saint-Aventin, had run from group to group to announce that the holy apostolic legate had done her the great honor of staying in the old Moustajon abode, in order to prepare the heretic's punishment. She lowered her voice to say that the punishment would be the most terrible that the Church can inflict, and murmured: "Excommunication!"

Alphonse Urraque! The man who had once refused me authorization to bury Raymond d'Alfaro! The Dominican of Avignonnet who seemed to have received the mysterious task of rediscovering the links uniting the present with the past and permitting the knowledge of how souls were linked to one another! The most terrible of tasks, that which prevented hatred from dying!

THE EXCOMMUNICATION IN THE MOUNTAINS

Summer was over. Strong winds blew from valley to valley. The foliage, the air and the waters changed color. The horns of shepherds sounded deeper notes.

Placide Escoube had come back several times since the day when he had warned me about the dangers that threatened me. He had not returned to Saint-Aventin, he said, with a certain embarrassment, and had not learned anything more. I expected to be summoned to appear before an ecclesiastical tribunal any day, but nothing happened, and I was beginning to think that Alphonse Urraque had renounced his intentions.

It was a Sunday evening when the events occurred. That day was doubtless chosen because of the market in Saint-Aventin, in order that all the inhabitants of the valleys could be impressed by the preparations for the ceremony

I remember that, on the day in question, I had discovered a clearing in the heart of the forest where wild rose-bushes had multiplied in large numbers, shedding so many roses round them that the ground was covered by their petals. That clearing was protected by the thorns of eglantines, but I had been able to get into it and I had seen, with surprises, that there was a very ancient square stone in the center, bearing on one of its faces a sign that I had seen before, made by a human hand and half-effaced by time.

The evening was stormy. The sun, as it disappeared behind the Peyresourde pass, tinted the low clouds with ruddy light. Night was approaching, the color of rust, full of disquieting warmth. I headed back to my cabin, promising myself to return the following day.

It was then that I heard a canticle, a sort of liturgical chant, a hymn of despair. It was sung by numerous voices, above me, and it gave the impression of falling lugubriously from the sky.

I raised my head. The part of the forest where I was standing was dominated by a great wall of stone covered by a

185

thick vestment of juniper and rosemary. I was climbing up along what woodcutters call a tree path, by means of which they slide trunks down to the valleys. But there was a stony path that, after having gone around the mountain, passed by higher up on its way toward the heights of Cabioules, where there was no longer anything but solitary eagles and dead lakes circled by frozen granite.

First I saw a tall cross that was advancing along the path, a cross that appeared to me to be immense, in spite of the distance. Then I distinguished a long procession marching behind the cross. There were priests clad in sacerdotal ornaments, striving to give their gait a certain solemnity. I counted them. There were twelve—which is to say, the ritual number for the ceremony of major excommunication, as it was practiced in the distant days of the Albigensians. Twelve! How had they been able to assemble so many?

There were the curés of all the neighboring parishes, that of Oo and that of Luchon. By his large nose and ears, I recognized a canon of Saint-Bertrand. A little old man with a stooped back and long hair was mounted on a mule; that was the curé of Saint-Aventin. The walk must have been judged too difficult for his great age. He had known me since my childhood. I knew his benevolence and I had no doubt that he was very sad to have to carry out a punishment. But behind him, by his tall stature, I recognized Domitien de Barousse, the magician priest. At first I had a frisson of horror on seeing him, but on reflection, his presence procured me an appeasement. If, under the impulsion of an ardent spirit full of faith, a ceremony of malediction could have an effect in the spiritual world, that effect must lose its winged force, since a soul possessed by evil was associated with it.

Bare-headed, in his white Dominican robe, Alphonse Urraque was marching at the head. He was not singing, like the priests who were following him and the peasants and woodcutters who were advancing behind the cortege of ecclesiastics. Sometimes he looked with an anxious eye at the forest that was at his feet, sometimes he turned toward the setting sun. Doubtless with the aid of impressing souls theatrically, he had associated the moment of the ceremony with that of the disappearance of the sun and the arrival of darkness. He consulted a man who seemed to be serving as his guide and who indicated, with an admirably precise gesture, the exact location of my cabin. It was with sadness that I recognized that man as Placide Escoube.

Alphonse Urraque raised his hand and the entire cortege stopped, interrupting the song. The curé of Saint-Aventine dismounted from his mule, with difficulty. A man set down a sort of bundle that he was carrying in his shoulders. There were torches tied together. A sacristan in a violet robe, who knelt down to pick them up, started running back and forth to distributed them to the priests. The peasants drew nearer. Some climbed on to rocks and arranged themselves in the manner of people who want to watch a spectacle comfortably. I saw faces agape with stupidity. I thought I recognized, among other women, the Dame de Moustajon, and next to her, pale in her white collar, I saw the pure oval face and empty eyes of Lucida de Domazan, the young woman devoid of a soul.

The peasants stood aside to let two of them, who had arrived last, pass by. They were carrying an empty coffin, which they came to deposit in front of Alphonse Urraque. According to the symbolism of excommunication, the coffin testified to the total death of the sinner, and if the sinner was docile, he came to lie down in the coffin.

The shadows were beginning to fall all around. The violet sacristan passed rapidly from one to another in order to light the torches. Then, placing himself beside the coffin, Alphonse Urraque advanced to the extremity of the ledge overlooking the forest and I heard his slightly muffled voice proclaiming toward me: "Michel de Bramevaque are you there?"

At the same time, the twelve priests raised their torches. From the Sacroux peak to Montarqué, the nascent stars recoiled. The hastening darkness seemed to catch fire, and it was as if there was a great red circle around me.

187

I had taken a few steps forward, and in spite of the foliage and the shadows, I distinguished the outline of Alphonse Urraque's head. He resembled me in such a striking fashion that I might have believed that it was me, a double in a Dominican robe, who had just pronounced my name.

I saw the gold of the stoles and chasubles of the past shining again, and the silhouettes of priests agitating. Gestures made to prevent the torches from going out stimulated them by shaking them. Those torches threw out great intermittent flames; one might have thought that they were making the mountains and the heavens tremble, that they were uprooting the oaks and firs in order to make a holocaust to God. The flame that Domitien de Barousse was holding seemed to me to be brighter than the others, to be the mother flame from which all those unexpected fires were springing. And suddenly, one of the first bats, with great maladroit wings, flew over the rank of priests, and it was necessary for the sacristan to chase it away with his stick.

I felt small, as if carried away with the trees by a force that swept everything.. But at the same time, there was a determination of resistance within me, a bitter desire to stand up to the power of the Church that had come, without reason or justice, to overwhelm me in my solitude.

"Yes, I'm here," I replied, and I perceived that my voice rose up and was heard by the man who resembled me in his external form of creature.

Doubtless he knew by heart the text of the accusation and the sacramental formulae of the malediction, for he did not read anything and he spoke abundantly. As he commenced, the evening wind that had passed through the gorges of Oo began to blow, and at the same time as it inclined the flames of the torches it carried away the Latin formulae and dispersed them.

Leaning forwards, Alphonse Urraque did not care whether or not the sinner that I was understood what he was saying. He was possessed by the hatred that I inspired in him and by a greater fury that embraced not only all living heretics but also those of the past, those who had died without having received the merited punishment.

By virtue of a strange phenomenon, his thought reached me and I perceived it easily. Without it being explained in his accusatory text, I understood that he was not excommunicating me for the reasons expressed, but because he knew that the ancient Albigensian belief had traversed the centuries, in spite of the Pope's Church, and was still alive in my heart, like an eternal flame.

The more he spoke, the more his voice, muffled at first, became emotional and forceful. I felt his exalted faith like a breath on my face. I suffered from its sincerity, the grandeur and beauty of which I was obliged to sense. Oh, how he believed! How he loved his Church and his God, to hate to that extent, how ready he was to shed my blood, that man in a white robe, so similar to me facially, that cruel brother who had placed is heaven higher than justice! His sincerity uplifted mine. I would have liked to speak, to defend myself, to fight. But how? I felt paralyzed, chilled to the bone.

I was attacked, just at the moment when the doubt that was in my soul rendered me most vulnerable. A great force fell upon me, crushing me. It was made of shadow. I had the sentiment that through all the corridors of the valleys, all the distributed darkness came flooding, penetrating my soul forever. My faith was annihilated. I had come here, among the old trees of France, to try to understand the divine mysteries thanks to the language of nature. But it was over. I was not to understand. My crime, in the eyes of the Church, was perhaps only that, of having tried to understand. And I would never understand now. By the power of its rites, the Church was condemning me forever to the darkness of evil.

Despair invaded me. If I had been able to cry out, my voice would have risen up to say that I would come to lie down in the coffin opened with my intention. I even attempted to climb the rock in order to reach it, to lie down between the planks and ask that I be buried alive.

Suddenly, Alphonse Urraque fell silent. The last formula of incantation had just fallen from his mouth

"*In nomine Patris et Filii et Spiritus sancti. Amen.*"

He straightened up and made an imperious sign. The twelve torches were lowered at the same time. They threw out a vivid glare, and went out. The twelve priests crushed them underfoot as the symbol of my soul, retrenched from the communion of creatures, of my spiritual life brought to an end.

And then, in the night that suddenly covered the forests and the mountains, a great light dawned within me and I suddenly understood everything that had seemed inexplicable to me, the silence of the gods and their speech more mysterious than their silence, the virtue of the Grail, its sacred beauty and its ungraspable character. I had searched for it and it was all around me. The emerald that now reposed beneath the Basilica of Saint Sernin only contained a drop of the blood of the world. The true blood of Jesus Christ was streaming all around with the redness of autumn in the foliage. It had tinted the old oaks and given that hint of rust to the junipers. It was in all of nature. I was living under a rain of divine blood. One could take communion in no matter what water from no matter what spring. The mystery of the spirit was accessible to everyone, and everyone could be saved. There was no need of a magic talisman, a liberating relic. Everyone had to make his own salvation. He had to find it in the depths of himself and ignite it, like a dormant candle from which he alone could bring forth the flame.

That verity was so explosive that it filled me with the suave delight that only the contemplation of what is true can provide. I raised my head and I saw an unknown star shining in an unaccustomed fashion, as if to give me a confirmation arriving from the immutable order of things. Never had the stars seemed as beautiful to me, and never as well distributed in the heavens.

Meanwhile I heard human voices calling to one another on the path. The cortege of priests resumed the route of return.

The curé de Saint-Aventin's mule refused to move at first. Then there was a sound of loud exclamations. Someone had dropped the coffin into the rocks, where it fell and broke. Voices lowered and became whispers. The last belated men must have been gripped by fear, and their silhouettes vanished.

The silent forest began to live again. I heard the sap flowing in the trees and I was sensible to the movements of roots through the earth. Flocks of birds woke up and took flight, soaring beneath the stars. Branches spread out in sheaves. And, filled with joy, I picked up my staff and started to walk.

I kept going. A little later, a bell rang in the distance, celebrating the mass for the dead. A long way away, like illuminations in the book of the night. I could see the stained glass windows of the church of Saint-Aventin, where, in accordance with the rite, people were praying for the death of the excommunicate, the man that no last judgment could any longer awaken. But the trumpets had already sounded for me.

I descended along the steep tree-path. Nature awoke as I passed. Badgers cleaved through the thickets with grunts of satisfaction. I saw the shrewd eyes of a fox fixed on me with an attention devoid of fear. Snakes and hedgehogs walked beneath the trees and caused stones to roll. As I jumped over a steam, a trout leapt and I saw its silvery body shining like the metal of a reliquary. An owl alighted close by. By virtue of my extraordinary faculty of perception I heard the ants emerging from ant-hills and I knew that they were raising their sharp lances in my direction as a sign of amity. I saw before me in the celestial azure, without adding any importance to it, a sort of turning wheel, which was the sign glimpsed during the day on a stone in the middle of a clearing full of roses.

I was dazzled by a light that came to me and gave me the joy of understanding. I understood the harmony that had enabled the Grail to be carried by the humblest creature on earth into the most sacred place on earth. The Grail I had sought was nevertheless in my heart. The blood of Jesus Christ was flowing within me. I was Jesus Christ.

THE ROSE OF THE FOUR HORSEMEN

In Isaac Andréa's garden there was an ancient altar with sculptures of gods that must have dated from a very remote era. It was placed at the extremity of a little cloister that bordered the garden, and anyone who stood in front of the altar saw before him the blue sinuosities of the Garonne, the vines on the hillsides and, when the weather as clear, the delicate shadow cast by the distant Pyrenees.

Isaac Andréa had welcomed me into his house not far from Toulouse. It was isolated at the extremity of a little path bordered by cypresses. It was full of books and manuscripts. On rainy days we deciphered certain Greek or Byzantine parchments that came from the ancient abbey on the site of which the house had been constructed. When the weather was fine, we discussed the problem of life and death along the cloister, in the quadrilateral of the garden, where there were tombstones bearing no inscription among the fig trees and eucalypti surrounded by wisteria.

Sometimes he said to me: "Good works are futile, you see." And I thought of what had become of my good intentions. "The only aid that the sage can give people comes from his active thought in solitude."

"Who is that goddess," I asked him, one day, pointing at a stone form on the altar with a very pure face, "and how was she able to remain in an abbey?"

"There were enlightened monks among the first Christians who understood the symbolism of the ancient gods. That goddess is Ilixone, the impetus of the soul toward the divine. One recognizes there the Pyrenean chamois and the otter that are to her right and her left. The primitive sculptor has polished the stone in a special manner, in order to conserve the whiteness, a sign of purity."

"And what does that stone there mean," I asked again, "which is carved like the indicative boundary-markers that one sees at crossroads?" I was pointing at a stone that had two lines broke into three sections, forming a sort of wheel. It was similar to the one that had intrigued me in the forest of Cabioules.

"It really does indicate a road to follow, but it is a road that does not go in any known direction. That sign is engraved all over the place by men who come from the Orient. It is sufficient to summarize an immense wisdom. But the meaning of the script is lost. The Holy Grail, also, is a living word in the same language. You see, a chamois and a white otter, a geometric design at a crossroads, and the divine blood of a perfect man at the bottom of a cup, are the same thing. Purity and detachment, that is all that humans have found, and what they transmit eternally."

I was sometimes astonished that no one came to visit Isaac Andréa. Was he never linked, then, to other men like himself?

One day, when we had made calculations related to the distance of the planets and we had talked about the voyages that the soul accomplishes after death, I asked him: "Are we alone in seeking?"

"There are other men," he replied, "but very few. The difficulty lies in encountering them." He stopped for a moment, and then added: "One never encounters them."

That same day, a little later, when Isaac Andréa had gone back into his library and I was walking in the garden alone, I saw at my feet a large fresh rose. The rose-bushes in the garden were entirely deflowered; the rose must have been thrown over the wall.

I suddenly remembered that I thought I had perceived the sound of hoof-beats a few minutes earlier. I ran to the altar of the goddess Ilixone and I saw in the distance, beyond the last cypress of the path, on the road leading toward the Garonne, the silhouettes of four horsemen, who had, it seemed to me, black cloaks floating in the wind.

I called to Isaac Andréa and I handed him the rose. He took it, raised it in the direction of the setting sun and murmured: "The rose!"

I showed him the horsemen who were drawing away and about to disappear along the road. He followed them with attentive eyes.

"Yes, there are those," he said, in a low voice. "They pass by without stopping. And there are also the others.

"What others?"

"Have you not woken up sometimes, feeling better, with the sentiment that life was more beautiful and also the sentiment that something sweet and admirable had passed by while you were asleep?"

"Yes, that has happened to me."

"I've often experienced it myself. It's because someone has thrown an invisible rose into our soul, by which it is embellished. But who was the being who threw it? Will we glimpse his silhouette when we are traveling, not along the bank of the Garonne, but along the river of death? Will it not be necessary to keep searching? Perhaps you'll perceive a new Grail, lifted up by a demented knight in mountains that are still distant. Who knows whether this is not the best, the unique, certainty in this redoubtable life, before the unknown death: this fragment of beauty, a rose, thrown in passing by a fraternal man that we shall never know?"

PREFACE TO *INVISIBLE BEAUTY*

I do not know whether there are people who escape despair, and if there are, I believe that they are not very numerous. I do not envy those people. There is in despair a bitter
substance, a fecund poison, the seed of a superior virtue that
one cannot find elsewhere. Everyone, sooner or later, ought to
aspire the juice of the hemlock that gives wings, the sacred
belladonna. But it is necessary to be able to drink the poison
and not die.

The greatest despair does not come from amorous disap-
pointment, nor from the sentiment of the impossibility of self-
realization, nor from the approach of death. It is a great force
of darkness that is sometimes reminiscent of an animate being,
a wave of negation that sinks over you and whose attack gives
the impression of being the result of a calculation. It is impossible, moreover, to affirm that the calculation in question does
not exist.

That force of darkness is more destructive than doubt. It
creates an anonymous void in the soul. All the fine monuments that one has edified in oneself and in the admiration of
which one takes pleasure, are transformed into phantoms, into
caricatures devoid of meaning. One has the sentiment of having loved fallacious figures, images of ugliness that one has
mistaken for beauty, gods without power, which suddenly
recover their veritable aspect under a tempest of desolation.
And one finds oneself alone on a desert rock, with all possibility of communication with living beings destroyed and, what
is more terrible, any determination to call for help. The image
of Hell has been justly represented by a solitary creature meditating on a bare stone.

In order for a man sitting down in the evening under his
lamp to be preserved from a danger that traverses the thickest

walls, in order for the columns of his interior temple not to be overturned along with the spiritual tabernacle, it is necessary that he has a few certainties, by means of which he can dissipate the menacing darkness as soon as it surges from the abyss, as the knight of legend has his fiery sword.

Those certainties one must cultivate within oneself. They are like precious plants that only yield flowers by virtue of the care and the love of the person who cultivates them.

There is no more solitude for someone who has found the hidden roots that connect humans to nature. There is no more discouragement for someone who sees the beauty of the world The fear of death does not exist and is even changed into hope for someone who, by the play and depth of contemplation, has been able to attain the first gleams of invisible worlds and their supernatural beauty. To change despair into beauty, to discover the secret of that transmutation, is perhaps the essential problem of human being.

For those who have glimpsed the presence of the enemy that has neither name nor form, who have felt the weight of mortal darkness and the treacherous bite that does not cause the blood of the soul to flow but corrodes it with the rust of annihilation, I have written this book, in which is reported what it has been given to me to discover about the invisible beauty of the world.

COMMUNICATION WITH NATURE

A MOTHER'S RING

When I was three, or perhaps four years old, I often asked my mother what he mysterious circle of gold was that she had on her finger. She invariably replied, with the same smile, in which there was a hint of pride: "It's a ring. A wedding ring. There's no jewel more beautiful in all the world."

I took that reply in its exact meaning. The most beautiful jewel in the entire world, an exceptional treasure, was in the little apartment in which I lived with my parents, in the form of a thin gold ring. That belief was forcefully engraved in my mind.

A little later, I acquired the faculty of comparison. I realized that in other apartments there was furniture much finer than that among which we lived—richer carpets, bookcases vaster than the few wooden shelves where I went to search for books—but I thought that difference came from unknown reasons that had nothing to do with wealth.

I had heard it said that a great fortune might be contained in a very tiny stone. The gold ring must be made of an inestimable metal, which gave it that unique value. If my parents' apartment was modest, it was doubtless because they preferred the narrow frame of those bare walls, cheered up by a few familiar objects. They had chosen those three rooms with a dark lavatory, at the top of a vast and sad house, by virtue of a special predilection. If I heard mention so frequently of difficulties with regard to the question of money, it was by virtue of an incomprehensible error on my part. Did not my mother wear on her finger the most beautiful jewel in the entire world?

197

The presence of that golden stripe reassured me for many years. It prevented me from sharing the dread of a poverty of which I did not even comprehend the threat. The sight of the light circle on the sacred hand sufficed to dissipate all anguish.

Later, I never saw that ring without emotion. Life informed me that my mother had not deceived me, and that my credence was just. Although I had acquired an exact knowledge of what the value of a few grams of gold represents to society, I knew that the ring in question was, for the person who wore it, the material symbol of an unlimited wealth.

Thanks to the treasure that she had, and the light grip of which she could perceive at every minute, my mother went through life, with its bitter shadows and its deserted paths, with the perpetual presence of a beloved possession.

In her final hours, I saw the magic ring on her emaciated finger again. She had been suffering intensely for several months. And looking back on the perfection of her life, her natural goodness, her quotidian pure intention, I wondered what incomprehensible, unjust law struck down the best, imposed unmerited suffering on them, without taking account of actions or thoughts.

If there is a justice, I thought, it escapes our conception, in which case one might as well say that there is none. How could the idea that I had of the goodness of the world be reconciled with the reality of that pain? And what cruelty there was in a deceit exercised throughout life. In that little ring, my mother had thought that she carried a talisman of good fortune, and here she was, on a bed, with a torture so great that she was not even permitted the consolation of a final adieu!

Later, I could not help thinking about what had become of that ring. It is a sadness of certain imaginations to possess an inexorable realism. Her hands clasped over her breast, my mother had been buried with her treasure, the treasure of her perfect love. I have reconstituted in thought the solitude of the body, I have pierced the darkness, imagined the drama of time, of the rain, of the wood that rotted, the roots that penetrated, the movement of the larvae and the germs, of the renaissance—and that with an acuity as heart-rending as the sentiment of sacrilege.

And in that slow mystery of the elaboration of atoms, in which the terrestrial form disappears, in which the tissues return to the primordial substance, in which the bones themselves become sodium and chalk again, in that chemistry of death, I saw the ring, which, by virtue of the power of its circle, the quality of its metal, the mystery of its occult genius, resisted the force of the mineral aids, the consumption of time, and survived, retaining it preservative force.

And one morning, a little before the appearance of daylight, I had a dream. Was it a dream? Was it not rather a creation of my mind, elaborated unknown to me in the midst of the unconscious agitation of my thoughts? Or was it not an apparition, a real presence of my mother, who, with the eternal fidelity of loving hearts, had not ceased to inhabit the air in which her son breathed?

My mother was standing before me and she was holding out the ring to me, the eternal ring. But what I saw of her was scarcely a form, and her representation is scarcely expressible in words. I certainly had before me a creature, but she appeared to me, so to speak, at the center of the relationships that she had with the rest of the world. She was like the middle of a star, or a living wheel, of which the multiplicity of natural things were the spokes. She retained nevertheless the maternal attributes of her tender gaze, of her beloved face, but she was confounded with the rest of the world.

There was nothing funereal in her appearance, even though it was the one that I had imagined in the narrow prison of the coffin. I could see the bones through the volatilized flesh, but they seemed to be made of an ideal substance, a cosmic essence, such as one sometimes imagines that there is in the center of the planet. The garments certainly had the corruption of damp cloth, but they had lost their quality of separate objects; they participated in a beauty that the elements have in their primal virginity.

I thought that because I had contemplated the mystery of the material transformation of the human form for a long time I was now seeing my mother participating in the diversity of the expanse of the realms. But although dispersed in the variety of things, she remained the creature from whom I had received the gift of existence and a gleam in her gaze reminded me that her love was fixed, like the pole star, and was not susceptible of being confounded with other loves.

She held out the ring to me with a silent ardor, and I took it from her hands: slightly luminous, slightly transparent hands; hands the shone in the twilight of the bedroom, and which only existed in order to be the support of that imperishable ring and the means of its transmission.

Only then did I understand the mystery that is hidden in a mother, of which every man ought one day to have the revelation.

A love more profound than that of her maternal love and my filial love united me with the person of whom I was born. She had given me blood: not her personal woman's blood but the blood that circulated in the veins of the planet. She was nature and I was linked to her. My proud thought urged me to detach myself, but I was linked. The ring was the symbol of the great terrestrial union. One can quit one's family, one can quit one's race, but there is a limit to human liberation. One cannot escape the law that directs all terrestrial forces, united in the maternal womb.

Like all visions, that one returned to oblivion, without me being able to tell in what measure it depended on my imagination, or on an exterior reality bringing that beloved presence from the distant realms of the afterlife.

Oh, what would I not have given, to see on my sheet, in the early morning light, the thin ring of gold, the most beautiful jewel in earth? I believe I searched for it at first, with a rapid but vain gesture; but then I said to myself: *What's the point? Have I not, in effect received it? Shall I not wear it on my finger henceforth?*

O my mother, you who have now resumed your place in the eternal rhythm, whose body has returned to the forms whose soul is following the route prescribed for it by its destiny, know that your son has received the revelation from you. Henceforth, his mother's face is inseparable from that of immense nature.

NATURE'S GRACE

There is a grace of nature that one receives, on a certain day, in an unexpected fashion, like an illumination. The grace in question is not of the same order as that of religion, but it has a certain resemblance to it, if only that of being accorded without reason, by virtue of a choice made by an unknown power.

For it is necessary to be chosen. Is it the consequence of a council held by the spirits of lakes, those of forests, and the more delicate spirits of flowers, creators of perfumes? Sometimes, woodcutters who have spent their life in the midst of trees, die without being touched by that grace, Perhaps that is precisely because they have been woodcutters. There is a great injustice in that descent of grace, as in all divine things. But it is necessary not to despair of being touched by it, and not to try to acquire merits for that reason, for the absence of merits sometimes gives an invisible title.

Perhaps the grace of nature is acquired by curiosity. It is strange that there are many marvelous gifts that are obtained by faults, or even by vices. Curiosity brings nature closer, and to be close is already to be loved. Perhaps it is also acquired by an extreme attention. To follow over the earth the march of a thousand animal feet, or to study in the sky the curve of a bird's dream, leads to a magnification of the soul that favors the descent of grace.

The greatest pleasures come from discoveries made by intelligence. But when that order of pleasure is mingled with the one that beauty procures, one attains the highest summit accessible to a human being. Now, it is only in the observation of nature that intelligence and beauty find their point of contact, and the play of grace favors that ideal rapprochement.

The individual who has received the grace is filled with admiration by the passage of a bee, and drinks like a beverage of joy a color in a landscape or a ray of moonlight; even the song of a solitary cicada communicates the desire to weep.

Fortunate is the person who can weep because an insect is singing! The grace is perhaps only a perfect emotivity which permits participation in all lives.

The individual who has received the grace of nature is not traversed through and through by a supernatural light. Neither forests nor seas are clad with a new appearance in his eyes. He does not know that he has received the grace, but nature knows, and she envelops him without his knowing it with her attentive love.

THE ANNUNCIATORY CRICKET

There are signs around us, warnings in nature. Certain images suddenly form in the most unexpected manner to warn us either of an imminent misfortune or, on the contrary, a happy event.

We refuse to think that nature occupies herself with us. It is always while laughing that we identify those bizarre connections, and if one wants to insist on them, the interlocutor declares that it is a matter of chance of coincidence. Here is one coincidence, among many others.

I was very ill and getting worse, I was at the point where there were conferences in my entourage, the sorrowful whispers that announce unexpectedly to the individual asleep in the quietude of fever that his hour might have come. A sage interior voice repeated to me that it was nothing of the sort, but does one ever know?

My illness was one of those that have a critical day—the tenth, I believe. When that day is past without an abrupt aggravation, it is considered that all will go well.

Now, to everyone's great surprise, on the tenth day, a cricket of whose presence no one was aware intoned a song. How had that cricket been able to penetrate into an apartment in a modern building in the heart of Paris? At any rate, its presence was considered as mysterious from the start, because it remained invisible.

Nothing is more difficult than to determine the exact location of the song of a cricket in the resonances of rooms; that one was eventually localized in a certain wall from which hot water pipes emerged.

The cricket did not cease singing, and a comforting delight was associated with that song for me, a delight that was linked to the decline of my illness.

As soon as I felt better, I delivered myself to an attentive investigation of the life of crickets, in particular the crickets that live in Pars. I interrogated individuals knowledgeable about crickets. It seems that there are a great many of them, without anyone being able to discover the origin of that competence. The insect that had just announced and celebrated my cure was a bakery cricket. Bakeries, I was told, are full of crickets. That one, animated by a liking for voyages and attracted by the warmth, had traveled along a pipe and reached me. There was nothing marvelous about it, competent people assured me.

I had offerings of salad placed at different opening where the cricket might appear when night rendered the house silent and full of security for a creature of its size. I thought that it was appropriate to nourish a messenger of good news, especially when, intimately, one considers it to be an envoy of a divine order. It seemed to me, without my being able to affirm it, that my salad was always intact the next morning. I was dismayed, but the same people assured me that a cricket is never in difficulty, that it finds microscopic creatures easily that serve as its nourishment.

I said to myself, what the hell, these people might be thus informed; but whatever its form of nourishment, the cricket intoned its song every evening with a regular force, and I might even have been able to be importuned by its nocturnal power if I had not firmly associated an idea of cure with that song. In truth, that bakery cricket must have enjoyed a perfect health, and if it did not do honor to my salad, it was only because the walls must indeed be populated by tiny creatures whose existence I did not suspect.

It was only much later, when I was completely cured, that it was given to me to perceive it. A housekeeper did claim to have encountered it early one morning, but as I had made many fruitless searches I ended wondering whether it really existed, and whether the song might be a collective hallucination.

I saw it, and that filled me with affection. It was a cricket like any other cricket, like those I had caused to emerge from their holes with the aid of a straw in my childhood. It was motionless and it had retained, in spite of living in Paris, a charming rustic quality. It was only a cricket that had come along a pipe, a bakery cricket, but personally, I could not doubt that it had been charged with a happy annunciation for me. Where had it come from? I didn't know. It had made a long tenebrous voyage, immense by its standards, guided by what beacon light? Unconscious of its message, it had come to bring it to me faithfully. Why had it not continued on its way? It knew that at some point, where there was a sick man, it ought to stop and intone a hymn of hope, with the same joy that it had found amid the clover and the poppies in the blessed lands where the races of crickets live.

I remained intimidated before it, fearing that I might frighten it by my gigantic proportions. But I firmly believe that it did not see me and did not establish any connection between me, the gifts of salad that it had been offered and the goal of its voyage along the pipes. Scarcely had I turned my back than it resumed its task of singing.

Spring arrived with its warmth and, as mysteriously as it had come, the cricket left again. Did it reach a minuscule flower-bed that is outside my window? Did it rediscover the route to the original bakery where, it is said, crickets and bakers live in perfect harmony? I don't know. I only know that in the great book in which the destiny of each man is traced, my darkest page bears the design of a black cricket and the poem of its song.

Thus, the world is full of correspondences. Certain images are reflected at considerable distances without our being able to know what the reflective mirrors are. All things are linked together and the souls of creatures vibrate in unison, in accordance with relationships that escape us. A human soul might have a liaison with the soul of an animal species, an amity of which it has no knowledge, whose bonds it has forgotten. But those bonds subsist, and the animal soul, perhaps more conscious in a certain domain than that of a human being, can remember them, and, at a grave moment, make the affectionate sign that manifests love.

THE YOUNG WOMAN AND THE FERNS

There came an hour when the first bats commenced circling the lamps in the garden. Then I pushed the gate, took the road already tinted by autumn and went down some way into the valley, in the midst of box-trees and wild laurels.

On a bench, alongside the line of cypresses standing erect against the wind, at the place where a field of wild ferns began, I saw a young woman sitting, who gave the impression of looking into herself.

Sometimes, she did not seem to see me, but at other times, she stared at me like someone that had just been recognized.

I did not speak to her. I have never spoken to her, but I felt better for having met her, and a great increase in wellbeing resulted from that. Her gaze seemed to me to be sometimes blue, sometimes mauve, in a frame of extinct gold, and the descending shadows gave the milky over of her face pastel tints.

I asked several times who she might be. One of the tenants of the villa at the end of the path replied to me once. But that young woman was tall, with red hair, whereas the one I encountered was of medium height. Another time, someone wanted to identify her with a Spaniard who had come to a farm at the bottom of the valley for the summer and who was very short and brunette.

I began to look forward impatiently to the time in the evening when I would see the unknown young woman sitting on the bench. And when I left at the end of the vacation I took with me the regret that the lost beauty left behind.

I saw her again the following year, and again the next, always in the same place, in the same attitude, and I don't know what timidity forbade me to approach her.

Then, I did not see her again, and the years passed. She became more beautiful in my memory, to the point where I wondered whether she had really existed, whether she was not a symbol, a living personification of the landscapes I loved, and among which nature had been revealed to me....

I have always thought about her, and once, much later, I found a fern branch in a book that I could not remember having put there. The fern had made a sort of colored bas-relief on the printed page of the book; it had traced unintelligible characters, the meaning of which I nevertheless understood: the melancholy of lost youth.

One always arrives at understanding the language of plants with which one is in sympathy.

I don't know why, but there was an association of ideas between the fern and the young woman of old, and I took pleasure in imagining, in spite of the implausibility of the notion, that it was her who had put the plant in the book.

I have kept that book preciously, with the fern and the mysterious characters it had traced.

And, still without the slightest valid reason, I think that there will come a time when I shall see the young woman again, and when she will hold out the fern branch to me, smiling: a branch of the road of youth, with which to perfume the road to death.

THE DISCOVERY OF THE DIVINE PLAN

There is only one essential problem, and if one succeeds in solving it, all the other problems are resolved at the same time. It is necessary to find the solution to that problem oneself, by means of one's own research in nature. All the scholars and all the observers of the earth and the sky, from those who study the motion of the Milky Way to those who occupy themselves with the intimate life of mites, have remained perplexed before that problem, and have different opinions about it. It is necessary to look oneself, to find material proof for oneself that will not be valid for others, which others will treat as poetic stupidity, or just pure stupidity, but which will be rigorously scientific in one's own eyes.

Are there traces of a plan in nature?

Can one see the presence, if not of an organizing will, at least the design of an architecture? It does not matter that the scale surpasses us. An ant wandering in the Sahara, even a patient one, might very well not succeed in imagining the structure and the diversity of the world, and yet that is perhaps possible for the intuition of an ant. But we have a field of experience much vaster in appearance than that ant.

If we succeed in discovering for ourselves, in the parcel of the universe we know, the trace of an organizing intelligence, then everything would be different for us. We would no longer have to fear the caprice of chance—for instance, the possibility of being tortured without reason for millions of years, an eventuality that would not be implausible if there were no order in the world. Chance produces all combinations, and that one might be produced.

The assurance of the order of nature removes from us the threat of annihilation. We would have the certainty of having time before us, time beyond death. For it is easy to see that nature transforms that which is material rapidly, but that qualities of duration are attached to the spirit. If she has created the complex bundle of spiritual elements that is the human soul, it is not to destroy it abruptly. Consciousness is, moreover, a nucleus of resistance that becomes increasingly lively as it develops.

It follows from the first glance at the divine plan that the plan in question has not been made exclusively for humans, and that they are merely a tiny component of it. Nothing is more contrary to reason than the infantile and poetic reveries of Bernardin de Saint-Pierre.[27] They were welcomed with enthusiasm because they flattered human pride by telling people that the heavens and the earth only existed for the expansion of their stupidity and cruelty.

The discovery of the plan leaves the mind stupefied before the vast play of combinations, the entanglement of causes and effects and the multiplicity of correspondences. It is something so enormous and so complicated at first sight that one is tempted to say that there is no plan. But laws, with their immutable character, contradict the explanation of the world by chance. They are like the general lines of the plan, lines so numerous and so contradictory that one never succeeds in discovering where they come from or where they go.

It is impossible to know the exact place we occupy in the plan, at our present degree of knowledge. In all times, humans have attributed themselves the first place. To legitimate such pride, they based it of the fact that they were the strongest of organized beings and had subjugated all that they saw on earth. But strength is only a sign of physical superiority. Nor are the superiority of intelligence and the complexity of organs absolute proof that humans are at the summit of the hierarchy of living beings.

As soon as the discovery of the plan has been made, it immediately becomes apparent that to want to go against the

---

[27] The reference is to the philosophy developed by Bernardin de Saint-Pierre in such texts as *Études de la nature* (1784) and *Les Voeux d'un solitaire* (1790) before being summed up in the posthumously-published *Harmonies de la nature* (1815; tr. as *The Harmonies of Nature*).

direction of its progress would be an insensate enterprise. Wisdom consists of discerning the primordial laws that direct the plan, the visible rules of its harmony, and conforming to those rules. If they seem rigorous to us, we will be sustained by the idea that they are ineluctable and that our faculty of modifying them to our advantage resides in the form of our resignation to their power.

A swimmer in a rapid river descends the current without fatigue, and his task consists of avoiding obstacles. We have only to allow ourselves to be drawn by the waters, since, in the distance, the best of us say that they have glimpsed, not a beach, but a place where the beach, the swimmers and the river all become one.

THE JOY THAT THE DISCOVERY OF THE DIVINE PLAN PROCURES

Understanding nature is the most important of preoccupations as well as the most passionate. There is no joy more moving than the discovery of the divine plan in the seemingly disorderly manifestations of the universe.

What is surprising is the large number of people who deprive themselves of that joy. But there is an hour of the search that sounds ineluctably for everyone. No one can escape the horror of his own ignorance, which surges forth sooner or later.

What is more surprising is that sincere people, full of attentive consciousness, can be inclined over nature throughout their lives without discovering the traces of the plan. For them, thought is an invisible sweat bound to return to annihilation, and chance alone is the primordial source of life.

It might be the case that the internal fulguration that gives the certainty of the plan does not spring forth for all gazes, and that observation itself, by limiting the field of study, does not permit the view of the whole that is necessary to distinguish the lines traced—all the more so as they are only broad lines that do indeed give the impression of being drawn at hazard.

For it is the disorder that is immediately striking, a dazzling disorder, perhaps voluntary, which fills the soul with delight because it is accompanied by a certain fantasy. There are oversights, negligences and, almost always, exceptions. It is necessary to say "almost always" because death, for example, does not appear to have any. But what would a world be in which there were no exceptions, and in which one felt surrounded by a machinery of stone?

One is also surprised and rendered indignant by a permanent absence of pity, an ignorance of any forgiveness in the exercise of the laws. An indifference and joyful ferocity is characteristic of the cosmic intelligence.

Good and evil are perhaps only givens of our scale. If, by an effort of consciousness, one succeeds in placing oneself outside the plan, one discovers that in many circumstances, our pity has cruel consequences and our justice unjust effects. No one would dare to remove a person's misfortune if they could see the chain of events that follow from that misfortune.

Pity, which has so much prestige for us, is perhaps only a sentimental and purely human aspect, and it is possible that every time a person wants to exercise it, he will encounter a superior law that surpasses him, an inhuman law but of a divine order.

Then again, one can ask oneself whether the creative intelligence, the author of the plan, might not, in spite of its vastness and its power, be the prisoner of certain immeasurable forces, with regard to which it is in the same position as we are in regard to it. In the framework of those forces, it might have realized the plan as best it could, while being hindered and sometimes impotent.

But one has a profound joy when one perceives that the beauty of the world is determined and prepared with care, the logic of which escapes us but the result of which is visible and indubitable.

One is tempted at first to think that the beauty in question has been distributed parsimoniously, and one accuses the author of the divine plan of avarice or poverty, but it might be the case that beauty is infinitely more abundant than the human faculty of admiration, and that it only seems so parsimonious because of the narrowness of human vision.

One might also say to oneself that perhaps beauty is proportional to certain capacities of the universe we are in. A vast scale of universes must exist, in which we elevate ourselves by grace of our desire for elevation, and there must be other worlds in which beauty is richer and more permanent, where it springs forth naturally, where it is a common property of things, which the inhabitants of those words perceive effortlessly by means of a direct communication. We would then be in a world regulate by a mediocre plan, dazzling in certain of its parts but imperfect in others, which would be what a student sketch is by comparison with a master painting.

It would then be necessary to excuse the author of the plan, who has been unable to realize his work without introducing oppositions into it, such as good and evil, and is preparing with this failed trial for a more perfect work, whose models exist elsewhere.

THE EXPERIENCE OF THE PIOUS FIR TREES

During my sixteenth year I had an experience of the fraternity of trees and the strange relationships they can have with human beings.

It was a summer night in the little town of Luchon, which is surrounded by mountains. I perceived, when the midnight hour arrived, that I had missed the last train capable of taking me back to the village where my parents had rented a house for the summer. On such occasions, one takes a room in a hotel, but I had spent all the money I had on me. That was not serious however. The night was warm and clear; I decided to spend it under the beautiful stars.

For that, I climbed a path that rose up above the town among dense trees. I went up high enough to be sure that no one would witness the quality of bed I had chosen, a choice I judged to be contrary to my dignity as a young man. I did not know that there would come a time when I would, by contrast, take pride in being able to sleep anywhere, on hard ground, with nothing but a felt hat for a pillow.

I turned when I encountered a path, and then I took an even narrower path, until I found myself under a vault of fir trees, in the midst of wild ferns. I installed myself as best I could, which was very poorly. But I did not render homage internally to the organization of rooms and the comfort of beds. I was charmed by the romanticism of the night. I had measured the petty dangers that might threaten me, which were limited to the passage of a rat or a snake. I was gripped by a certain anguish on contemplating the immense circle of trees above me, through which the moonlight filtered with difficulty, but I ended up going to sleep.

I was woken up with a start, as if someone had called to me or touched me with a finger. Why does one wake up at one moment rather than another? That mystery is inexplicable for everyone.

I was surrounded by a light that seemed to me to be supernatural and fantastic, because I had not yet seen the pure light of the sun rising under a vault of trees. And I perceived with an indescribable astonishment that I was surrounded by monks. I was in an immense convent. Were they really monks? Upright, similar to one another under the flow of their robes, which widened out, the fir trees that stood round me were, at any rate, individuals of a religious order.

Surprise made me leap to my feet. I realized then that those beings of meditation were thinking about me. They were a trifle severe, their gravity unfathomable, and yet they were fundamentally indulgent. But how distant they were from my own thoughts! I understood that they expected something from me, without perceiving what it was.

I sat down again in great perplexity. And I perceived that the ferns that were at my level were full of fantasy and poetry themselves, and that we were in complete sympathy. I extended my hands to touch them. They were damp, and although I was frozen, that freshness seemed delightful to me, as if I had touched the tears of poets or musicians.

I had lowered my head. When I raised it again, the monks had disappeared, as well as the artistic personalities hidden in the ferns There were only ancient fir trees, upright in the morning light, and at their feet, a young man numb with cold, who forgot that rapid vision in order to remove the traces of the night from his clothing.

Many years later, having acquired knowledge of the souls of plants, I wondered whether the firs I had seen one morning in the Pyrenees might not have had a special character. I went back to the same place and followed the same paths. The firs were still there and the ferns too, at exactly the same height.

But I appealed in vain with my soul to the mute trees. They remained silent, uniquely endowed with the quality of fir trees. They had manifested themselves to an ignorant young man full of futile preoccupations, but they remained indifferent before a man informed of their personality, who invoked them with sincerity.

Is the light of the rising sun necessary to the appearance of the true nature of trees? Or is a receptacle of youth that I no longer possessed necessary to perceive it? I knew that the mountain was a vast monastery of pious fir trees, but I could no longer obtain the proof of it.

THE AMITY OF A LIZARD

The amity one experiences for certain species of animals can become perceptible in certain cases and permit the establishment of a temporary communication with creatures of those species.

I have always had a desire to fraternize with lizards, to study their mores, to see their haunts and their amours. In my childhood, I was very impressed by the words of a comrade of my own age. He affirmed that it was very easy to domesticate lizards by whistling. He claimed to be able to make them emerge from their profound dwellings, and make them run over his hand, merely by the charm of a light whistle.

I often attempted to employ that method, in vain. It produced no result, either because the sounds I made were imperfect or because of the natural dread experienced by lizards at the sight of a man, which the fact of whistling was insufficient to attenuate.

However, to attract animals and establish the state of sympathy with them that must be primordial, there are certain means that can be exercised without our being aware of it, and which do not depend on our will. I once possessed one of those means for a few minutes, without suspecting it, but virtue of the play of a faculty that I did not know I had.

I had gone out at about five o'clock under pine trees on a summer day, not far from the sea. I was thinking about lizards, what was charming in their aspect, their marvelous faculty of letting half their body drop without suffering as a result, and their inoffensive nature for all beings that are not little insects susceptible of adhering to a long wet tongue.

I regretted for the thousandth time the separation between them and me created by differences of nature and dimension. Perhaps that regret was one of the subtle elements that determined what happened.

Nothing happened, in any case, in the domain of facts.

On a sandy area, a lizard slid in front of me. A desire was formulated confusedly in my mind to see it stop, and, to my great surprise, it stopped. I stood still, waiting for it to disappear, prey to the fear that all small creatures experience when the accursed shadow of a man extends over them. As it did not budge, and it was only fifty centimeters away from me, I bent down as slowly as possible and leaned toward it until I was very close to it. Then it turned in my direction and it seemed to consider me attentively. My head must have appeared to it as an immense smiling ball, in which it doubtless perceived all that was engaging in the smile. But in its attention I discerned, without the possibility of any mistake, a sympathetic consideration, which was not far removed from the sentiment of a familiar cat that is about to leap on to your knees.

It seemed to me to be expecting something that was not forthcoming—perhaps a gift. Relationships between primitive beings always commence with gifts. It yawned twice in succession, which permitted me to see the projection of its tongue and might have been an invitation to a gift of nourishment. What I took for yawns might also have been a mode of expression appropriate to lizards. In order to demonstrate its perfect ease, its absence of dread, it was satisfying a physical need, but it did not have any insulting thought in my regard.

Then, without any haste, and even with a certain slowness, it drew away and headed for one of the holes that were some distance away amid stones and roots. It hesitated. It looked back at me, as if for an adieu, and then it disappeared.

I confess that I was gripped at first by an extreme pride. So I could charm lizards! I possessed that magical virtue, and did not know it. Perhaps it only depended on me to be followed by a group of those animals?

I was soon undeceived, for I wanted to know the extent of my power right away. I had continued my walk and arrived near a wall bathed by the evening sunlight, on which several lizards were resting. I could not count them. I only saw several little gray jets, fleeing. I tried in vain to project a current full of amity toward them. It appeared that my proximity had no sympathetic significance for them. I even attempted to emit a few whistles, in accordance with my childhood friend's method, but it had no result.

It was the same the next day and the days that followed.

It seemed to me that I had enjoyed a richness as fleeting as it was agreeable. I returned to the same place fruitlessly. The familiar lizard did not reappear. There were others, which slid away fearfully at the sight of me. But where was the charming friend? I never discovered the secret of the rapport that existed between us. Having given me what might have been a manifestation of a lizard's amity for a human, it had reentered into the immensity of the earth.

THE MYSTERY OF FIRE

How mysterious fire is. If I understood fire I would understand the world. The physical science of all the scholars is no use to me. It is because of a great habitude that one is not perpetually astonished by the apparition of fire. It emerges from nothing; it returns to it. What is it?

And what prestige it has! Once, humans adored it, and even today there is no joy without fire. Animals are hypnotized by it and even though insects burn their wings on lamps they prefer to lose their capacity for flight, and even their life, rather than draw away from a flame.

A flame springs forth with its power of heat, light and destruction, and then it disappears. Where does it go? Is there an abode of fire? But no, fire is unaware of space. Can one even measure the dimension of a flame?

There would be an attraction to being consumed by fire, to becoming fire oneself, if it were not for the acute pain. But perhaps that pain is only the evil inherent in any admirable transformation.

In the same way that what we call nothing conceals that destructive force, it must have another power, which ought to be creative. But we do not know how to make it appear. There is no match to cause the force of life to spring forth. That force will be found when the impenetrable and divine mystery that is fire is finally understood.

HESITATIONS AND IMPERFECTIONS
OF DIVINE LAW

Why do certain insects, like millipedes of the myriapodan genre, have as many as five hundred pairs of legs? Are so many necessary in order to run rapidly? Is it not a slightly crazy superabundance of nature that has determined that that category of creatures should move rapidly and has given it exaggerated means?

Such profusions occur frequently. The female of the aphid, contrary to the general law of generation, gives birth to an immense number of tiny living aphids without having been fecundated. Nature seems to have feared that the precious species of aphids might diminish, and in order to avoid that disaster, she has suppressed the embarrassment of couplings. Since that means of reproduction, known as parthenogenesis, is possible, and is evidently the simplest, why has nature not employed it for all species and has gone to so much trouble, in certain cases, to permit the male and the female to come together?

She spares no effort when it is a matter of the perpetuation of life. One might think that she fears beg caught in a trap coming from higher up than herself. Or perhaps she has to obey laws that she has put in vigor and no longer wants to oppose. At any rate, she yields constantly to a preoccupation with general equilibrium.

In order to arrive at her goal of procreation, nature offers intense pleasures like that of sexual intercourse. There is enjoyment every time there is a development of life. Plants must be recompensed for growth by a pleasure of which we have no idea.

Nature provides even more intense pleasures for the realizations of a spiritual order that are the final word of her effort on earth. But those intense pleasures are not much sought after, in spite of their intensity. Although there are multiplications of aphids, there are no multiplications of ecstatic ascetics. Their rarity is a sign of the slowness that individuals bring to their progress.

The further one rises in the spiritual order, the more a quality of personal effort intervenes as a necessary element. Progression must be accompanied by effort. There is a genius of nature, an occult force that impels individuals to improve themselves, to have more complete organs, more apt for survival, which have spiritualization as their supreme goal, but that goal can only be obtained if individuals extract it from themselves by a constant effort, and there is only amelioration in proportion to that effort.

That genius of nature has in its essence a transformative force. That force, which seems limitless to us, has limits that escape us, and which are in the capacity of the effort of the engendering beings. We are the ones, with our inertia and our love of ignorance, who put limits on divine law.

Perhaps there are others, coming from a higher source, but about which it is impossible to know anything. There are limitations that give to the work that apparent incoherence in the laws of generation, which are the cause of its numerous exceptions and its inexplicable regressions. It has hesitations and instances of puerile awkwardness.

One can say, for instance, that after the creation of the earth, nature did not decide, for a long period, on the measure of grandeur that she would give to the inhabitants of the earth. She decided initially on beings of gigantic size and extravagant gait, and there was an expansion of life that brought the dinosaurs into the world, formidable vertebrates with reptilian bodies, salamanders standing upright on short, thick legs, snakes with canine heads, fabulous dogs with the horns of bison, and pterodactyls resembling flying crocodiles.

Then the expansion of life had a sort of regret. Nature observed an error of proportion. Although she went a long way into the infinitely small—or what appears as such to us— she limited herself in the infinitely large. She allowed the enormous species to die in order to restrict herself to a moderate measure, or what our human intelligence finds moderate.

Why that limitation in dimension? The limit of growth is a subject of astonishment that remains unexplained. It is only our habitude that prevents us from being astonished that every seed carries an innate faculty of growth that ought not to be exceeded. Even by the title of exception, no human attains a height of several meters, no cat can succeed by carelessness in attaining the height of an elephant. There is a constant and eternally manifest power of measure in that—but the scale was not determined without groping.

Is there not similar evidence of research in the fact of having placed the eye of a snail on the end of a horn, of having developed a mobile nose in the elephant, of having placed the mouth of a sea-urchin at the summit of its body and its eyes on its back, in spite of the difficulty that entails in steering?

The imperfection of nature is more moving than a perfection that would be crushing if it were absolute. At any rate, no sun will be detached, by virtue of divine forgetfulness, in the celestial world. No excessively striking anomaly will intervene in the human world that might create belief in the advent of disorder. But by virtue of the knowledge of a weakness in divine law, of a research in its immense labor, we are less lost in her immensity, and we feel closer to her.

THE LIFE OF OBJECTS

The fraternity of things is attested by the amity of familiar objects. Those objects store the strength and thought of those who possess them and become the receptacle of a life of their own, in which a confused consciousness is condensed, infinitesimal but real. They return in a certain measure the sentiments that one has for them, and if one loves them, they manifest in their turn a love that can become perceptible.

It is necessary to be good to animals, it is said, but it is also necessary to be good to objects. Like us, they know fatigue, and they need rest. Everyone has been able to observe that a costume, after a period of slumber in a cupboard, renders a more active, more joyful service than if it is worn every day.

A notebook in which one has written notes contains a condensation of intellect such that, in touching it, one recovers the order of one's own thoughts. A paper-knife that lives in the proximity of books is more intelligent than other objects, and more deserving of attachment and the honors rendered to intelligence.

There are hostile objects. I would not trust a knife whose provenance I did not know. It might be ill-intentioned. Between itself and me, it might create a disharmony that would provoke a maladroit gesture on my part, leading to a shock that would not be produced with a known and amicable knife.

What is surprising is the fashion in which objects render love to those who carry them.

Once, when I was a child, there was an alpenstock in the house that we took with us to the Pyrenees every vacation. Everyone agreed in saying that it was made of a particularly hard and marvelous wood. What wood? No one knew. That stick was an object of particular veneration. A family legend said that my grandfather had climbed a mountain with it in his youth. Perhaps the stick had saved his life on the edge of some abyss.

225

I remember that one summer, in order to climb a mountain that was not very high, I wanted to make use of that alpenstock, but scarcely had I leaned on it than it broke like glass. Alpenstocks are like humans, and the most robust become debilitated as they grow old. There was general consternation. It was given to a specialist, who fitted it with another iron tip. When it came back, however, it had lost a considerable part of its length; it was even shorter than an ordinary walking-stick. But such is the blindness of love that no one in my family wanted to recognize that diminution. "It's almost the same," they said, although only a dwarf could have used it for mountain-climbing.

I believe that the veneration even increased, and there was a question of enveloping it in cloth during the course of the year.

Now, that venerable but henceforth small alpenstock returned the love that was given to it and it did what a former branch can do—for every cane has a sylvan origin.

One day when, I don't know for what reason, I had taken it in my hands, I was very surprised to notice a certain transformation in it. At each knot in the wood there was a slight swelling, the trace of a burgeoning. It was a spring burgeoning that had cracked the varnish. Amazed, I pointed it out to various members of my family. But my amazement was not shared. In spite of the evident of the transformation, the phenomenon was denied and considered as an illusion on my part.

I invoked the testimony of several friends, but as they were first told that the alpenstock had belonged to my grandfather they only cast a rapid glance at it. They recognized that there was something bizarre about the knots in the wood, but they declared that there could be no burgeoning without sap.

There was, of course, no bursting forth of foliage and flowers, and in any case, I no longer gave any thought to that marvelous expansion, the reason for which escaped me then, but was an indubitable reality.

I thought about it again much later. The love that had surrounded that fragment of wood had restored a lost warmth to it. It had gone all the way to the heart of dead sap and had rendered a little life to it. The object had testified its gratitude in its own fashion. It had done what it could, within the frame of the natural laws that fix the death of wood. It had manifested for its friends the debris of youth that it retained within it.

THE SADNESS OF GROWING OLD
AMONG THE INSECTS

I saw an enormous and singular insect with a body in velvet damask, a helmet of rubies, vast bright wings and two long sharp lances. I did not know its name, being ignorant of the scientific classification of insects. Perhaps it did not have one and was a phenomenon never seen before. I ought, in that case, to have embalmed it respectfully and tried to attach my name to its discovery.

Its phenomenal character permitted me to recognize it immediately. I had seen it the previous year in the same garden in Provence. It was flying around the same clump of geraniums, while making a formidable buzz. The power of its flight and its audacious confidence made it understood that it was a king among the population of insects and in the realm of geraniums.

It did not even fear humans, for it came to buzz around my face in an irritated manner. It obliged me to move away precipitately because of the threat of its two long lances, which my inexperience of insects caused me to fear.

I recognized it perfectly, the king that had astonished me by its solitude and its pride. I had not seen it with any family. It was unique. It must have survived the winter sheltered in some hidden dwelling under the large stones that served as a support for the geraniums. It had escaped all the enemies of insects. No bird's beak had seized it. Perhaps it was sufficient for it to buzz to inspire terror.

But it was no longer the same. It had surpassed the cycle of time reserved for its peers, if it had any. The first suns of spring had not returned its lost strength. It was trailing its body of velvet and crimson silk over the sand. I saw the futile effort of its wings. It was making leaps instead of flying. Its lances were soft and curved inwards, and seemed incapable of pricking.

I had at my feet an aged insect. I leaned over and listened to its buzz. It still filled the garden, but it had an entirely different character. It was a dolorous buzz. The insect made it resound while it went about painfully on foot, or even when it was motionless, meditating on the power of flight forever lost, in front of the geraniums that had known its splendor and witness to its decrepitude.

Beneath the metallic tissues and the fantastic armor, beneath the mute mask of chitin, the dolor that one divined was more oppressive. But could the insect truly measure the place of its dust in the forest of eternal geraniums? How can one know the idea that insects have of death? In the most elevated of them, the ants and the bees, there are sometimes funeral honors rendered to certain corpses, and gestures of lamentation and despair have been distinguished. On the other hand, an insensibility has been distinguished that is incomprehensible to us. Bees of the same hive, encountering the cadaver of a dead sister, continue to gather nectar as if nothing had happened. And what indifference to their own death in certain cases! Insects abruptly cut in two have sometimes continued a meal commenced, even though they are separated from their organs of digestion. Their sensibility has no relationship with ours.

Do they have a notion of time? Yes, since they hurry or slow down in accordance with events. But do they establish, with regard to time, the relationship that permits them to measure the duration of their own lives?

The collective soul of an ant-hill ought not to be more saddened by the loss of an ant that we are when we cut a fingernail. But among species that have not attained the prodigious development of ants, there ought to be individual developments, and if the insect is a phenomenal insect, like the one I saw, its case is perhaps similar to that of certain old and solitary elephants, in which old age and solitude have developed exceptional faculties.

The insect inhabiting the forest of geraniums had acquired, among the various prerogatives of intelligence, the faculty of discerning the impotence of flight, the incapacity to prick an enemy, the decreased enjoyment of living, and the inexorable sadness of growing old—and that was translated by the melancholy of its buzzing, which was like a funeral chant beside the hollow stone and the desiccated petals where its skeleton was going to repose.

THE ANIMAL SOUL

Often, a human being suffers because he believes himself to be alone and the wickedness of other human beings confirms him in his solitude. But if he knows how to look at nature, he will perceive that there is an astonishingly varied host of creatures with which an affectionate communication is possible.

It is necessary to discover those creatures. It is necessary first of all to believe in their existence, for some are invisible. To approach those requires a great deal of time and reiterated appeals, and perhaps it is not even possible without a special grace of nature.

But the number and diversity of visible animal creatures is immense. Our relationships are only rendered difficult by the idea that we have of hem. Christian theology found it convenient, in order to regulate questions of mortality regarding the human soul, only to accord the animal soul a simple mechanism. Philosophers like Descartes and Malebranche gave a philosophical gloss to that affirmation. It is necessary to reach Bergson in order to see this opinion emitted:

"The capital error, transmitted since Aristotle, that has vitiated the majority of philosophies of nature, is to see in vegetative life, in instinctive life and in rational life three successive degrees of the same developing tendency, when they are three divergent directions of an activity that is split in growing."

The animal soul is not, therefore, an inferior way for the spirit to be manifest, but merely a different way. The direction of its development escapes us. It is a feature of ignorance to deny what cannot be understood. Humans have found it more convenient to deny the animal soul.

An individual of an animal species is certainly inferior to a human individual. That inferiority is betrayed by the religious admiration that is seen, for instance, in the gaze of a dog fixed upon its master, even though, in principle, an admirer can be superior to the object of admiration. Nature has employed different methods with regard to animals than those she has utilized or humans. There is no more reason for that difference than there is in the fact that our planet posses four elements, whereas divine experimentation could certainly be exercised with seven or twelve, perhaps more, on other less known planets.

While human beings, in a first stage, seek perfection in the development of their individual intelligence, animals are subordinate to a collective group soul. Their experience makes a contribution to a total experience. And what is called instinct in an animal is the manifestation of the knowledge acquired by the collective soul of the group.

We only have a vague idea of the extent and the possibilities of that collective soul. The magnification of consciousness does not seem to be its ideal, as in humans. It has in certain domains a wisdom that appears far superior to that of the wisest human. That wisdom is not transmissible immediately to the individuals of the group. They can only benefit from it at length and what they succeed in possessing is infinitesimal.

There are hierarchies in the collective souls of species, some being a thousand times more developed than others, and there are also hierarchies in the souls of groups that are subdivided among those of species. Thus, dogs, elephants, bees and ants occupy a superior degree. Among the bees, for example, some groups have retained primitive mores, while others have an advancement whose extent we cannot measure, nor, above all, know the goal.

Certain small collectivities of ants have arrived, as Maeterlinck[28] has demonstrated, at an organization and, at the same time, a disinterest so absolute that they seem to have attained the highest realization possible on our earth.

---

[28] Author's note: "It is to the intuitive genius of that great writer that it is always necessary to return in order to study all these problems. He is the only one to have explored them profoundly."

We believe that we have glimpsed the goal assigned to humans by the law that moves all things. That goal is to spiritualize the soul and then make it return to the divine soul of which it is the issue. The great religions, whether they make saviors intervene or prescribe finding the truth in oneself, are in accord on that essential given. But it might be that the animal soul has another task, for which it must follow another path, with other modes of development.

Whether their supreme goal is the same, or different, humans ought to be the allies of animals. They ought to renounce the pride of the master and the bloody lust for destruction. And if they take the first step, if they seek to understand, if they make the initial contribution of amity, they will receive immediate compensation by way of a love of a different quality from human affection, but perhaps having a more moving resonance in the interior domain.

THE BENCH OUTSIDE THE INN

In order to understand nature it is necessary to have killed within oneself the appetite for possession. Although it is difficult to prove by experience, I do not believe that a rich and miserly man can communicate with things.

The smaller the inn is at which the traveler stays, the narrower the communication with the surrounding nature will be. Everyone can verify that easily. The person who is staying in a large hotel has other relationships with the fields and trees than the guest of a village inn. Wealth implies an enjoyment of cities that is contrary to the soul of nature. Without there being valid arguments, one can be certain that the naturalist Fabre would not have realized his observations if he had not inhabited the poor little house that he has described. Can one imagine a Rothschild dreaming on the edge of a wood?[29]

There is no pure enjoyment of the earth and the sky unless it is realized in conditions of modest existence. Fortunate is the person who does not have to contemplate on waking the hostile or merely indifferent face of a servant, and makes his own shutters click as he opens them. For the prayer of the soul after slumber—the one into which it launches itself with lucidity—ought not to be troubled by the presence of any creature.

In order to hear the musicians of the woods or the beach, the cantors sitting in the foliage and on rocks, it is necessary to go there alone. It is necessary, however, to have a staff on which to lean, because the staff is the son of the tree, and in touching it one shakes the hand of a fragment of the great vegetal force and communicates with it.

Books are perhaps harmful. Those mirrors in which the truth is expressed in characters, those vivifying springs of beauty, are deformed mirrors, springs that, like ferruginous

---

[29] Author's note: "I am not designating any particular member of that family; the name is used in the symbolic sense with which common usage has dressed it."

waters, have a fortifying but very particular taste. Nature only admits books like the Vedas, which are written in the heart, the Bible secretly composed by her own inspiration.

There is an inspiration that is only found on the wooden bench that is outside the door of every inn. There, a peace of a superior quality descends upon the person who is sitting there at dusk. In general, there is a tree some distance away, and on that tree an owl has just uttered its cry when the shadows descend. As is commonly believed, that cry has a certain connection with the presence of misfortune. But the misfortune is uniformly spread over the earth, and there is no need to be disturbed by it.

The voice of the last cicada mingles with that of the first owl. The more detachment the person of the bench has, the better he will understand how those voices mingle and the harmony that they form.

THE TEMPLE OF SPACE AND TIME

How many secrets are buried behind the motionless veil of things! How many beauties are hidden in the intermediary world of refractions and images, in which it is first necessary to believe in order to have the faculty of perceiving them.

In the depths of a forest in the land of India there is a temple, or perhaps the appearances of a temple. The traveler to whom it is given to see it is astonished that in the midst of such prodigious vegetation, behind the circular expanse of marshes in which pestilence reigns, people were able in ancient times to carry huge blocks of granite, superimpose them and sculpt them according to the rules of a lost art.

Furthermore, what is visible of that monument is only the vestige of its summit, the fragments of a mysterious crown. For the temple is subterranean. One descends into its depths by means of three vast staircases, the triangular disposition of which ends at high collapsed doorways. Those doors are guarded by stone gods whose faces and forms reveal, according to those who have tried to decipher the enigma, gods anterior to those of the most distant mythologies.

Millennia-old roots have split the mosaics of ceilings and the arches of vaults; water has invaded the galleries and no one knows what mysteries were celebrated in the rooms lost under the ground. A few wise men, however, among those who possess the science of recognizing a total truth in a fragment of truth, claim that it was a temple erected—or rather hollowed out—in order to symbolize space and time and the divine Unity. They say—and perhaps they are right—that a superior geometry presided over the conception of that subterranean work, that the distances of the earth from the moon and he sun, the number of planets and that of galaxies, as well as the givens of a superhuman metaphysics are inscribed in the interior figures formed by the galleries, their angles, their circles and the succession of rooms. They say many other things, and do not add that the prodigious constructors of the temple of space and time had not foreseen the destructive movement of the waters in that space and the inexorable labor of time on the symbolic stones.

But the man full of faith who has come into that forest in the land of India one day in spring fixed by the evolution of the moon—or perhaps by another planet, or some star—and who gazes at the broken crown of the temple with the triple stairway sees and hears this:

First, there are slight sounds, muffled and distant, which rise toward him. And as those sounds come nearer, forms emerge from the triple stairway, the symbol of the three sects of the divine manifestation. Those forms are infinitely light, and if the observer had more attention and less surprise, perhaps he would be able to notice that the feet of the men who are emerging from the temple are not touching, or hardly touching, the paving stones split by the succession of sun and water.

There are tall and short ones, handsome and ugly ones, smiling and sad ones. The one who is in the lead causes minuscule cymbals to resonate, made of a substance that resembled copper. Behind him, there are tambourine players striking their instruments with the regularity of automata. Then come those modulating sounds as thin as tapering glass on reed flutes, those who are drawing colored silken musical waves from lutes, harpists who are producing cloudy trailing vapors and those who are striking the parchment of large oval drums with violet sticks.

Thin men whose only vestments are a high tiara—perhaps in gold or perhaps in a metal whose alloy is forgotten—and a purple loincloth, march with arms extended. On their features is a hallucination as old as the temple itself, and they are modulating syllables whose meaning is:

I am Him! He is me!

Two of them are carrying a naked child on a shield, but a child of wax, the one that is placed at the very bottom of the temple in the hall of Unity.

Now, the sky, which openings in the trees permit the observer to glimpse, has a dull, opaque density and gives the impression of descending. Without knowing why, he thinks that it is twilight. A monkey has uttered a cry of terror. There are whistles in the thickness of branches, suave glow-worms are born from the putrescence of the humus, while others, possessors of wings, are carrying the glow of their little lamps here and there. Flocks of parrots rise up. A peacock appears and deploys a sun of plumes. A panther has sighed somewhere with an infinite sadness.

The procession advances with a light solemnity. And suddenly, a musician, as if by mistake, bumps into a branch with the extremity of his flute. The flute remains attached and becomes a branch without interrupting he sounds that it emits. Another flute is detached from the distracted fingers of the man holding it, who does not try to pick it up. It has become a snake with a striped back, which glides like a living and sinuous arrow under the lianas, leaving behind it the tones of a flute.

At the same time, the zithers fly away and perch in the branches. They have changed into birds. The drums model beehives in certain hollow trees, and swarms that must be awaiting them take their place there with ease. The harps have placed themselves behind the peacock and have become other peacocks, all of whose plumes resonate.

"I am Him! He is me!" the thin men with extended arms are still saying, but their voice is analogous to that of the broad leaves of clove trees and camphor trees. They are covered with bark. They are trees, and they are already learning to exhale crystals of camphor and produce the ashy berries of cloves.

The last ray of sunlight slides obliquely to stain the two eyes of the child of wax and cause him to melt. Nothing remains of him in the long grass but a few dead droplets.

Oh, the marvels of the forests of India!

THE ARTISTIC ALLIANCE
OF VEGETABLES AND HUMANS

As soon as I bend over a flower to admire it and as soon as I experience the enjoyment of its colors I cannot help wondering about the origin of that beauty. Who created it? Who worked on those combinations, that order, that harmony of colors?

That is the work of the creator, or the work of nature, reply those who are content with very little in the satisfaction of their curiosity.

But in the same way that humans model themselves, the features of their faces with the development of their thought, so that the ensemble of the form is the result of their hereditary heritage and their personal creation, plants and flowers are the product of a primitive gift and a patient personal modeling, a faculty appropriate to changing terrestrial juices extracted by the roots into bunches of stamens and surprising colors.

Flowers are not uniform, because there is an individual composition of each species and there is even an individual composition particular to each plant that produces flowers. Life is manifest in vegetal forms, but the soul of each species has wrought a particular creation with a will of its own. And those various souls have given different results by virtue of a variable power that results from their energy, their idleness, and perhaps their ambition.

Those vegetal souls propose an ideal goal for themselves, and they can only realize it by virtue of certain limited possibilities. Wild flowers are often less beautiful than a species whose flowers are obtained by the art of the gardener. That is because they need, in order to attain their goal, a combination of watering, compost and temperature that nature does not give them. For the realization of their interior plan they need the collaboration of creatures with a different development. In order to build a house, humans call upon the aid of vegetables for its roof or its door. In the same way, the plant needs humans to realize its disinterested artistic dream.

There are admirable creations in wild forests that have no necessity of human intervention, but for certain refinements, certain mixtures of colors, vegetables utilize the aid of humans.

Thanks to that mutual aid, great results of beauty are obtained. Every plant has its ideal of art, but when it is united with other plants in the harmony of gardens, it collaborates in a more complex ideal, which is realized by the proximity and combination of flowers. And that union perhaps creates, unknown to us, a competition that we do not perceive because of its slowness, but whose result is an even greater beauty in nature.

VEGETAL SENSIBILITY

I have read somewhere that the Hindu scientist Bose had arrived at his marvelous discoveries about the sensibility of plants after an illness.[30] Finding himself in a clinic, he had only had, during the long days of convalescence, the vision of a single tree standing outside the window near his bed. Unfortunately, I do not know the species of that revelatory tree.

By dint of contemplating it, involuntarily, he arrived at an intimate penetration, a kind of communion. Then he saw it living, expanding and suffering. He had the perception of the currents animating it, circulating in its trunk and in its branches, and all the reactions of an emotive nervousness.

The link that existed between the tree and the man was so narrow that when the savant Bose was nervous and agitated, the branches of the tree quivered with the same agitation, and when he was sad, a branch, elongating enormously, came into the clinic and posed on the invalid's bed.

That amity was the point of departure of studies that lasted a quarter of a century, which permitted Bose to prove that the tree was endowed with a sensibility absolutely identical to that of an animal, that it possessed a nervous system animated by the same influxes as that of a human being.

He made a demonstration of it by means of recording apparatus that produced graphic traces, complicated and indubitable apparatus. For there is no truth more certain, for men of science, and for people in general, than that demonstrated by the intermediary of machines in which there are needles and balances, and in which velocities are inscribed in diagrams.

---

[30] The reference is to the physicist and plant physiologist Jagadish Chandra Bose (1858-1937) and his work in plant biophysics, which led him to hypothesize that plants can feel pain.

The initial discovery of vegetal nervous systems—which is to say, subtle organs of perception and suffering—was due to an attentive examination, a faithful friendship realized in observation and solitude.

For any science, whatever the number of its classifications and subdivisions, only has true value, and is only creative, by virtue of the attentive love of the person who studies for the object of study.

It was an immense discovery that the Hindu scientist Bose made in contemplating the trunk of his vegetal friend. He informed people of the relationship of structure that united them with trees; he told them that they were, like them, animate beings with the rudiments of a similar organization, and that, within the immobile wood, forever linked to the earth, circulated not only life but the aptitude to experience life.

THE HIDDEN COMEDY OF CREATION

It is something worthy of astonishment to see human profiles in the profiles of fish, to rediscover expressions already seen on human faces in animals, in crocodiles or certain snakes. Is that a fortuitous encounter, an aberration of the person making comparisons, or can another hypothesis be formed?

If one looks at a photograph of the gorilla that died in 1935 in the zoological gardens in Berlin,[31] one sees an old man irritated at not having profited from his past lives in order to develop himself, an old man containing his rage in a being with a retarded spirit. Purely human stupidities, frivolities and fantasies are betrayed in the ridges of birds' beaks and I know not what bewilderment in their round eyes.

The great and small carnivores reflect the ferocity of humans. And if one descends in the scale of dimensions, one sees that the thing is even more striking the smaller creatures are, as if the jesting creator had given himself free rein in his reproductions of images because he knew that no intelligence would be able to see his joke without the aid of a powerful microscope. Perhaps, in those distant times, he did not foresee the invention of the microscope.

Earthworms of an inferior species have the silhouettes of pitiless and limited magistrates. The Blepharopsis, a species of mantis of minuscule size, resembles unmistakably a dancer disguised as Mephistopheles who dances on four limbs, and, during one period of its movement, its dances affect all the characteristics of those of the Théâtre de l'Opéra. Certain aquatic coleopteran larvae are the portrait of Molière's caricature physicians, with their bonnet and syringe. There are

---

[31] Author's reference: "*La Terre et la vie*, 1936." The reference is to the pioneering ecological scientific journal that still exists today; six issues were published in 1936.

243

among insects, nuns with their head-dresses, redskins with their crowns of feathers and ascetics sitting on meditation.

It is as if, at the origin, at the time when the spirit commenced moving over the waters, all the images that were to succeed one anther during the millenarian periods had been seen in advance and distributed by means of a game of correspondences in the diversity of animate creatures.

And perhaps those images only had a limited number. They were the fruit of an imagination evidently prodigious but which nevertheless had limits. In the same way that in a conversation, we sometimes repeat the same words too frequently, the creative imagination reproduced the same images.

One can tell that that did not happen by chance. There is an immense comedic taste in the distribution of silhouettes and glacial expressions. Our narrowness of vision prevents us from seeing the whole of that comedy, but we can interpret the ridiculous resemblances of creatures to one another as the sign of the immense, transcendent joy, immoral according to our human conception, that the creative force experiences in imagining earthquakes, plagues and the sexual mingling of species.

Perhaps, if we could grasp the interior gaiety of the world, all noises would be bursts of laughter and we would rediscover in ourselves the joyous essence that is that of the divine spirit.

A STORMY NIGHT

The closer one approaches the equator, the more humans are bound to the earth.

A few paces from the dwelling, as we arrived, we saw a tall naked negro, lying on his back, asleep in the setting sun. His hair was white and extraordinarily frizzy. On his broad breast sat an enormous motionless toad, the life of which was visible in the movement of respiration in its throat, hanging down like a goiter. The negro's little finger was touching the toad lightly.

A bell rang. I heard a voice say: "Take care of the lame mule."

The owner of the dwelling appeared on the threshold. He was fat, he gave the impression of just having woken up from a profound slumber, and he was holding an extinct cigar in his left hand.

I followed him. He took me further on, behind the trees. He showed me a barn. Doubtless I was supposed to make astronomical observations, or he believed that I was, for he said to me: "I've prepared this barn in order for you to dispose all your instruments there."

A little later, when the sun had set, I asked someone: "Why are there so many toads here?"

He did not reply.

A child who was running back and forth was charged with attaching my hammock to two tree branches, and he laughed, lingering, sitting astride the trunks.

"You see," said my companion, indicating the master of the place, who was drawing away wearily, "he's installed you in that barn so you won't see a fifteen-year-old half-breed girl who is very pretty, and whom he hides from everyone."

And a little later, when alcohol and rice had been served to the exceedingly thin Indians, he said to me again:

"He's a man who's afraid. Every evening, over there, at the foot of the old tree, he goes to deposit goat's milk and a portion of nourishment for a negro murderer who lives in the forest, and by whom he fears being killed. Only sometimes, instead of the negro, it's a panther that comes and eats the food."

For a long time, an Indian played a bizarre instrument, and then everything fell silent. I had a fever. The hammock swung like a bridge of lianas over a torrent that I had traversed during the day. When I sat up, I thought I saw a multitude of toads, which had formed a circle around me, heads raised, agitating their goiter.

"Beware of vampires," I had been told. "One doesn't hear them flying, and they settle on you like a very soft piece of felt."

Late in the night, someone threw a heavy cloak over me. "It's because of the rain...."

The weather was fine, but a few minutes later, there were metallic explosions in the foliage on all sides, and a hot droplet fell between my eyes.

Suddenly, there was a mighty clap of thunder, followed by several others, and I thought that the world was about to end. That thought was not exempt from pleasure. The water ran over the cloak without traversing it. There were flashes of light such as ought only to occur on certain very distant planets. Suddenly, I saw a great jet of fire, but it was only a single tree, lit up from the roots to the topmost branch, and all of its leaves had a glare of silvery phosphorescence, so luminous that one could distinguish the smallest veins, like minuscule rivers of fire.

Everything was extinguished, and there was a great silence. Then, somewhere in a room of the house, a profound voice began to recite a prayer, which resembled the prayer for the dead.

Time went by. The rain had stopped. I heard a sound of nourishment being swallowed precipitately. In the direction of the tree that had been pointed out to me, I distinguished confusedly a wooly head and a squat body. It was the man, not the panther, who had come. The stars had become bight again.

A window opened slightly. There was a slender silhouette, which made signs in the direction of the man. Was that the fifteen-year-old half-breed girl, only visible shortly before dawn, and for a negro assassin of the forest?

It seemed to me that the daylight, in rising, lifted the fever from me like a delicate cloth. The air was soft, calm and full of resonances. People were hurrying to quotidian occupations. Oxen were pawing the ground. Whips cracked.

There were no more toads, but their presence was perceptible, like that of vampires, the panther, ants on the march, hidden snakes and all the invisible beasts of the forest.

And in the utmost depths of myself, I sensed that everything, humans and animals, the house, the stables and the forest, was only a single organism and that the movement of its life was rotating round a central point, which was its soul, the little hidden half-breed.

"There's a mule that will never get to the end," said a voice.

The end! I wondered whether I would ever arrive there myself.

The proprietor with the extinct, indifferent eyes was standing on the threshold. He lifted his lighted cigar....

AN ANONYMOUS LANDSCAPE

I know two cypresses on a hill with a bench in the space between them. Had someone, in a distant epoch, planted the cypresses around the bench, or, on the contrary, had someone taken advantage of the space between the trees to place a bench there? That question occurs naturally to the stroller, but its solution is, in sum, of no importance.

The only thing that matters is the placement of the bench, which is turned toward the setting sun, in a position such that one can see from there the extent of a peaceful valley, with little groups of houses, woods of laurels and gardens separated by white walls.

Anyone who sits down on that bench cannot despair of life, giving himself as a reason that all immediate beauties will disappear from the earth. He knows that, great as human wickedness might be, no one will ever overturn that bench and destroy the two cypresses, that nothing will be able to alter a softness that is produced by the purity of the air and the harmonious relationship of things.

The road that leads there, without being rough, is narrow and not accessible to vehicles. It does not connect important routes. It is not a short cut for people in a hurry, and the location cannot be considered as a viewpoint for tourists. There is, in truth, little to contemplate from that bench. It is a perfectly ordinary landscape that unrolls; it has a beauty that the soul needs to identify for itself.

One cannot even perceive the sea, which is hidden by another hill. The bench is deserted at all hours. No one knows why it was placed there for the contemplation of things. No one knows that nature is more beautiful there than elsewhere, with her costume of modest gardens, ordinary houses and perfect laurels. That landscape is reminiscent of a discreetly beautiful young woman whom men cannot designate in conversation because she has no name.

GAMAHEUS

O secret law of creation, how can one succeed in grasping you in your profound essence? It is necessary that there is a primordial thought behind forms and before they become manifest, in order to imagine them. In order for the first rose or the first oak to bloom, even through multiple transformations, it is necessary that the perfect rose and the perfect oak have been conceived and seen in the world of the spirit.

Now, creative thoughts of a divine order are wandering in space, and one can sometimes glimpse them before materialization. In Algeria and Tunisia, roses that are sometimes of an extraordinary perfection are formed in the sand by the caprice of the wind, under the action of the sun. Those flowers are made with petrified sand. But whatever the fantastic play of nature might be in order to produce that circular order and that resemblance to a flower, which a human artist would find it very difficult to obtain, it is necessary for a directive will to have been present. Custom alone enables one not to be astonished by it. In those places, in order for the result to be obtained, thoughts of roses have floated and have made use of the plastic sand and some creative solar element is order to be realized.

There are other traces in nature of the mysterious labor of an invisible artist outside the ordinary laws. Those creations are called gamaheus.[32] In his *Unusual Curiosities* Gaffarel identifies a large number of them that were known in his day.

---

[32] Gamaheu [gamahé in French] has been dropped from most English dictionaries, but was borrowed from French in the seventeenth century to designate a stone bearing a semblance of an image and considered for that reason to have talismanic properties. It was popularized by Jacques Gaffarel's *Curiositez inouyes* (1629; tr. as *Unheard of Curiosities* in 1650), an unorthodox astrological text that enjoyed an extraordinary success in its day.

In the Church of Saint George in Venice there was a marble plaque bearing in relief a crucifix with the nails, wounds and drops of blood, which was the work of nature. In a mine near Forcalquier in Provence, a number of stones were found representing figures of all kinds, and even characters.

The objection will inevitably be raised that all of that comes from human art and had been previously buried, but images have been found of great perfection inside certain pieces of marble, as if a creator had wanted to sculpt in relief without paying any heed to the destiny of the material. These images can only be seen by sawing the marble in two.

Gaffarel remarks that these creations are discovered more frequently in very hot countries and he attributes a creative action to the ardor of the sun. According to him, agate and cornelian are more apt than other stones to become matrices of forces avid to perpetuate an image or a sign. More-or-less complete portraits and formulae found thus are always portraits of famous persons or oft-repeated formulae, as if nature only created in that unusual manner images corresponding to frequently-expressed thoughts.

In the presence of that surprising game of nature, people begin by denying it, and then they say that it is an effect of chance. But how can a representation of Apollo, surrounded by the nine muses, depicted on an agate, be attributed to chance? All facts that are manifested by unknown laws are considered as legendary and denied. Gamaheus are, however, frequent in nature and there are collectors of gamaheus who marvel at their collections without seeking an explanation.

The spirit moved over the waters, says the ancient book. One can say that with the primitive waters, the spirit created in those remote times a complex and immense work. On examining that work with a human attention, one can distinguish immense imperfections and errors are great as the successes; but one has the sensation at first that the spirit has done what it could, and then that a part of the task is over, that there has been a deceleration, an abandonment of self-created forces.

But fragments of the spirit till move over the waters and over the land.

In the cemetery of Lisieux in 1923 someone picked up a rose-petal and saw with surprise that there was a face of Christ very clearly designed thereon. The petal was photographed, but it served immediately as religious propaganda and that was harmful to its sincerity as a true gamaheu. I ought to add that it is impossible that Christ had such a charming and banal expression. The creative force that imprinted it on the petal must have been emanated by a believer who imagined the incarnation of the Word like a melancholy and not very poetic pupil of the School of Fine Arts.

Perhaps the Tibetan characters seen by Père Huc on a tree near the monastery of Koumboum were gamaheus.[33] The fashion in which Père Huc, in his celebrated voyage in Tartary, described the tree and its ten thousand images is well-known. The wood and the leaves of the tree were completely covered in characters "that are part of the leaf, like the veins and fibers. If one detaches a fragment of old bark one perceives on the new the indeterminate forms of characters that are already beginning to germinate and, singularly, they quite often differ from the ones that were above."

It seems that there, all the ordinary laws of the planet have been forgotten by the creative force. The excellent Abbé Huc, who sees nothing anywhere but a struggle between two clergies, adds: "We sought everywhere, but always in vain, for some evidence of trickery. Sweat rose to our brows." One reflection, he was obliged to conclude a little later that it was some "barbaric and diabolical ruse of Lamaism."

Recently, one of my friends, the writer René Silvy had the good fortune to be at a winter station in the Alps immedi-

---

[33] The French missionary Évariste Huc published his memoir of his 1844-46 voyage through Tartary, Tibet and China in 1850; it was translated into English the following year. It proved very popular and became a key source for works of imaginary literature set in the Far East.

ately after the passage of a certain force of divine nature. That force, if one admits that it was one and not a creature from the beyond, a dev air unknown entity, had just modeled in the snow the form of the poet Paul Verlaine on his deathbed.

The creation had been made on a corrugated iron roof with melted snow, thanks to an easing of the temperature. It is noteworthy that a little solar force is always an element in the creation, as well as a certain solitude. By virtue of what whim, what coincidence, was the image of the dead Verlaine recovered from the universal memory and reproduced there rather than elsewhere? René Silvy was wise enough to take a photograph of that gamaheu and it was reproduced in *L'Illustration* in 1935. But his camera was unable to glimpse the invisible power that was its author.

Just as surprising are certain correspondences of images. The image of a human hand is found in pine cones, and children call it the hand of Jesus, finding it natural to attach the play of nature to the idea of the divinity. In the pips of grapes and grains of wheat there are figures and signs. A cross and a snake's head are found in seeds of rue. There are Rosicrucian emblems in the middle of marine jellyfish and a crucified Christ is designed on the abdomen of certain spiders. It is remarkable that it is generally the sexual organs of plants that contain these figures, as if their generation was prepared therein, the creative force being obliged to pause longer, having had more time for the modeling of a familiar form.

Thus, the person who scrutinizes nature cannot fail to encounter the divine spirit there in its virginal surge.

But the great enigma remains. It is in the fact, profoundly illogical and unjust from our human viewpoint, of having placed at a certain level of the great tree of creation, at the human level, conceptions of merit and justice that are never found in any other part of that rich and surprising tree.

The human spirit is also creative. It is similar to the divine intelligence, but with something more: pity. It suffers in seeing what it has created perish. And the certainty comes to us from the profound depths of ourselves that that pity is the most beautiful creation on earth. By an impulsion of admiration, one would like to say that the divine spirit must have a reason for ignoring pity or putting off its settlement indefinitely, which is equivalent to not having any; something cries out to us incessantly that it is superior, as perishable as us, and that only destruction is eternal.

THE SECRET OF THE BERMUDAS

O beauty of the isles of the Bermudas!

There are several, they are very small and they form a minuscule archipelago in the confines of the Sargasso Sea. There are no ships in their narrow harbors. But if one gazes into the depths of the transparent waters that surround them, one perceives that there is an immense fleet there, with ships of all models.

Except that the fleet in question is beyond harbors and under the water instead of above it, contrary to what happens in all the other maritime regions of the world.

That is because the coraline sea-bed that surrounds the Bermudas is made of sharp reefs where innumerable ships have been wrecked since there have been navigators in search of new islands, and those ships have stayed there.

A man animated by the genius of invisible worlds named William Beebe has descended, in a luminous tube of his fabrication, through the waters that surround the shores of the Bermudas, and by projection the beam of a powerful electric lamp he has seen those dead ships lined up around him.[34]

There were some similar to that of Christopher Columbus, but had less luck—or perhaps more, according to whether one places the happiness of a ship on the waves or in the calm depths beneath them.

There were great caravels with their masts and forecastles almost intact, where iridescent fish were wandering. There were Carib pirogues gone astray, made of gigantic tree-trunks

---

[34] The American naturalist William Beebe (1877-1962) conducted explorations off the coast of Bermuda from 1930-34 in a bathysphere invented by Otis Barton, which obtained huge publicity when it was displayed at the Chicago World's Fair in 1933. It was the first time that a biologist had been able to observe animals living at considerable depths in their native environment.

patiently hollowed out. There were Spanish galleons with enormous hulls, on one of which the skeleton of the captain was still standing, with his hand over his eyes in order to see better in the distance—the pose in which death had surprised him. How had that skeleton been able to remain upright in spite of the centuries, submarine currents and redoubtable fish? And how did his hand of bones maintain itself at the level of his eyes? Does the firm will of a Spanish captain permit the defiance of natural laws beyond death? O marvel of William Beebe's submarine lamp!

And there were also corvettes with hatchways open on rows of cannon, the luggers of filibusters that had resembled seagulls but had dived instead of flying, fluyts upright on long keels, cutters with high hulls, clippers so slender that, deprived of their rigging they gave the impression of the carcasses of dried fish, and even bombards without decks, with stone mortars.

Through the gallery of nautical specters, that panorama of mineralized, corroded, rusted phantoms clad in seashells and studded with starfish, evanescent jellyfish floated like great gelatinous sails, and fish streaming with phosphorescence swam under tresses of magical plankton. Pale sponges gave the impression of moons forgotten in the submarine desert. Trees of scarlet coral expanded on mauve sands visibly painted with human hands and ostentatiously allowing the sight of their perfect beauty. To the side, uncanny silver crayfish played with golden crabs. And in the waters into which the light of the projector put emerald incandescence, inoffensive sharks passed by, with delicate fins and magnanimous eyes, sharks that one would have liked to love for a lifetime.

The silence was only troubled by the phantom detonation of one of the bronze cannons confusedly awakened, but the resonance was both muffled and sweetly musical. The invisible projectile traversed the water slowly, leaving something like a wake of colored ash, and went to strike in the heart a large deep-water cephalopod, which was perhaps awaiting martyrdom in one of those meditations of which only creatures made of cartilage are capable.

As soon as it was light, the octopus deployed its tentacles and became a luminous star with eight branches in the twilight of the waters.

Then millions of eels with cylindrical bodies, which had come from all parts of the planet, slithering and leaping, in other to reproduce in the Sargasso Sea, arrived in haste, quivering, and beating the water with their varnished tails. They formed a great circle around the cephalopod that had become a star. All the suckers of the tentacles were as many blue lamps, and the silently spinning octopus made a great circle of phosphorescent light, which was lost to the visible confines of the sea.

It was given to me to encounter one of the rare men who have spent time in the Bermudas. He was a young French scientist who had a job in a museum. I thought at first that he only knew the exterior part of the Bermudas and that he had not been under the water like William Beebe. He was a young man like any other, correctly dressed, with a moustache and smooth hair.

With great precaution, avoiding showing too much credulity, I made a few allusions to the sunken vessels; I indicated that one can sometimes see strange things under the sea—but I avoided talking, of course, about the cephalopod in the form of a star.

The young scientist suddenly looked at me like a freemason who discovers that his interlocutor is also a freemason. He lowered his voice, even though we were alone, and moved his chair closer to mine.

"There are great submarine mysteries. But there are those who know and those who remain ignorant. The revelation of those mysteries is not good for everyone."

And he looked at me intently in order to discover the category in which I ought to be placed. I noticed for the first time that his eyes had a roundness unusual in human eyes, and that his moustache was singular.

"Evidently," he went on, "it is a matter that humankind will perhaps never be able to elucidate. Why is there one place on the globe, a unique place, where all the eels that exist, even those of the altitudes, must go to accomplish the work of generation? Why is that place the Sargasso Sea? That sea was visibly prohibited in the course of the ages by an occult force, as the Himalaya still is today. The proof is in the cadavers of ships that have sunk in the circle of its waters. Such a great quantity of catastrophes cannot be explained by the rocks or the winds. The advance of humans must stop there.

"One becomes habituated to enigmas so easily that people have become habituated to that one as to so many others. The prohibition must have been lifted, for unknown reasons. People have also become habituated to the idea of a sea half-liquid and half-vegetal, a grassy sea, as Aristotle said. What was hidden in the vast regions where algal vegetation, the foliage of a prodigious submarine forest, mingled with the debris of submerged mountains, which made an amalgam with the waters with no analogy elsewhere on the Earth? Creatures lived there that humans ought not to see.

"The entire Sargasso Sea is covered by volcanoes and the creatures of which I speak were only the inhabitants of that sea because of the volcanoes, because via them they were able to communicate with their natural homeland, the interior of the Earth. But there have been great cosmic upheavals and an intermediary form of matter, more fluid than the land and denser than water is no longer necessary. The beings that ought not to be seen by humans have returned to their original places. The prows of ships now cleave through less dense Sargassos, conformed more like ordinary seas circumscribed by the continents."

Giving my face the most knowing expression that was possible for me, I asked the young scientist whether he had seen with his own eyes the submarine marvels that surround the Bermudas: the dead vessels, the immense medusae, and the benign sharks.

The roundness of his eyes made me understand that such a question was unnecessary. He had seen everything. And he had a personal proof of the quality of a certain attractive force that rendered the waters ensorcelled on certain moonlit nights. Perhaps the attraction that possessed the eels was of the same quality.

"At the prow of the vessels there is always a figurehead. It is an individual, sometimes of metal but almost always of sculpted wood: a saint, a heroic mariner, a ship-owner or some ancient goddess, on whose head a crown is placed. Those figureheads were solemnly blessed by bishops and they were the object of mariners' adoration. They were invoked during tempests. Experience demonstrates that they did not prevent vessels from being wrecked. I even believe that they led them to it deliberately when it was their destiny. For those figureheads were inhabited by entities in the service of providence. And providence reserves for some a fortunate voyage, and for others a descent under the waters.

"Well, this is what I have seen. Those figureheads are detached on certain nights from their ships and they go to join others, by virtue of hidden affinities. Under the waters of the Sargasso Sea, there are strange meetings of those emblematic beings. Note that one can find an explanation for that fact, which does not offend reason, which is almost scientific. A great force has been accumulated in those figures by the faith of men. That force is in contact with another prodigious force, the force of that submarine environment, the issue of the volcanoes. Those forces communicate a temporary life to certain material bodies."

Doubtless my face reflected the uncertainty that agitated me with regard to the seriousness of the young man. I remembered the importance of the post he occupied, while wondering in what measure the love of poetry might impinge upon reason. I even judged that the poetry of submarine things is more powerful than any other.

But the young scientist must have read that in my features. He had stopped, and resumed in a sarcastic tone:

"Have you ever heard mention of the Tetraodon of the tropical seas? It's necessary before anything else to know that globular fish, which has the faculty of enlarging itself in a circle and simultaneously capturing a light from the depths, come from who knows where."

I made a sign that I was familiar with it. But he could see that I was not. Decidedly, I was not an initiate. His eyes became even rounder. His face closed forever.

And as if the word "globular" had been a revelatory key, I perceived that he resembled a Tetraodon—or, rather, the idea that I formed of the tropical fish in question. His face had a faculty of enlargement and rounding out, and the hairs of his moustache, which were not very numerous, were like the flexible antennae of a crayfish.

THE BEAUTY OF HUMMINGBIRDS

Nature composes certain marvels with love, and no one knows why she concentrates so much application on certain points and so little on others.

Anyone who has seen a hummingbird fly will never forget it. A hummingbird is the condensation of the beauty of colors, the mystery of precious stones, combined with the intoxication of artistic enjoyment, and the exaltation of life.

It is the smallest of birds. Certain gifts consume. The larger the size, the more apathy there is. The fever of life reduces forms. Even in humans, one never sees a giant in the nervous disorder that sometimes possesses individuals who are almost always of small stature.

A hummingbird is a living ruby, a flower endowed with wings animated by a folly of amorous activity. What nature has produced with precious stones in the mineral realm and with certain vividly colored flowers in the vegetal realm, has its correspondence in the society of birds in that creature, which carries the rainbow in its plumage. Emeralds, sapphires and rubies represent the summits of realization in the creation of stones. Flowers are also the summits of geometrical art, of suavity and splendor. The hummingbird has attained a more elevated degree. It has conquered movement, and its exaltation toward pleasure is in direct proportion to its beauty.

In the same way that the nightingale is consecrated to musical genius and the swan to religious purity, the hummingbird has no other concern than a magical beauty of vestments, an insatiable appetite for the sensuality of sunlight.

It can only live among flowers, in hot lands where they spring forth in abundance from the soil. It is the most rapid of all birds, and each of its movements has the nervousness that only the avidity for pleasure gives. Its life goes by in a state of constant intoxication: a delirious intoxication that humans can never know, which gives it the delirium of colors, causes it to precipitate itself hither and yon over the great pulps of tropical flowers, holds it in suspense over a leaf, or impels it to describe great circles in space.

It is a strange thing that the love of beauty is always coupled with an excess of amorous sensuality. Apart from the time consecrated to the projection of its tongue into the corollas of flowers, the hummingbird has no other preoccupations than those derived from sexual attraction. The amorous act of birds is always described as perfectly rapid and one can take account of that rapidity by means of the most superficial observation. But the hummingbird prolongs the duration of sexual voluptuousness curiously.

Before the wonderstruck female the minuscule male causes its plumage to glitter, vibrates its wings, rotates like a sun and traces circles, augmenting the innate intoxication in which it lives with an intoxication of hectic movement. And when that intoxication has attained its maximum, the two creatures of color and pleasure adhere to one another tightly, raising themselves up by means of the invisible beating of their wings, abandoning themselves to the winds, rising higher than the trees and the clouds, in an indefinite flights whose duration can only be limited by their exhaustion and the impossibility of experiencing a greater voluptuousness.

It is surprising that the admiration for living beings does not diminish in the slightest the natural desire that humans have to kill. Perhaps, when it is a matter of animals, the appetite for murder is even increased by admiration. People are not content to see a creature of supraterrestrial beauty flying through the air; they prefer to touch it and handle it, and if they do not kill it by ripping out its plumage, those who flatter themselves that they love animals lock it in a cage, where it is condemned to suffer the most frightful torture, the loss of liberty, in order to please those affectionate animal-lovers.

In the lands where hummingbirds pullulate, people have sticks covered with birdlime, special blowpipes, and all sorts of means to capture and kill them. The essential thing is that those flying marvels are stolen from the air.

In Paris there is a commercial collector who possesses, in glass cases and display cabinets, sixty thousand humming-birds! He is waiting for the cruel stupidity of women to bring back into fashion the wearing of birds on hats. How can he not dread his nights being troubled by sixty thousand phantom wings?

The naturalist Audubon, who has inspired a universal respect for his love of nature and living things, made a description of hummingbirds interrupted by exclamations and lyrical effusions. That description is so enthusiastic, so full of love, that after having read it, one wants to live exclusively with those tiny creatures. That model lover of the works of nature concludes thus:

"I had the habit of killing them by loading my rifle with sand instead of lead. I have renounced that method."

And he prescribes, at length, others more efficacious.

ERRORS OF SCIENCE

There are implausibilities in many affirmations of science relative to natural laws as striking and sometimes as risible as those off Bernardin Saint-Pierre in *The Harmonies of Nature*.

For nearly a century the law of selection has been considered as absolute. If that law were true, how is it explicable that certain species are entirely deprived of means of defense by nature, while others that are equipped with breastplates, carapaces and armor, like the armadillo of South America, are in danger of extinction?

The South American armadillo is covered with shields and bears a helmet on its head. When an enemy appears, it rolls up into a ball and forms an inaccessible sphere of lead. It is specially selected, like a knight of the Middle Ages whose armaments came from Toledo. Now, there is no multiplication. Almost invincible, the armadillo is dying out in its fortress.

Why are butterflies, devoid of stings or poison, so slow in flight, which are signaled to the attention of their enemies by bright colors, not entirely absorbed by birds? Many other unarmed insects continue to perpetuate themselves, thanks to an invisible shield.

It is the same for nightingales. All the owls of the woods ought have eaten that musical prey, which proclaims it presence when all the other birds are nestling silently, a long time ago. Their imprudence does not prevent nightingales from multiplying.

Science has recently discovered that the colors of the plumage of birds and the costumes of insects are due to certain metallic secretions of their insufficiently functional kidneys. It is rather as if the genius of a painter were attributed to the quality of his brushes and the acidity of his paints.

An act of scientific faith consists of thinking that all animal songs are appeals of the male to the female, with the objective of bringing them together for reproduction.

The naturalist Fabre has devoted himself to attentive experiments on cicadas and has observed that in no circumstances has their song any connection with sexual appeal.[35]

Like crickets, cicadas have developed musical organs of a marvelous complication. Although those insects only attain, for the moment, a rather simplistic rhythm, perhaps, in a few million years, they will have a more complete knowledge of the musical art. Insects employ an immense time in their transformations.

It is the same with birdsong, where the composition of a more savant art is perceptible. Birds sing by virtue of a love of music conceived by the animal soul. Secondarily, the song is used by the male to intoxicate the female. In the same way, a human male might, in order to seduce a woman, play a muscle instrument before her, without that implying that for him, music is uniquely a means of seduction.

There is a power in the scientist's microscope that, but the enormous magnification of detail, prevents in many cases the seizure of the law of the ensemble. Furthermore, the essential element of nature, which is the beauty concealed beneath things, is not visible through a microscope, whatever the quality of its lenses.

One can even say that beauty escapes any overly attentive research. In order for beauty to be perceived, it is necessary that a spark springs between the soul of the individual perceiving and the mysterious rhythmic element emitted by things. Beauty is manifest by virtue of an occult operation that is defined well enough by the popular expression of the operation of the Holy Spirit. No scientific analysis can observe that operation.

---

[35] Author's reference: "Fabre, *Souvenirs entomologiques*, 5th series."

Beauty is an invisible fire, a divine force, of which everyone carries the seeds but which is only realized by union and in the ineffable delight of love.

THE DESTRUCTION OF ANIMAL SPECIES

The comprehension and the love of nature cannot go without a certain negation of human genius. Even if one admits that human beings are at the summit of terrestrial creatures, one is obliged to observe that they have made a barbaric use of their superiority and have used it for entirely egotistical ends. They have resembled a brother who, having weaker brothers, has reduced them to slavery and, without caring whether they live or die, makes them serve for the augmentation of his pleasures.

Although it appears that humans are the strongest species on the earth, it is not absolutely proven that they occupy the summit on which they have placed themselves, and that there is no other scale than that of force, or even intelligence. The indisputable superiority of humans comes, above all, from the fact that they have always refused to debate it and have considered it as absolutely evident.

But who can say that the artistic ideal of flowers is not leading vegetal life toward goals that we do not know, but which are perhaps as high as those to which human consciousness is aiming. Insects occupy the planet with a total ease, and if they do not know that humans exist alongside them, can that ignorance be considered as an inferiority? At any rate, humans, if they wished, could not exterminate the insects of the world. The study of ants has shown, as it has developed, that those insects have created unusual social organizations and have acquired, in certain respects, a material wellbeing and a progress equal, if not superior, to those we know. An idea of justice similar to ours sees to reign in certain tribes with innumerable units. A goodness extended to its utmost limits is practiced there.[36] Observers search obstinately and blindly in ants for an intelligence resembling that found in

---

[36] Author's reference: "See Maurice Maeterlinck, *La Vie des fourmis*."

human; they do not encounter any, but that is not the mark of an inferiority on the ants' part. They have developed a completely different psychology, which can lead them by other paths to goals superior, or at least equal, to those that human intelligence can attain.

Is there not, in any case, in the profound love of destroying the nature of which they are the issue, a revelatory sign that humans are not the rulers of creation that they claim to be? If the earth had really been made for them, for their perfection, as theologies inform, would they be systematically destroying its beauty and its life?

The history of what we call civilizations shows us the destruction, almost always futile and even dangerous to the destroyer, of the great forests that covered the land. Immense regions where trees grew freely, extending around them the benevolent influence of vegetal souls, are no more now than denuded rocks. Two thousand years ago, Greece, France and North Africa were lands of immense forests. We are witnessing at present the death of the few woodlands that subsist on the shores of the Mediterranean. Everywhere, venerable trees that have traversed the millennia and represent qualities of shade for humans and shelters for birds and thousands of smaller creatures, not to mention their permanent beauty and their radiant wisdom, are being destroyed under the most futile pretext. That pretext is, in general, human cupidity. But it may be that it is a natural hatred of vegetal life and its expansion.

The destruction of animals gives a greater joy, and the pleasure of the hunter, consciously or not, is singularly augmented by the sight of blood. With the improvement of weapons, the greater facility that hunters have for transporting themselves, and the augmentation of the liking for hunting, under the magical name of sport, a large number of animal species have been on the point of disappearing in recent years.

The bison of North America have been completely annihilated, to the point where it has been difficult to find a few survivors in order to put them in parks under the title of a curiosity. Beavers have been almost exterminated for their fur, ostriches are in the process of disappearing because of the quality of their feathers, rhinoceroses because their powdered horns are used by lustful Chinamen as an aphrodisiac, the giant tortoises of the Galapagos Islands because of the taste of their flesh. The great auks of the north have now disappeared entirely because of their innocent souls, which led them to manifest too great an amity for humans, which was not reciprocated.

That amity has caused the death of a host of animal creatures. A large number of voyagers of the last century recount that when they arrived in lost islands, flocks of birds came toward them fraternally, perching on their shoulders and fluttering around their heads. "One could stun them with sticks, grab them in the hands and wring their necks without difficulty. They were so stupid that they offered themselves to death." Launches were filled with eggs, and when there was no wood to burn, fires were built with the bodies of birds.[37]

The number of elephants killed every year in Africa can be estimated by means of customs records. "At Matadi alone in 1911 thirty thousand tusks were embarked, which represents fifteen thousand elephants killed exclusively in the Congo."[38] One can foresee, in a very short time, the extinction of the African elephant, forty thousand of which are killed every year.

Many animal species disappear silently. Naturalists have given them mysterious names, as for the okapi, a variety of antelope, or the tuatara, *Sphendodon punctatus*, a strange lizard from New Zealand. One learns of their extinction from the premiums offered by zoological gardens to acquire a final example of the model that nature has created and humans have exterminated, which the Earth will never see again.

---

[37] Author's reference: "See Dr. Robert, "Le Grand pingouin" (*La Terre et la vie*)." The great auk was known by that name in France.

[38] Author's reference: Edmond Perrier, *À travers le monde vivant*." The book cited was first published in 1916.

Thus humans diminish life because of their love of killing. It is not even out of cupidity or the desire for wellbeing; most of the time it is a game. The most civilized go to massacre the large species of savage lands with redoubtable weapons, devastating explosive bullets that eliminate danger and leave the stirring joy of causing death. They then give themselves the name of sportsmen.

In any case, they are within the rules of their morality. No prescription of the religion of Christ forbids killing animals. The prophet of Galilee did not given them a place in the circle of his love. Mohammed imitated that abstention. Those great men thus perpetuated, by the prestige of their incomplete religion, an injustice never punished in the human domain.

And if one questions those who rise above religion in order to regulate their conduct, they are able to cite philosophers like Descartes and Malebranche and affirm in the name of a superior speculation that there is no importance in killing beings that are only machines.

What singular machines, though, whose mechanisms sometimes seem to surpass those of Christian men and are capable of a despair a thousand times greater by virtue of the impossibility of expressing it!

The monkey that a bullet has just caused to fall from branch to branch often does not think of fleeing and falls to the ground. It cannot believe that the being it judged stronger than itself, and superior in a confused hierarchy that it imagines, has been capable of causing it that immediate suffering, since it was chattering in a tree without doing any harm to anyone and was perhaps proffering words of amity in its own language. Even mortally wounded, it still believes in an error. It takes the blood from its breast in its hand and holds it out to the hunter, in order to say: "See what you have done!"

Futile testimony! That gesture, often reported in many stories, merely permits the hunter to save another bullet, and the monkey is killed by blows of the butt.

Machines! How faithful they are, too! I cannot forget an episode in the voyage of an explorer in South America. While traversing an immense forest with a little caravan he killed a monkey, a male, and loaded it on to his mule, desiring to conserve it as a specimen. Throughout the time that the traversal of the forest lasted, a troop of monkeys followed the group of men in the trees with cries and impotent threats. They redoubled their fury by night and prevented the voyagers from sleeping. When the latter emerged from the forest the monkeys did not quit their domain, sending maledictions from a distance. But in the plain, the explorer perceived that there as a silhouette of a monkey in the distance walking behind him, waiting when the caravan toped and the resuming its march. He thought that it was the female of the dead monkey, which did not want to quit her husband, even dead. He saw that silhouette for several days. Then he noticed that it was tottering. And on the third evening, he saw that it was lying on the ground and no longer moving.

That is reported in his story without commentary, as one petty fact among others. Doubtless he had read Descartes.

Machines! And what mutual aid there is between them! What friendship between companions! A wounded elephant is not abandoned to the terror of firearms, to the fury of the beings that kill at a distance with implacable certainty. Two elephants of the herd hasten to frame it, sustain it and draw it along, pushing it far from the danger.

That mutual aid is not limited to the species. The parasitic birds that live on a rhinoceros warn the monster by flapping their wings that an enemy is advancing stealthily carrying the murderous tube from which death springs. Bubal antelopes watch for hunters, follow them at a distance and take advantage of their rapidity in running to warn herds of zebras or impalas, less perspicacious and more imprudent animals, of the danger. Some of those antelopes seem to be consigned to that mission and have a special call that serves as a warning.[39]

---

[39] Author's reference: "See Dugmore, *Les Fauves d'Afrique photographiés chez eux*." The book in question, *Camera Adventures in the African Wilds* by the Irish naturalist Radclyffe

Machines! What a dolorous sentiment of death their mechanism contains!

A hunter killed a large female elephant accompanied by a young calf scarcely a meter tall. Hidden in the bushes, he watched his victim die. This is what he saw. First the calf sniffed its mother, and then pushed her with its foot and its trunk. It required a moment to realize the mystery of death. It trumpeted in a manner so infantile and so heart-rending that the hunter's blood was chilled. It started circling the body rapidly, but sometimes interrupted its course to rear up on two feet and—which is exceptional—executed strange movements that could have been interpreted as sketching a dance, fixed in advance, like the celebration of an animal rite—one of the rites that, according to legend, elephants practice in inaccessible solitudes.

Machines that take mutual love as far as humans, and do so outside the sexual appeal of generation. Cases of dying for love among animals are countless and it would be fastidious to cite examples. One finds affection even among species that are on the lowest echelons of the scale of beings.

Darwin reports that two snails, one vigorous and the other weak, found themselves together on a terrain that did not contain any nourishment for them. The stronger of the two quit its companion, went over a wall and, having found a garden, it returned twenty-four hours later to search for its companion. "Both of them, following the same route, disappeared over the wall."

Machines of dolor that, in proportion to their faculty for love, suffer from the hatred that pursues them! In spite of the effort of nature and perhaps her immeasurable sadness in seeing her work compromised, species are diminishing everywhere, creatures bleeding and dying. Cavalcades of zebras and antelopes, increasingly less numerous, run over savannahs in bewilderment. Birds fall from branches. Wild beasts no longer

---

Dugmore, was published in English in 1910 and translated the same year.

have secret caves. Stags bell toward the sky. Polar bears search vainly to the north of deserted icebergs. Whales wandering in the tranquility of the depths know that if they come up to breathe they will hear harpoons whistling. All the beasts await with anguish the nocturnal hour when they must come to drink at the pool or the river, because the hunter knows that rendezvous with thirst and has made it a rendezvous with death.

There is no longer any inaccessible peak where the eagle can sleep in security, and no matter what country migrating storks fly over, they are not preserved by their immaculate plumage, a symbol of purity. Neither running, not wings, not burrowing underground will any longer permit animals to preserve their lives. They are condemned to the torture of fear. Tracked relentlessly from one end of the earth to the other, they are put to death by their pitiless elder brother, whose role was to love them and to favor their elevation.

THE CRUELTY OF BEASTS

It is a paradox to sustain that terrestrial evil comes from humans by virtue of a fall and that innocence is in a virgin state in the soul of animals. Animals are as cruel as humans.

Certain snakes wait for crocodiles to yawn, launch themselves into the depths of their bodies, devour their entrails and take advantage of the spasms of agony to reemerge with that living nourishment.

A tiger follows large herds of elephants and waits for an imprudent calf to move a little way from its mother. It bounds forward, snatches away with a single thrust of its jaws the calf's trunk and goes to settle down some distance away, in accordance with the wind, the direction of which it has calculated, far from the gaze of the myopic giants. The hemorrhage kills the little elephant instantaneously. The herd reassembles, utters lamentations, discusses the cause of the death, and makes futile searches. At length, it continues its route. Then the tiger comes back and eats its victim.

A tiger often kills without appetite, for the pleasure of killing. People in Indo-China recall an irruption on the first floor of a kind of boarding-house where the tiger killed a dozen sleeping children, and another irruption during a theatrical performance in which thirty people were slain without any of them being carried away for a meal.

A wasp, by means of a prodigious surgical knowledge that is innate in its wasp soul, pierces a cricket with its sting at the central point of its nervous system, where the sting paralyzes it without killing it. It transports the paralyzed creature, still alive, to its nest and conserves it there in order that its larvae will have the nourishment of an animate being later, which will see itself slowly eaten after an interminable torture.

Many insects, including spiders, kill and eat their mates after the sexual union, in order that the pleasure in question should be followed by another of a different order. The males of many species willingly eat their children and the females are obliged to defend their progeniture against them ferocious-ly.

Evil is inherent in terrestrial creation. It is part of the law, like love. But a moment comes when it appears, with a certainty that cannot be denied, that love ought to triumph over hatred, and there is an orientation of the world of which everyone must extract the secret for himself. And when a glimmer of that secret, however tiny, has shone, it is necessary to march toward it ineluctably.

PRAYER FOR SEEING
THE BEAUTY OF THINGS

O Beauty, let me see you, you who are everywhere and whom my eyes only perceive at are moments, under certain solar influences, in the deployment of certain particular landscapes.

You are the greatest mystery that exists. You live under stones, in the sap of trees, in the play of light and shadow, and you only appear in a fugitive manner to privileged souls. By what grace have souls received the gift of contemplating you? I have often thought that there is among those who strive only to see the virtue and good intentions of people, by virtue of a mysterious mechanism of the soul, a transposition of those virtues into a delight that seems to emerge from things. But no, you reveal yourself directly to those you have chosen, without any consideration for virtue, by a caprice that has no fixed law,

O Beauty, make me one of your elect! Since you do not care about justice, having set aside the most worthy, teach me the means of acceding to your perception. Is there a magic formula that it is necessary to pronounce at dawn? Are there sacred flowers that only flourish in certain places of predilection and of which I must make you an offering? Must I fast and lie on a hard bed, like an ascetic, in order to have a light body and a blank mind? Ought I to run at dawn to the summit of a mountain in order for you to appear to me and touch my heart with your finger?

But do you have a form susceptible of appearing? You have been represented as a goddess with a beautiful face inhabiting a divine abode. How much more convenient it would be if that were the case! I would have set traps for you like those wily Greeks whose stories I learned in school, and I would have ended up gaining your amity on the beach of a gilded isle alongside a wood of lemon trees. But you are a distributed force, a hidden essence, an immaterial presence.

The hollow of your hand is that of all valleys, every tress of your hair is a forest of the earth and there is a little of the aquamarine of your gaze in the limpidity of every spring.

Let me see you, you who make the trees talk most fluently than the wind and who gives the shadows of reeds more mystery than any spring moon! If I am afflicted, you console me and if I am hurt because of a memory you make me forget better than the bewitchment of any drug.

Sometimes, in the evening, I only have to open the window and look out and I perceive you all the way to the horizon, and beyond the stars. You envelop everything with a robe of splendor; you are the joy and the wonder of my soul.

But at other times, I open the same window and there is a gaslight trembling, a road winding along a somber wall and an automobile drawing away. And I could call you a thousand times, dragging myself on my knees and begging you, but there would still be the gaslight and the auto and you would not make the slightest drop of your light shine for me over that dead landscape.

O Beauty, I know that I bear you within me and that it is me, by the accumulation of my aspirations, who has created the faculty of seeing you. May my most ardent aspiration rise incessantly toward you like the prayer of the believer toward the mute God of the tabernacle! May my desire to see the spirit behind forms appear, and cause the spiritual genii that live behind things, awaiting the signal of souls to appear, to emerge a little more every day. May the sage retribution of the law give me the quotidian beauty that is as necessary to me as bread!

THE DISCOVERY OF THE NEW WORLD

Every man is like Christopher Columbus; he has a new world to discover. Once, he must embark on a marvelous caravel, like him, without knowing whether he has seventy days of navigation before him. Standing at the prow, the silent and motionless voyager will scrutinize the immense sea of serene contemplation. He will also see the stars rotating like mute wheels and the blue-tinted phosphorescence of tropical seas will be signs on the waters before him. He will sense his reason weaken when the great terrifying silences hasten from the depths of the horizon, float and draw away slowly, like immense creatures.

But in the end, he too will distinguish floating vegetation and drifting tree trunks, which will indicate to him that land is not far away. Mysterious flowers will emerge from the empire of darkness. Birds with multicolored plumage will pass over his sails and he will salute them as the annunciation of the promised realm.

The realm is that of the ideal archetypes, the dreams of God, the refractions of which in matter have created forms. That is the divine beauty that it is necessary to attain.

The great artists, the great visionaries, have glimpsed the sublime world of creative thoughts, of ideal images, and they have transmitted reflections of it in their terrestrial works. Toward that kingdom, of which only a few lightning flashes are transmitted, there are narrow paths that it is necessary to discover.

Those paths are well hidden, and before undertaking the voyage, it is necessary to wonder whether the departure is even possible in the tumultuous word in which Occidental man lives.

Do not the noise of cities and the radiation of evil men, or only agitated and vain ones, constitute invisible and insurmountable barriers? Is it necessary to exile oneself to solitary mountains? And where are there solitary mountains? Is it necessary to quit one's father and mother, as it was prescribed by Jesus, and if one has lost one's parents a long time ago, is it necessary to make an equal sacrifice?

The realm is very close, with its real phantasmagorias and its miracles of verity. We are only separated from it by a very light veil, but it is more opaque than a wall of lead for the person who does not make the gesture that will tear it. And there is not even a gesture to be made; perhaps it will be sufficient to add a slight coloration to the soul, as slight as that given to the blue of the ocean by the fall of a grain of rose pollen. Perhaps a slight shock will suffice, like that produced by the antenna of a irritated bee on striking the Great Pyramid.

It is necessary to depart. The caravel is here, the sails are inflated, and the wind is blowing. Will the voyage be long or brief, fortunate or terrible? And when one has meditated for a long time on the possibilities of the departure, when one is on the point of renouncing it, it sometimes happens that by an implausible play of nature, one suddenly perceives that one has arrived without having departed.

www.ingramcontent.com/pod-product-compliance
Lightning Source LLC
Chambersburg PA
CBHW030355020726
47493CB00003B/830